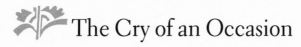The Cry of an Occasion

The Cry of

an Occasion

FICTION FROM
THE FELLOWSHIP OF
SOUTHERN WRITERS

Edited by Richard Bausch

With a Foreword by George Garrett

 Louisiana State University Press   *Baton Rouge*

Copyright © 2001 by Louisiana State University Press
Manufactured in the United States of America
First printing

10 09 08 07 06 05 04 03 02 01

5 4 3 2 1

Designer: Erin Kirk New
Typeface: Electra
Typesetter: Coghill Composition Co., Inc.
Printer and binder: Thomson-Shore, Inc.

The editor gratefully acknowledges the authors, editors, and publishers of the following books and periodicals, in which the stories noted previously appeared. Madison Smartt Bell's "The Naked Lady" was first published in *Crescent Review* (1983) and then appeared in *Harper's Readings* (1984), *Best American Short Stories* (Houghton Mifflin, 1984), and *Zero dB* (Ticknor & Fields, 1987). Doris Betts's "Three Ghosts" appeared in the Raleigh *News and Observer* (1999). Fred Chappell's "The Encyclopedia Daniel" appeared in *100 Menacing Little Murder Stories* (Barnes & Noble, 1998). Ellen Douglas' "About Loving Women" has appeared in *Texas Review* (1991) and in *That's What I Like (about the South) and Other New Southern Stories for the Nineties* (University of South Carolina Press, 1993). Shelby Foote's "The Sacred Mound" appeared in *Jordan County: A Landscape in Narrative* (Dial, 1954; Vintage, 1992). George Garrett's "Feeling Good, Feeling Fine" was published in *Meridian* (1999). Allan Gurganus' "Reassurance" appeared in *White People* (Knopf, 1991). Barry Hannah's "Death and Joy" was published in *Le Monde* (2000). William Hoffman's "The Secret Garden" has appeared in *Virginia Quarterly Review* (1991) and in *Follow Me Home* (LSU Press, 1994). Madison Jones's "Sim Denny" originally appeared in *Season of the Strangler* (Charter, 1983). William Henry Lewis' "Germinating" was first published in *In the Arms of Our Elders* (Carolina Wren, 1994). Jill McCorkle's "Life Prerecorded" appeared in *Final Vinyl Days* (Algonquin, 1998; Fawcett, 1999). Lewis Nordan's "Tombstone" was published in *Some Southern Stories* (Columbia College Chicago, 1998). Louis D. Rubin, Jr.'s "The Man at the Beach" appeared in *Virginia Quarterly Review* (1982). Lee Smith's "Between the Lines" has appeared in *Carolina Quarterly* (1980) and in *O. Henry Awards Prize Stories, 1981* (Doubleday, 1981), *Cakewalk* (Putnam, 1981), and other anthologies. Elizabeth Spencer's "The Everlasting Light" was published in the Raleigh *News and Observer* (1998).

Library of Congress Cataloging-in-Publication Data

The cry of an occasion : fiction from the Fellowship of Southern Writers / edited by Richard Bausch ; with a foreword by George Garrett.
    p. cm.
   ISBN 0-8071-2635-7 (alk. paper)
    1. American fiction—Southern States. 2. Short stories, American—Southern States. 3. Southern States—Social life and customs—Fiction. 4. American fiction—20th century. I. Bausch, Richard, 1945— II. Fellowship of Southern Writers.

PS551.C79 2001
813'.54080975—dc21
00-063288

Contents

Foreword

The idea of the Fellowship of Southern Writers came from the late Cleanth Brooks, who had been thinking of the need for some sort of organization aimed at encouraging Southern literature in general and, especially, offering some kind of formal recognition to young Southern writers. In 1987 while Brooks was visiting Chapel Hill, he talked about the idea at some length with scholar Louis D. Rubin, Jr., and together they decided to begin. On September 18, 1987, Brooks sent out a letter to a varied group of Southern writers, saying: "For some time several of us have been discussing the need for, and the possibility of founding, a society or fellowship of Southern writers." The writers were invited "to meet and establish an organization to encourage and recognize distinction in Southern writing." The meeting was scheduled for and held on October 30–31 in Chattanooga.

Why Chattanooga? First of all, because it already had a highly successful Biennial Conference on Southern Literature, created by the Arts and Education Council there, one which had built up the widespread support of the local community. Louis D. Rubin, Jr., who, together with George Core, editor of the *Sewanee Review*, joined Cleanth Brooks in arranging the first meeting, says that Chattanooga and its conference seemed especially appropriate because of "the fact that it was a civic and not an academic undertaking and equally that it was not identified with any one school or group or coterie or a particular kind of Southern writing." This latter goal, literary neutrality, was more important than one might have imagined: "The two universities most active in contemporary Southern letters, Vanderbilt University and the University of North Carolina at Chapel Hill, were good possibilities for a home. But each of them was associated with a particular group of writers, and we did not want the Fellowship to fall under the aegis—no matter how benevolent—of any one group." On June 22, Rubin, Brooks, and Core met with Chattanooga community leaders at the offices of the Lyndhurst Foundation, from whom the Fellowship received both an organizational grant and, later, a development grant. The organizational meeting of the Fellowship took place in October 1987. Those present included Cleanth Brooks, Fred Chappell, George Core, Shelby Foote, George Garrett, Blyden Jackson, Andrew Lytle, Lewis P. Simpson, Elizabeth Spencer, Walter Sullivan, C. Vann Woodward, and Louis D. Rubin, Jr. Not present at the meeting, but already committed to support of the Fellowship were Eudora Welty, Robert Penn Warren, Peter Taylor, Walker Percy, Ernest J. Gaines and John Hope Franklin. Says Rubin:

> We wanted to encourage and stimulate good writing in the South. While we didn't think of our group as competing with any of the national academies and institutes—to which many of our group already belonged—we wanted the work of young Southern authors to be read and evaluated and recognized by other Southern writers for whom the region and the subject matter would not seem 'quaint' or 'exotic.' But at the same time we wanted to recognize and encourage only work of the highest quality, free from insularity and localism. And we wanted our members to include not only novelists, poets, dramatists and critics, but writers of history and other genres whose work displayed literary excellence.

Cleanth Brooks was chosen to be the first chancellor of the Fellowship; Louis D. Rubin, Jr., was named chairman of the executive committee; George Core was chosen to be secretary-treasurer; and George Garrett became vice chancellor. In addition to the eighteen writers already committed, James Dickey, Ralph Ellison, Reynolds Price, and William Styron joined the others and all were constituted as founding members of the Fellowship.

At the outset the Fellowship agreed to hold a meeting and an awards convocation in conjunction with the regular Biennial Conference on Southern Literature. The University of Tennessee at Chattanooga offered to house the archives of the Fellowship at the Lupton Library. The Fellowship set out to secure endowments from which prizes would be awarded to younger Southern writers. One form of recognition of distinction would be membership in the Fellowship. And the highest award, given for a lifetime's achievement in letters, would be a medal which the original membership, without consulting its first chancellor, named the Cleanth Brooks Medal.

Soon the Fellowship was incorporated under the law. It received a development grant from the Lyndhurst Foundation to cover operating expenses and such incidental costs as the casting of bronze medallions for the individual Fellows. Photographer Curt Richter was commissioned to photograph each Fellow, and the photographs are on display in the Fellowship's Archive Room, renamed in 1997 the Arlie Herron Room in honor of the professor of Southern literature at the University of Tennessee at Chattanooga. And in the months prior to the first full-scale meeting and convocation of the Fellowship, endowments for the various awards were secured. The Hillsdale Foundation created the Hillsdale Prize for Fiction. The James G. Hanes Foundation offered a Hanes Prize in Poetry. Chubb Life supported the Robert Penn Warren Award in fiction, and the Bryan Family Foundation financed an award in drama. The Fellows themselves contributed funds for an award in nonfiction and for the Fellowship's New Writing Award.

After two terms of two years as chancellor, Cleanth Brooks was followed, in turn, by Louis D. Rubin, Jr., George Garrett, and Doris Betts. Elizabeth Spencer is now vice chancellor. The full membership of the Fellowship now includes A. R. Ammons, James Applewhite, Richard Bausch, Wendell Berry, Doris Betts, Joseph Blotner, Fred Chappell, George Core, Ellen Douglas, Clyde Edgerton, Horton Foote, Shelby Foote, John Hope Franklin, Ernest J. Gaines,

George Garrett, Gail Godwin, Allan Gurganus, William Hoffman, Josephine Humphries, Blyden Jackson, Madison Jones, Donald Justice, Yusef Komunyakaa, C. Eric Lincoln, Romulus Linney, Bobbie Ann Mason, Marsha Norman, Reynolds Price, Louis D. Rubin, Jr., Mary Lee Settle, Lewis P. Simpson, Dave Smith, Lee Smith, Elizabeth Spencer, William Styron, Walter Sullivan, Henry Taylor, Eudora Welty, and Charles Wright.

In the decade since its beginning, a number of Fellows have died: Cleanth Brooks, James Dickey, Ralph Ellison, Andrew Lytle, Walker Percy, Monroe K. Spears, Peter Taylor, Robert Penn Warren, and C. Vann Woodward.

Beginning with the first formal convocation of the Fellowship in 1989, awards have been presented to the following Southern writers: Hillsdale Prize for Fiction—Ellen Douglas (1989), Richard Bausch (1991), Josephine Humphreys (1993), William Hoffman (1995), Lewis Nordan (1997), Bobbie Ann Mason (1999); Hanes Prize for Poetry—Kelly Cherry (1989), Robert Morgan (1991), Ellen Bryant Voigt (1993), Andrew Hudgens (1995), Yusef Komunyakaa (1997), T. R. Hummer (1999); Chubb Award for Fiction in Honor of Robert Penn Warren—Lee Smith (1991), Cormac McCarthy (1993), Madison Smartt Bell (1995), Allen Wier (1997), Barry Hannah (1999); Bryan Family Foundation Award for Drama—Jim Grimsley (1991), Pearl Cleage (1995), Naomi Wallace (1997), Margaret Edson (1999); Fellowship Award for Nonfiction—Samuel F. Pickering, Jr. (1991), John Shelton Reed (1995), Bailey White (1997), James Kibler (1999); Fellowship's New Writing Award—William Henry Lewis (1997), Michael Knight (1999); Special Achievement Award—Andrew Lytle (1995), James Still (1997); James Still Award—Charles Frazier (1999); Cleanth Brooks Medal for Distinguished Achievement in Southern Letters—John Hope Franklin (1989), Eudora Welty (1991), C. Vann Woodward (1993), Lewis P. Simpson (1995), Louis D. Rubin, Jr. (1997), and Shelby Foote (1999).

In addition to their biennial meeting and the public awards convocation, the Fellows are active participants in the Chattanooga Conference on Southern Literature. They join in panel discussions, readings, and lectures, and the keynote address for the conference is given by a member of the Fellowship. In 1997 the speaker was novelist Ernest J. Gaines. Prizewinners visit local and area high schools and meet with students there.

The Fellowship has now been in existence and active for ten years. "We are beginning our second decade in excellent shape," Louis D. Rubin, Jr., says. "We are now firmly linked to the Chattanooga Conference and we have high hopes that we can play an ever more active part in recognizing and honoring achievement and encouraging excellence in Southern letters."

This anthology is made up of fiction both by members of the Fellowship of Southern Writers and by the prizewinners of the Hillsdale Prize for Fiction and the Chubb Award for Fiction in Honor of Robert Penn Warren. The work has been selected by the writers themselves, in conjunction with the editor of this volume, member Richard Bausch. It will be followed, in due course, by an anthology of poetry edited by Fred Chappell and, finally, a gathering of nonfiction edited by George Core. Members and prizewinners have agreed that any and all earnings from this book and the others will go to the Fellowship as a contribution to its modest endowment. It is our hope that this book, these books, will give to the reader a sense of the direction and development of Southern writing in our time.

— GEORGE GARRETT

Preface

I have always considered that an editor's job is to efface himself as much as possible and simply put forward the work of the writers who have his enthusiasm. That is my purpose here. But I would not be able to live with myself if I did not say, at the outset, that to be associated with this group of writers, as advocate and editor, makes me more proud than I can say. Many of these people are heroes of mine, and have been since I first started trying to write, now almost thirty-five years ago. In every single case, with every single story, the author has my awe and wonder. I think it comprises indeed "the cry of an occasion," a phrase I first heard Allen Wier use. I think it is a hell of a collection. I believe you will, too.

— RICHARD BAUSCH

MADISON SMARTT BELL

 The Naked Lady

for Alan Lequire

This is a thing that happened before Monroe started maken the heads, while he was still maken the naked ladies.

Monroe went to the college and it made him crazy for a while like it has done to many a one.

He about lost his mind on this college girl he had. She was just a little old bit of a thing and she talked like she had bugs in her mouth and she was just nothen but trouble. I never would of messed with her myself.

When she thrown him over we had us a party to take his mind off it. Monroe had these rooms in a empty mill down by the railroad yard. He used to make his scultures there and we was both liven there too at the time.

We spent all the money on whiskey and beer and everbody we known come over. When it got late Monroe appeared to drop a stitch and went to thowin bottles at the walls. This caused some people to leave but some other ones stayed on to help him I think.

I had a bad case of drunk myself. A little before sunrise I crawled off and didn't wake up till up in the afternoon. I had a sweat from sleepin with clothes on. First thing I seen when I opened my eyes was this big old rat setten on the floor side the mattress. He had a look on his face like he was wonderen would it be safe if he come over and took a bite out of my leg.

It was the worst rats in that place you ever saw. I never saw nothin to match em for bold. If you chunked somethin at em they would just back off a ways and look at you mean. Monroe had him this tin sink that was full of plaster from the scultures and ever night these old rats would mess in it. In the mornin you could see they had left tracks goen places you wouldnt of believed somethin would go.

We had this twenty-two pistol we used to shoot em up with but it wasnt a whole lot of good. You could hit one of these rats square with a twenty-two and he would go off with it in him and just get meaner. About the only way to kill one was if you hit him spang in the head and that needs you to be a better shot than I am most of the time.

We did try a box of them exploden twenty-twos like what that boy shot the President with. They would take a rat apart if you hit him but if you didnt they would bounce around the room and bust up the scultures and so on.

It happened I had put this pistol in my pocket before I went to bed so Monroe couldnt get up to nothin silly with it. I taken it out slow and threw down on this rat that was looken me over. Hit him in the hindquarter and he went off and clamb a pipe with one leg draggen.

I sat up and saw the fluorescents was on in the next room thew the door. When I went in there Monroe was messen around one of his sculture stands.

Did you get one, he said.

Winged him, I said.

That aint worth much, Monroe said. He off somewhere now plotten your doom.

I believe the noise hurt my head more'n the slug hurt that rat, I said. Is it any whiskey left that you know of?

Let me know if you find some, Monroe said. So I went to looken around. The place was nothin but trash and it was glass all over the floor.

I might of felt worse sometime but I dont just remember when it was, I said.

They's coffee, Monroe said.

I went in the other room and found a half of a pint of Heaven Hill between the mattress and the wall where I must of hid it before I tapped out. Pretty slick for drunk as I was. I taken it in to the coffee pot and mixed half and half with some milk in it for the sake of my stomach.

Leave me some, Monroe said. I hadnt said a word, he must of smelt it. He tipped the bottle and took half what was left.

The hell, I said. What you maken anyway?

Naked lady, Monroe said.

I taken a look and it was this shape of a woman setten on a mess of clay. Monroe made a number of these things at the time. Some he kept and the rest he thrown out. Never could tell the difference myself.

Thats all right, I said.

No it aint, Monroe said. Soon's I made her mouth she started in asken me for stuff. She wants new clothes and she wants a new car and she wants some jewry and a pair of Italian shoes.

And if I made her that stuff, Monroe said, I know she's just goen to take it out looken for some other fool. I'll set here all day maken stuff I dont care for and she'll be out just riden and riden.

Dont make her no clothes and she cant leave, I said.

She'll whine if I do that, Monroe said. The whole time you was asleep she been fussen about our relationship.

You know the worst thing, Monroe said. If I just even thought about maken another naked lady I know she would purely raise hell.

Why dont you just make her a naked man and forget it, I said.

Why dont I do this? Monroe said. He whopped the naked lady with his fist and she turned into a flat clay pancake, which Monroe put in a plastic bag to keep soft. He could hit a good lick when he wanted. I hear this is common among scultures.

Dont you feel like doen somethin, Monroe said.

I aint got the least dime, I said.

I got a couple dollars, he said. Lets go see if it might be any gas in the truck.

They was some. We had this old truck that wasnt too bad except it was slow to start. When we once got it goen we drove over to this pool hall in Antioch where nobody didnt know us. We stayed awhile and taught some fellers that was there how to play rotation and five in the side and some other games that Monroe was good at. When this was over with we had money and I thought we might go over to the Ringside and watch the fights. This was a bar with a ring in the middle so you could set there and drink and watch people get hurt.

We got in early enough to take seats right under the ropes. They was an exhibition but it wasnt much and Monroe started in on this little girl that was setten by herself at the next table.

Hey there Juicy Fruit, he said, come on over here and get somethin real good.

I wouldnt, I told him, haven just thought of what was obvious. Then this big old hairy thing came out from the back and sat down at her table. I known him from a poster out front. He was champion of some kind of karate and had come all the way up from Atlanta just to beat somebody to death and I didnt think he would care if it was Monroe. I got Monroe out of there. I was some annoyed with him because I would have admired to see them fights if I could do it without bein in one myself.

So Monroe said he wanted to hear music and we went some places where they had that. He kept after the girls but they wasnt any trouble beyond what we could handle. After while these places closed and we found us a little railroad bar down on Lower Broad.

It wasnt nobody there but the pitifulest band you ever heard and six bikers, the big fat ugly kind. They wasnt the Hell's Angels but I believe they would have done until some come along. I would of left if it was just me.

Monroe played pool with one and lost. It wouldnt of happened if he hadnt been drunk. He did have a better eye than me which may be why he is a sculture and I am a second-rate pool player.

How come all the fat boys in this joint got on black leather jackets? Monroe hollered out. Could that be a new way to lose weight?

The one he had played with come bellyen over. These boys like to look you up and down beforehand to see if you might faint. But Monroe hooked this one side of the head and he went down like a steer in the slaughterhouse. This didnt make me as happy as it might of because it was five of em left and the one that was down I thought apt to get up shortly.

I shoved Monroe out the door and told him to go start the truck. The band had done left already. I thown a chair and I thown some other stuff that was layen around and I ducked out myself.

The truck wasnt started yet and they was close behind. It was this old four-ten I had under the seat that somebody had sawed a foot off the barrel. I taken it and shot the sidewalk in front of these boys. The pattern was wide on account of the barrel bein short like it was and I believe some of it must of hit all of em. It was a pump and took three shells and I kept two back in case I needed em for serious. But Monroe got the truck goen and we left out of there.

I was some mad at Monroe. Never said a word to him till he parked outside the mill. It was a nice moon up and thowin shadows in the cab when the headlights went out. I turned the shotgun across the seat and laid it into Monroe's ribs.

What you up to? he said.

You might want to die, I said, but I dont believe I want to go with you. I pumped the gun to where you could hear the shell fallen in the chamber.

If that's what you want just tell me now and I'll save us both some trouble.

It aint what I want, Monroe said.

I taken the gun off him.

I dont know what I do want, Monroe said.

Go up there and make a naked lady and you feel better, I told him.

He was messen with clay when I went to sleep but that aint what he done. He set up a mirror and done a head of himself instead. I taken a look at the thing in the mornin and it was a fair likeness. It looked like it was thinkin about all the foolish things Monroe had got up to in his life so far.

That same day he done one of me that was so real it even looked like it had a hangover. Ugly too but that aint Monroe's fault.

He is makin money with it now.

How we finally fixed them rats was we brought on a snake. Monroe was the one to have the idea. It was a good-sized one and when it had just et a rat it was as big around as your arm. It didnt eat more than about one a week but it appeared to cause the rest of em to lay low.

You might say it was as bad to have snakes around as rats but at least it was only one of the snake.

The only thing was when it turned cold the old snake wanted to get in the bed with you. Snakes aint naturally warm like we are and this is how come people think they are slimy, which is not the truth when you once get used to one.

This old snake just comes and goes when the spirit moves him. I aint seen him in a while but I expect he must be still around.

DORIS BETTS

 Three Ghosts

I hurried from bed thinking Mama had called; she often does. But instead my Aunt Jean was standing in the hall, still wearing very black hair in a coil wrapped on what they called a "ratt" in the '40s—still tall and slender, having no face wrinkles, with a jaw line that had not sagged.

I didn't blink. I don't believe in ghosts.

She was wearing a pale blue dress with gold buttons and a brooch at the neckline. I hadn't thought the word "brooch" in so long that it sounded mispronounced in my mind. "Hello! Hello, Hallucination!" I called to her, using all I've learned about false cheer.

She didn't move—her silence was a bit unnerving—but only fixed on me those overly big blue eyes I had almost forgotten. Aunt Jean had that combination of bright blue eyes with black hair years before entertainers created this striking effect using contact lenses. From puberty on, though, her eyeballs had always bulged. Perhaps in life she'd had a thyroid problem.

But tonight I knew Jean had not been "in life" since the late '70s, after three minor husbands and one major car wreck. When her body lay reassembled and sculpted together in her coffin, thinner and faded hair had hung beside those rebuilt cheekbones like a pair of shingles. This younger face she showed now I only knew from photograph albums: the pretty girl entering nurse's training, the pretty woman posed beside various young men under flat straw boaters like bottle caps, the pretty nurse in her dark cape swirling off to World War II and the bedsides of wounded soldiers.

(All they taught Mama was how to cook and to half-sole a shoe.)

But like Jean and Mama, I'm Scots-Presbyterian and hard to fool. I stepped smartly down that hall carpet runner I got overcharged for, demanding, "Aunt Jean? What are you doing here?"

She spoke in the old way—that twangy edge-of-the-Blue Ridge way. "How's my sister?"

I said, "She's 92, how do you think she is?"

Jean would be, if alive, 97. If she hadn't died when she did, I'd be looking after them both.

"Does she hurt?"

That stopped me. Was she sick, old, failing—I could have answered those. Did she limp, fall, suffer from nightmares, wet the bed—I knew these answers as well.

"Probably so," I said. But then I took a deep breath, shook all confusion out of my head, and slotted this very vivid, multicolored Jean into the figment category. I declared her to be no more than a figment of my imagination, perhaps my resentment, certainly my fatigue. She'd had husbands to spare while I never married. In the South, marrying is what determines which old invalids women will care for—male or female.

Immediately I knew I'd robbed power from this image of Jean by reducing her to size, cramping her inside my head where she was no bigger than a brain cell. I took a firm step or two closer down the hall, confident. In fact, my real self was probably two doors back, in bed and sound asleep, merely exaggerating her dream until it swelled to the size of Mama's nightmares in which she killed hogs and wrung chicken necks.

But Aunt Jean, still looking solid, kept backing ahead of me down the hall, at last resting her firm white fingers with too many rings against Mama's door. It's an unnatural gait, to go backward for more than a step or two, and her easy movements made my stiff knee hurt.

"Let Mama alone; she's had her medicine, let her sleep!" I said, springing forward.

As if Jean had turned into Mama's figment instead of mine, she half-opened that door and half-melted into its edge and corners, then disappeared into the dark.

I dreaded to follow! Mama would be lying on her back, her mouth empty and open. Dentures were soaking nearby. Ears empty, too— her hearing aids now in their moisture-absorbent jar. If it was much after midnight, her diaper would be wet and the rubber sheet below would only have trapped the wide stain. Unless recent, it would smell. A wen growing by one eye looked like old chewing gum. If startled awake, Mama would scream. Long minutes of soothing would be required.

I whispered, "Oh, please!" but Aunt Jean was already at the bedside, drawing off the sheet Mama always wrapped around her face because breathing downward warmed the bed.

I slumped in the doorway.

In a shocked voice, Aunt Jean exclaimed, "But this isn't Lucille!"

And her words answered, perhaps, my questions about whether we die by degrees or all at once, whether the soul seeps across by drips and spiritual leakage or only departs with a single thump when the bottom drops out of the heart. Jean, of course, stabbed by a steering column, fled in the second way.

I managed to answer her, pointing. "It's what's left." My hand wavered.

But Jean's revelation that Mama's best, true, and barely remembered self had not already left this room to squeeze by stages into the hereafter was harder to endure than all the surgeries and bandages and bedpans combined.

I wanted to kill Aunt Jean a second time.

"You go back!" I ordered her, feeling my teeth sharpen themselves on my lower lip. "Who do you think you are to come back here making trouble after all these years?" I moved past the bed where Mama lay like a white apparition herself.

Now I could accuse Jean by shaking my finger hard in midair. "Lucille has forgot you, forgot you were the prettiest, forgot Jerry boy, forgot your mother and your papa, forgot my daddy, forgot me most of the time! So you've got no business here, get away! go on!" An ancient word rose in my mouth. "Begone!"

Aunt Jean, again backing away in an effortless slide I doubted, a gait so artificially smooth I might have invented it, touched the back bedroom window.

She said in some wonderment, "You love your mother!" and half raised the frame, became half transparent against the glass. Now I could not separate her gold buttons from gold stars beyond.

I hurried quickly after her to slam down the sash against cold air. She was gone. I worked the lock shut against dried paint.

What do they know about love—the dead? Who have escaped it?

I checked my watch, its stretch-band too loose on a wrist growing rapidly thin itself. Soon Mama would wake and need her pill.

FRED CHAPPELL

The Encyclopedia Daniel

Yesterday *cows* and the day before that *clouds*, but today he had skipped all the way to *fish*.

"What about *dreams?*" his mother asked. "What about *dandelions* and *dodo* and *Everest* and *Ethiopia?*"

Danny's reply was guarded. "I'll come back to them. *Fish* is what I've got to write about today. Today is fish day."

"Do you think that's the best way to compose an encyclopedia? You're twelve years old now. That's old enough to be methodical. You were taking your subjects in alphabetical order before. When you were in the *b*'s you didn't go from *baseball* to *xylophone*. Why do you want to jump over to *fish?*"

"I don't know," Danny said, "but today is fish day."

"Well," she said, "you're the encyclopedia-maker. You must know best."

"That's right," he said and his tone was as grave as that of an arch-

11

bishop settling a point of theology. He rose from his chair at the yellow dinette table. "I have to go think now," he announced.

"All right," his mother said. "Just don't hurt yourself."

Her customary remark irritated Danny. He didn't reply as he tucked two blue spiral notebooks under his arm and headed toward his tiny upstairs bedroom. Going up the steps, he found his answer but it came too late: "It doesn't hurt me to think, not like some people I know."

He closed his door tight, dropped his notebooks on the rickety card table serving for a desk, and flung himself down on the narrow bed. Then he rolled over, cradled his hands behind his head, and watched the ceiling. It was an early May dusk and the headlights of cars played slow shadows above him.

He tried to think about fish but the task was boring. Fish lived dim lives in secret waters and there were many different kinds and he knew only a few of their names. People ate them. People ate a lot of the things Danny wrote about in his Encyclopedia: apples, bananas, beans, coconuts. Cows too—Danny had written about eating cows in a way that distressed his mother. "Slaughterhouses!" she exclaimed. "Why write about that? You don't have to put that in." He had explained, with a patient sigh, that everything had to go in. An encyclopedia was about everything in the world. If he left something out, it would be like telling a lie. He wrote what was given him to write.

Yet today he had skipped from cows to fish, leaping over lots of interesting things. He would come back to *daredevil* and *Excalibur*, *eclipse* and *dentists*, but it wouldn't be the same. His mother was right. It was sloppy, zipping on to *fish*; it was unscientific. He said aloud: "This method is unscientific."

Then another sentence came into his mind. He could not keep it out. It was like trying to hold a door closed against someone bigger and stronger and crazier than you. You pushed hard but he pushed harder, swept you aside and came on in, sweaty and purplefaced and too loud for the little bedroom. This sentence was as audible in his mind as if it had been spoken to him in the dark and lonely midnight: "He tore the living room curtains down and tried to set them on fire."

He sat up on the edge of the bed and gazed out the window above his table. The dusk had thickened and the lights made the houses on

Orchard Street look warm and inviting. But that was only illusion. They were not inviting, all full of people who whispered and said ugly things. They lived happy lives, these people, you could tell from the lights in their windows, but you were not to be any part of that. Those lives were as remote and secret as the lives of fish in the depths of the ocean.

He turned on the dinky little lamp with the green shade and sat down in the creaky wooden chair. Dully he opened a notebook and began to read what he had written in his encyclopedia about cars:

> The best kind of car is a Corvette. It is really flash. Lots of kids say they will buy Corvettes when they grow up but I dont' think so. You have to be rich. Billy Joe Armistead is not going to be rich, just look at him. Anyway by the time we grow up Corvettes wont' be the hot car. The hot car will be something we dont' know about yet, maybe it has like an atomic motor.

Danny flipped the page. He had written a great deal about cars; that was his favorite subject. He had learned all about them by looking at magazine photos and articles and talking to the guys in the neighborhood. Corvette, they all said.

He turned through the scribbled pages until he came to a blank one to fill up with the facts about fish. Except that he didn't know any facts. Well, a few maybe—not enough to help. And then while he was looking at the page with its forbiddingly empty lines another sentence sounded in his head so strongly that he reached for the green ballpoint: "Then he vomits a lot of red stuff, yucky smelly red stuff." But he couldn't write and dropped the pen.

The house began to tang with kitchen smells and Danny understood they would have spaghetti for supper, he and his mother chatting at the dinette table. He understood too that he had better write at least a paragraph about fish because it would soon be time to go down. With a heartfelt groan, he began:

> Fish have gills so they can breathe water. They are hard to see but fisher men find them anyhow with radar they have. Some fish are real big like whales but most are not as big as people. When the police men come he tries to hit them all and then they put hand cuffs on him and drive off.

Three times he read the last sentence and then slowly and with close deliberate strokes marked out the words one at a time. Then he used his red ballpoint to make black rectangles of the canceled words. Red on green makes black.

He had interpreted the smells correctly. Supper was spaghetti and meatballs with his mother's pungent tomato sauce. She offered him a spoonful of her red wine in water but he preferred his Pepsi. There was a green salad too, with the pasty raw mushrooms he would avoid.

His mother raised her glass in his direction. "So—what is your schedule tomorrow? After school, I mean."

"Baseball practice," Danny said. "I'll be home about five."

"Homework?"

"I don't know. Math, probably. Maybe history."

"How about tonight?"

"None tonight."

"So you can go back to writing The Encyclopedia Daniel. How is *fish* coming along?"

"Not so hot."

"That's because you skipped," she said. "You were going like a house afire when you wrote the entries in order. Now you've lost your rhythm."

"I'll come back," he said. "I'll pick up *doors* and the *Dodgers* and *elephants* and *engines* and *farming* and *falcons*. I'll do *fathers*."

Her eyes went wet and she set her glass down as gently as a snowflake. "*Fathers*," she said. "That's what you skipped over, isn't it? You didn't want to do that part."

"I don't know. I guess not."

"Maybe you'll be a writer when you grow up," she said. "Then you'll have to write about sad things whether you want to or not."

"No. I'm not going to be a writer. Just my Encyclopedia. When I get it finished I won't need to write any more."

"Maybe I could be a writer." His mother spoke in a murmur—as if she was listening instead of talking. "When I think about your poor father I believe I could write a book."

"No," he said. His tone was imperious. "Everybody says they could write a book but they couldn't. It's real hard, it's real real hard. Harder than anybody thinks."

"Are you going to finish your Encyclopedia?"

"I don't know. If I can get past this part. But it's hard."

"Maybe it will be good for you to write it out."

"It makes me scared," he said. "Stuff comes in my mind and I'm scared to write it down."

"Like what? What are you scared to write?"

New sentences came to him then and Danny couldn't look into her face. He stared at his cold spaghetti and recited, "He said he would kill her no matter what and she said he never would, she would kill him first. If that was the only way, she would kill him first."

"Oh Danny," his mother said. "I didn't know you heard us that time. I didn't realize you knew."

"I know everything," he said. "I know everything that has already happened and everything that is going to happen. When you write an encyclopedia you have to know everything."

"But that night was a time when we were both pretty crazy. I wouldn't hurt your father. You understand that. And he's never coming back. They won't let him. You understand that too, don't you?"

"Maybe. Maybe if I write it down I'll understand better."

"Yes," she said. "Why don't you write it all down?"

But it was coming too fast to write down. Already there were new words in his head, words that spoke as sharply as a fire engine siren:

"Then in August the father got away and came back to the house. It was late at night and real dark. He didn't come to the front door. He went around back. He was carrying something red in his hand."

ELLEN DOUGLAS

 # About Loving Women

I

It was after the fight, walking home from school, that I remembered what had happened—such a long time ago I can hardly believe I remember it.

You know how there are some memories you're sure belong to you—because you've never shared them—like standing by the basin when you were three and watching the old lady who was live-in housekeeper the year your mother broke her pelvis and had to stay in traction for two months. You're leaning against the basin. Your head comes up just high enough so you can rest your chin on the cool smooth curving surface. You're looking up and she (the old lady) opens her mouth and *takes out her teeth*. And then, while you're watching (you can't believe it's happening—she never says a word the whole time and seems not to know you're there), she dips her tooth-brush in a can of powder and brushes the fronts and sides and corners and then she rinses them off and *puts them back in her mouth.* How is such a thing possible? Does anyone else know about this weird and scary, this magical skill of hers? You believe without even thinking about it (can you think at all when you're three?) that no one is supposed to know. Something awful may happen if you tell. You slip away—it still seems to you she hasn't noticed you standing there—and you never, never tell anyone what she can do.

And then there are others, stories you've heard people repeat so often you think what you know may be the memory of someone else's telling—like the time on vacation in Colorado when you fell in the Roaring Forks River and almost drowned and your mother ran downstream and threw herself on a log and wiggled out and grabbed you as you went tumbling by underneath. Is that her memory or yours? Because it's like you feel her terror more than the choking and drowning and banging against rocks that went on with you.

The third kind, the kind you must have tried to lose, is what came back to me the other day, sort of during and sort of after the fight. It's been there all my life, just waiting.

It even seems as if some people look at me in a special way because they remember, too. But they're not sure I do and so they never say. My grandmother looks at me like that—as if we have a secret. She wants to talk to me about it, but she sees it's impossible. I even think sometimes that because of this secret she wants to stand between me and my own life, as if I'm not up to it by myself and she has to protect me, and that makes me feel, no matter how much I love her, like I'm trapped in an elevator between floors or nailed in a packing crate or locked in the trunk of a car. Sometimes Uncle Alan looks at me that way, too, but his eyes are—not pitying, but sad and—I don't know— detached maybe.

I could be imagining things about both of them. They may have forgotten. My grandmother may never have known.

So I got in a fight after school last week.

I fight a lot.

I was small for my age until this past year—shot up last summer between sixteen and seventeen—and I've always had to either fight or be sharp enough to stay out of fights if I didn't want my face rubbed in the dirt. It's great when you're little—I mean littler than the other guy—to turn things around, to make him look like a fool in front of his friends for wanting to fight you, to make him have to laugh it off. And fighting's been okay, too, when I've had to do it, even when I got hurt. I've got a fucking terrible temper, and a point comes when I'm so mad I'll pick up anything handy—a stick or a chain or a tire tool—and no matter how much bigger the other guy is, he better watch out. Goddamn it, they're not gonna push me around, I don't care how big they are, that's what I'd say to myself. I'll kill any fucking bastard thinks he's gonna push me around. And I'd forget everything. Nothing hurt. No matter how hard a guy might hit me, I would barely feel it. And so I'd keep coming back.

And then, too (before I grew), if I could scare somebody who was bigger than me or walk into the gym and know they might be saying to a new kid in the class, Yeah, he's a little bitty honky, but don't mess with him, man, just don't mess with him. . . .

But I'm tall now—six-one. I can jump up and touch the ceiling in the hall at school. Not that I'm invincible; everybody else is taller, too, and in the school I go to, you're always having to prove yourself. Some of these black guys. . . . Last time it happened—cornered behind Renfro's Bicycle Shop—I picked up a broken bicycle chain from the trash heap and. . . . Well, I got out alive.

The way it is, you see, your parents have these convictions about public education and maybe you do, too—I'm not a racist, understand. But I'm the one who gets cornered behind Renfro's or has to walk home late, not knowing who's waiting or where. One time, seventh grade, I got held out the window of the third-floor john by my feet. That's helplessness. I kidded this seventeen-year-old eighth-grader into pulling me back in. As a matter of fact, he was white.

Then, last September, everything changed. The truth is I just completely forgot about being tough or not being tough, about being little or big, about fighting or studying or playing ball, about everything but Roseanne. It was like I turned into another person.

I still want to think and talk mainly about Roseanne and I can't seem to stop or even to want to stop, no matter how bad it hurts. I'm driving along in the car and I'll turn the radio off so I can think about nothing but her. Or walking to school. . . . I walk along and imagine I see her. She has a way of walking, a little bit slew-footed and tomboyish . . . and her legs, just so trim and beautiful (she swims a lot) and brown, and her little ass, as round as apples, and her face and her hair.

Her hair is real thick and lots of times she wears it in one of those French braids that look so hard to do, and the wispy curls that didn't get braided in fuzz up around her face like a baby's hair. Her eyebrows are straight across instead of curved and somehow to me that gives her a more serious and honest look. I imagine her coming toward me along the sidewalk, glad to see me, smiling. She has a kind of doubtful smile, as much as to say, Here I am and I like you. Okay?

But mainly, of course, I didn't think about what she looks like or how she walks or smiles. Instead, I go over and over in my mind the times we've been together. I feel her breast under my hand and the littleness of her waist and the way her hips swell out in such a neat curve. She's my love, I say to myself, my only, only love.

Not that I hadn't fucked a few girls before her. Well, two, to be exact, and one of them it was only one time and didn't work out too well. But I wasn't a damn virgin just screaming for sex, ready to be made a sucker of. All the same, virgin or not, I will never in my whole life love anybody like I love her. Laugh if you want to. Tell me I'm a kid. Tell me I don't know anything about love. But I never will. I know.

So the fight was about Roseanne.

We'd been going out together since September. I knew I wanted to go out with her the first time I saw her. To begin with, she went out with other people, too, but then later only with me and we got serious. She wasn't a virgin either, she said. She'd been with a guy in Birmingham, where she used to live, and she really cared about him, but that was over and now they were friends, but nothing else, and anyhow it hadn't been like us, she said. She was *really* in love with me.

II

Before I knew who he was, he told a couple of friends of mine at school that he was going to fight me, that he was going to *kill* me, for Christ's sake, and of course they told me. People always tell you things like that. He said something about beating me up with one arm tied behind him—he'd been watching me, he said, and I was so clumsy I stepped on my own feet. Well, sometimes I do miscalculate. When you grow nine inches in a year and your feet go from nine C to twelve D, it takes a while to get everything under control again.

Of course he didn't know anything about me either. He'd just moved to town.

His name is Henry.

What happened was that he—his whole family—followed her over here.

The reason Roseanne's folks moved here in the first place was that the company her dad worked for sent him to open a new plant. And Henry—the one who was so crazy about her, the one she was "just friends with" now—his dad worked for the same company, and six months later when the plant got revved up, he was transferred, too.

These are some questions I don't know the answers to: Had they been writing to each other? Maybe talking on the phone? Did he know about me? Were they really just friends now? Does Roseanne even care about me at all? Would she have left me and gone back to Birmingham and him if she could have?

Anyhow, his first day in school he heard about me. He told somebody that he knew her, that they came from the same town, that they'd been tight (this is the way I heard it) and the other guy said, "Yeah, well, she's Charles's girl now." And he said, "Who's Charles?" And when the guy points me out, he looks at me for a while and then he says, "That clumsy big-footed sucker? I don't believe it." And in about three days it went from there to I could murder him with one hand tied behind me. All without our ever saying hello or fuck you.

Where was Roseanne? She could have settled the whole thing with a word.

She had the flu, that's where she was. Or something. Anyhow she stayed out of school all that week.

Every day on the country music station I hear songs about how you can love two people at the same time, not be able to choose between them. Maybe that's what gave her the flu.

So inside a week it gets to the place where he's said so many things at school I can't let another one pass by. It's not that I was thinking maybe she cared about him instead of me. I didn't. I thought she was sick. And she was. Maybe she was. But at some point you know if you let a guy say one more thing like he'd been saying about me, you're going to be in trouble. You're going to lose it—everything you've fought to prove.

I held back as long as I could and then one day after school I waited for him and he knew I was waiting for him and we went out back of the gym where there's a storage building that cuts off the view of the street—a place where you can fight without anybody seeing you—me and three or four friends of mine and him and a couple of the guys he'd been talking to—he hadn't had time to make any friends yet.

I suppose I was half mad and half sad already. What's he thinking? He must be thinking Roseanne is going back to him. He *must*. All he's got to do, he's thinking, is show me up and humiliate me. And what am I thinking? I'm thinking he's made it pretty clear how tight he and Roseanne were in Birmingham and that he's expecting to move back in. And also I'm thinking that the last two days she wouldn't talk to me when I called her. Once her mama said she was asleep and the other time she said her fever had gone up and she felt too bad to talk. That didn't get it. She could talk, for Christ's sake. She wasn't in a coma.

He came at me without saying a word. I looked at him and my arms felt like they'd gotten almost too heavy to lift, like I didn't want to hit him.

To begin with, he was a good bit smaller than me, five-seven or five-eight, and stocky. But it wasn't that—he looked like he was strong enough and he held his fists and moved like he could handle himself. It was the look on his face. He came at me like he really did mean to kill me, to wipe me off the planet—or anyway, out of his mind—forever. His face had that tight look that makes you know somebody is feeling the prickly beginning of tears in the back of their nose and behind their eyes, and a rock in the bone at the top of their throat.

How do you see pure hatred in somebody's eyes? You read in a story that somebody's eyes "twinkled" or "shone with desire" or "glinted with rage." I never have seen anybody's eyes twinkle or glint. But I knew from his eyes that he hated me. He was keeping his face blank because if he didn't he'd start crying, but he hated me so much he couldn't even blink. He just stared at me like a crazy person and came at me.

I'd had a plan for the fight from the beginning. I've got these long arms now and big hands as well as big feet and I figured I could just hold him off. Make an ass of him by keeping him from hitting me. After everything he'd said about beating me with one arm tied behind him, why not put one hand in my pocket and show him who can fight one-handed? I've already said I've been fighting ever since I was in first grade. The truth is, it hasn't all been just crazy, show-off, or mad fights, or self-defense. I went out for golden gloves one year and picked up a few pointers. I figured I could keep out of his way and teach him not to mess with me.

But it didn't turn out the way I thought it would.

I had my left hand in my pocket and when he came at me the first time I put my right hand against his chest and gave him a shove and said something like, "You want to see who can fight with one hand tied behind him?" and he didn't seem to hear me or feel the shove, he just came in again, flailing, and said, "Roseanne."

"Man, you're tough," I said, "but tough don't necessarily get it."

And he came at me again and that time he got past my arm and hit me pretty good, but you could tell he didn't know how to fight worth a shit. All he knew was to keep coming and flailing, so it wasn't any trouble to stay out of his way.

I hit him a couple of times—now his nose is bleeding and his lip is cut a little bit. So maybe he's ready to quit.

"Look, man," I said, "I'm too big to be fighting you. Let's quit. Okay?" Unfortunately I dropped my guard when I was saying that and he came plowing in and the next thing I know he's kneed me in the balls and I'm doubled up rolling around on the ground.

Jesus Christ! That motherfucker kneed me in the balls. I was goddamn near paralyzed. And then he's all over me, on top of me, straddling me, pounding at my ears and my face like a maniac, and my mouth and eyes are full of dirt, but I'm hurting so bad I hardly even know it.

Somebody dragged him off and said, "Hey, man, you kneed him in the balls." And it took two of them to hold him until I got myself together and stood up, and then they let him go and he came at me again.

I wasn't feeling so cool by now, as you can imagine, and I didn't put my hand back in my pocket after that.

I hit him as hard as I could in the belly and he didn't seem to feel it, just came at me, and said, "Roseanne," one more time and the water began to pour out of his eyes and he was crying and trying to kill me at the same time. He grabbed me by the arm where I was holding him off and for a minute, for Christ's sake, I thought he was going to bite me.

That's when the heaviness in my arms got heavier. My hands were as heavy as bricks and I tasted dirt and blood in my mouth and something was floating into my mind and I dropped my hands and he hit me in the face and in the belly, but he couldn't knock me down. And it was almost like I forgot about him, and instead I was watching one of those stick and mud and rock dams—the kind you build across a creek when you're a kid—and I saw it break up and wash away, and I let him hit me again and then again. And afterwards I just turned around and walked off and old Henry was still coming after me and he got me pretty good in the kidney, but a couple of the guys grabbed him and held him and later they told me they picked up a hose by the outside hydrant there and hosed him down and then he left, too.

III

My Uncle Alan and his girlfriend Betsy came to visit us the year I was five. They came again later, of course, and I'm sure they'd come before, but the memory is from the time when I was five. They spent three weeks with us and all that time she loved me—not like I was her kid—not that kind of grumpy bored love like your mother's, the surface part of something so powerful it scares you, but another kind. Maybe, I think, now that I've started thinking about it, remembering it, maybe it's the kind a woman has for a kid who's not hers, when she wants a kid real bad and doesn't have one and no prospect of having one any time soon.

Because they weren't married, and they didn't get married for two years after that, and she wasn't young—at twenty-eight or twenty-nine, probably. I remember later when they finally got married hearing my mother say, "Well, I hope they go on and have a kid. Betsy's getting along, and God knows she's wanted one long enough."

I've asked myself what I was thinking when they were with us that summer. But you can't go back to what you thought and how you thought when you were five and time was just starting to tick and people beginning to be separate from you. You felt and saw and smelled, you felt pain, but if you *thought* the way you did it gets buried. I see myself and remember myself, but the memories are like this: I'm sitting on the ground under a sycamore tree with long bumpy roots on each side of me and I've built a tiny little house out of curly pieces of bark. My butt is against the rough bumpiness of a root and the ground is dusty and I feel the powdery warm dust under my legs and on my fingers and I smell the air—it must be late summer because the smell is the sharp, sad smell of goldenrod. I've scraped a road in the dust leading to my bark house and I've maneuvered one of those big black carpenter ants onto my road with a stick and I'm trying to get him to go into the house I've built for him, and finally he goes in and I'm really pleased. But then another one of those big ants is crawling on my leg and I squash him with my fingers and afterwards I lick my fingers and taste the formic acid (delicious, like pickles or sour grass) and that's what the memory of being five is like—never of thoughts—or not for me, anyhow.

So I'm walking home after the fight with my arms and hands feeling heavy and my balls hurting and dust and blood in my mouth, and the memory floats up—first her face, Betsy's face, floating up in my mind like a face through water, and then her hair, the smell of her hair like the smell of the rosemary bush by the kitchen door, and colors, lavender and pale green and blue; and she's sitting on the side of my bed telling me a story and knitting and the colors are the skeins of yarn around her—she's making something soft and stripy in those colors—and it's after bedtime and she leans over me and kisses me good-night and I'm pressed against her, feeling the softness of her.

And then it's daytime. I'm out in the yard by the driveway and my Uncle Alan and Betsy are loading the car getting ready to leave and my dad is helping them and I see the suitcases going into the car and a box packed with jelly and pickles she and Mama have been making and Uncle Alan's fly rod and the basket full of yarn and knitting needles. Everything is vanishing into the trunk of the car and then the lid is slammed down and there is nothing of theirs—of hers—left in our house, just as there was nothing of hers before they came. And then she's kneeling down beside me in the grass with her arms around me saying, "Good-bye, Charles. Are you coming to see us next year? Next summer?" I hear her voice, as soft as silk and her long hair is falling around my face and shoulders, smelling like grass and like rosemary and my face is against her and her arms are around me, holding me. She loves *me, me*. But her clothes and her knitting basket and the blue and lavender yarn are in the trunk of the car and the lid has slammed and she is saying good-bye, as if she can abandon me and I can go back to being the same one I was before she came.

And Uncle Alan is saying good-bye, too, and his hand is on my head and then his hand is under her arm making her stand up and leave me and I look at him and see the sadness on his face, but the other thing, too, that I put down earlier—the detachment or knowledge or whatever it is. And Betsy is crying, and she gets in the car and he pushes the lock button down and shuts the door and shuts her away from me and starts around to the other side.

I go after him and he's huge. I'm hitting him as hard as I can on the legs, reaching up, trying to hit him where I know how bad it hurts, and to climb up his legs so I can hit him in the face and choke him and bite him and kill him.

And then he has put me aside and he's in the car and I feel my father's arms holding me and I'm trying to pull free. I hear his voice very low and deep: Charles! Charles! They'll be back, son. Don't cry. They'll be back. The engine starts and the car begins to roll, slow and then faster, and dust spurts out from behind the wheels and gets in my mouth, and then she's gone.

She's gone, Henry. The blue and green and lavender yarn, the hair that smells like rosemary, the breasts as soft as down. Hit me again, if you want to, but it won't help. Still, she's gone. And you and I, Henry—we can't go back to being the ones we were before she came.

SHELBY FOOTE

 The Sacred Mound

Province of Mississippi, A.D. 1797
Number 262: CRIMINAL

Against the Indian, Chisahahoma (John Postoak) *of the
Choctaws, self-accused of the grisly murders of* Lancelot
Fink *and*_____Tyree (*or* Tyree_____) 1796.
Master Fiscal Judge, Mr John the Baptist of Elquezable,
Lieutenant Colonel and Governor.

Scrivener,
Andrew Benito Courbiere.

DECLARATION: HEREIN SWORN & SUBSCRIBED. In the town of
Natchez and garrison of St Iago, on the 23d day of September, 1797,
I, Mr John the Baptist of Elquezable, Lieutenant Colonel of Cavalry
and Provisional Governor of this said Province of Mississippi, proceeded to the house Royal of said town (accompanied from the first
by Lieutenant Francisco Amangual and Ensign Joseph of Silva, both

of the company of my office, as witnesses in the present procedure) where I found the prisoner Chisahahoma, a young man of the color of dusky copper, smallpox pitted, with hair cut straight along his forehead and falling lank to his shoulders at the back, who having been commanded to appear in my presence and in that of the said witnesses, before them had put to him by me the following interrogatories:

Question. What is he called, of what country is he a native, and what religion he professes? Answered that he is called Chisahahoma, that he is native to a region six sleeps north and also on the river, and that he is a Roman Catholic these nine months since the turning of the year. *Q.* Is he sufficiently acquainted with the Spanish language, or if he needs an interpreter to explain his declaration? Answered that he understood the language after a fashion and that if he doubted any question he would call for the advice of the interpreter. *Q.* If he would promise by our Lord God and the sign of the Cross to speak the truth concerning these interrogations? Answered that he would promise and swear, and did. And spoke as follows, making first the sign of the Cross and kissed his thumbnail:

Lo: truth attend his words, the love of God attend our understanding: all men are brothers. He has long wanted to cleanse his breast of the matter herein related, and has done so twice: first to the priest, as shall be told, then to the sergeant, answering his heart as advised by the priest, and now to myself makes thrice. His people and my people have lived in enmity since the time of the man Soto (so he called him, of glorious memory in the annals of Spain: Hernando de Soto) who came in his forefathers' time, appearing in May two sleeps to the north, he and his men wild-looking and hairy, wearing garments of straw and the skins of animals under their armor; who, having looked on the river, crossed westward and was gone twelve moons, and reappeared (in May again) three sleeps to the south, his face gray and wasted to the bone; and died there, and was buried in the river.

Desecration! his forefathers cried. Pollution!

So they fought: the strangers in armor, man and horse looking out through slits in the steel—of which he says rusty fragments survive in the long-house to commemorate the battle where the Spaniards (he says) wore blisters on their palms with excess of killing—swinging their swords and lances wearily and standing in blood to the rowels of their spurs: and at last retreated, marched away to the south, and were seen no more.

Then all was quiet; the young ones might have believed their fathers dreamed it, except for the rusting bits of armor and the horse skulls raised on poles in the long-house yard. Then came other white men in canoes, wearing not steel but robes of black with ropes about their waists, and bearing their slain god on a cross of sticks, whose blood ran down from a gash in his side: saying, Bow down; worship; your gods are false; This is the true God! and sang strange songs, swinging utensils that sprinkled and smoked, and partook of the wafer and a thin blood-colored liquid hot to the throat; then went away. But the Choctaws kept their gods, saying: How should we forsake the one that made us of spit and straw and a dry handful of dust and sent us here out of Nanih Waiya? How should we exchange Him for one who let himself be stretched on sticks with nails through the palms of his hands and feet, a headdress of thorns, pain in his face, and a spear-point gash in his side where the life ran out?

Q. Was he here to blaspheme?—for his eyes rolled back showing only the whites and he chanted singsong fashion. Answered nay, he but told it as it was in the dark time; he was the Singer, as all his fathers had been. And continued:

Then came others down the years, also in boats—all came by the river since Soto's time—but bearing neither the arquebus nor the Cross: bringing goods to trade, beads of colored stuff and printed cloth and magic circles no bigger than the inside of a hand, where sunlight flashed and a man could see himself as in unspillable water; for which, all these, the traders sought only the skins of animals in return. Now of all the creatures of the field, only certain ones were worthy of being hunted by a man: the bear, the deer, the broad-wing turkey— the rest were left for boys. Yet the traders prized highest the pelt of a creature not even a boy would hunt: the beaver: and this caused his people to feel a certain contempt. Lo, too, these strangers placed an undue value on women, for they would force or woo a man's wife and lie with her, not asking the husband's permission or agreeing before-hand on a price or an exchange, and though they were liberal with their gifts when the thing was done, there began to be not only con-tempt but also hard feelings in the breasts of his people.

So much was legend: he but told it as his father before him told it, having it from the father before him, and so on back. Yet what follows, he says, he saw with his own eyes and heard with his ears; God be his witness. And continued, no longer with his eyes rolled, speaking singsong, but as one who saw and heard and now reported (making once more, in attest of truth, the Cross upon his breastbone):

Two summers back, in the late heat of the year, spokesmen arrived from many sleeps to the south, near the great salt river. Three they were, the sons of chiefs, tall men sound of wind and limb, sent forth by their fathers, saying: We have a thing to impart. Will our brothers hear? That night they rested and were feasted in the long-house, and runners went out to bring in the chiefs. Next day as the sun went bleeding beyond the river all assembled on the sacred mound, the leaders and the singers (himself being one) and the three came forward, lean with travel, clean-favored and handsome in feathers and paint, upright as became the sons of chiefs, and the tallest spoke. It is transcribed.

—Brothers: peace. We bring a message and a warning. May you hear and heed and so be served. The white ones speak with forked tongues, no matter what crown they claim their great chief wears beyond the sea. We bring a warning of calamity. It will be with you as it was with us, for they will do as they have done. Thus. First they came boasting of their gods and seeking a yellow metal in their various languages: Or, they call it, or Oro. Then, in guile, they exchanged valuables for the worthless pelts of animals, calling us Brother, and we believed and answered likewise, Brother. And they lived among us and shared our pipe and all was well between us. So we thought.

—Then, lo, they began to ask a strange thing of us, seeking to buy the land. Sell us the land, they said: Sell us the land. And we told them, disguising our horror: No man owns the land; take and live on it; it is lent you for your lifetime; are we not brothers? And they appeared satisfied. They put up houses of plank and iron, like their ships, and sent back for their women. Soon they were many; the bear and the deer were gone (—they had seen and known in their hearts, without words; but we, being men with words, were blind) and the white men sent forth laws and set up courts, saying This shalt thou do and This shalt thou not do, and punishment followed hard upon offense, both the whip and the branding iron and often the rope. And we said, Can this be? Are we not brothers, to dwell in one land? And they answered, Yea: but this is Law.

—Nor was it long till the decree came forth, in signs on paper nailed to the walls of houses and even on trees, and the chiefs were called into the courts to hear it read. Go forth, the judges read: Go forth from the land, you and your people, into the north or beyond the river; for this land now is ours. And our fathers spoke, no longer trying to disguise the horror: How can this be? Are we not brothers? How can we leave this land, who were sent here out of Nanih Waiya to dwell in it forever down through time? And they answered, Howsomever.

—So it was and is with us, for our people are collecting their goods and preparing for the journey out. So too will it be with you. And soon; for this was all in our own time, and we are young.

I have spoken, the tallest said, and rejoined the circle. The chiefs sat smoking. Then another of the young men spoke, asking permission to retire to the long-house to sleep, for they had far to go tomorrow. And it was granted; they left, all three; and still the chiefs sat smoking.

The moon rose late, red and full to the rear of where the chiefs sat passing the pipe from hand to hand. But no one spoke, neither the chiefs on the mound nor the people below, their faces back-tilted, looking up. Then one did speak—Loshumitubbe, the oldest chief, with the hawk beak and thin gray hair that his ears showed through, a great killer in his day, and lines in his face like earth where rain has run: saying, Yea, the moon be my witness; we have offended, we have strayed. This is not the cunning of the white man. This is anger from the gods. They want it as it was in the old time.

So saying, he made a quick, downward motion with the pipe; it might have been a hatchet or a knife. Some among them understood, the older chiefs and the singers—he being one—and nodded their heads, saying Yea, or smoked in silence. And down at the base of the mound the people waited, faces pale in the moonlight, looking up. After a term the chiefs spoke in turn, grave-faced, drawing out the words, some for and some against. By morning it was decided; they came down off the mound with their minds made up.

Runners were sent one sleep to the north: five they were, strung out along the river bank, a hard run apart. Three weeks the people waited.

It was cold and then it faired, the air hazy, leaves bright red and yellow though not yet brown; it was nearing the time of the corn dance, when a man's heart should rejoice for the fruits of the earth. And the people said to one another behind their hands, Can this thing be? (for such had not been done since far before the time of the man Soto; not even in that hard time, he says, was such a thing considered) but others answered, not behind their hands but openly, proud to have gone back: Yea, can and shall: Loshumitubbe says it.

Then came one running, the nearest of the five posted along the river bank, running with his legs unstrung, and knelt before Loshumitubbe, unable to speak but holding up two fingers. Then he could speak, panting the words between breaths: Two come by water. Trappers, O chief. In buckskin.

Here was a halt, the dinner hour being come. Next morning, again at the house Royal, immediately I, the said Governor, together with the aforesaid witnesses of my company, commanded to appear before me Chisahahoma, whom I found a prisoner in the care of the guard as before and still in bonds, who once more subscribed and swore the oath and resumed as follows, confronting the witnesses and Benito Courbiere, scrivener:

That night in the long-house they played the drum and painted, himself among them. Next morning they waited in the willows down at the river bank, again himself among them. For a long time, nothing. The sun went past the overhead; they waited. Then two together pointed, raising each an arm: Lo: for the trappers were rounding the bend in a canoe. Still they waited, knee-deep in the water, screened by willows, watching. The trappers held near to bank, seeking signs of game—one tall and slim; he sat in the stern, and the other short and fat; he was the older. They wondered if they could catch them, for his people had only dugouts: when suddenly the man in the bow stopped paddling. Lance! he shouted, and pointed directly at the willow clump. So he and his people bent their backs to launch out in pursuit. But the one in the stern changed sides with his paddle and the canoe swung crossways to the current, approaching. A sign from the gods, his people thought; their hearts grew big with elation. And when the two were within arm's length they took them so quickly they had not even time to reach for their rifles. Truly a sign from the gods! his people cried, and some began to leap and scream, squeezing their throats with their hands to make it shriller.

So the two were bound at the water's edge and brought up to the town, walking hunched for their wrists were strapped with rawhide at the crotch, one hand coming through from the rear and one from the front so they could not stand upright, though the tall one almost could; his arms were long. They were marched the length of the street, the smell of fear coming strong off the short one. Bent forward—his arms were short, his belly large—he turned his head this way and that, watching the gestures of the women hopping alongside, the potbellied children staring round-eyed, and skipped to save his ankles from the dogs; twice he fell and had to be lifted from the dust. The tall one, however, kept his eyes to the front. The dogs did not snap at him, for even bound he was half a head taller than any Indian.

Hi! the women shouted: Hi! A brave! and made gestures of obscenity, fanning their skirts. Hi! Hi!

The chiefs sat in the council room, wearing feathers and paint in gaudy bars, and the two were brought before them. Now they looked at each other, chiefs and trappers, and no one spoke. Then Loshumitubbe made a gesture, the hand palm down, pushing downward, and they were taken to the pit room at the far end of the long-house. It was dark in there, no fire; the only light was what fell through the paling disk of the smoke hole. The cries of the women came shrill through the roof, mixed with the yapping of dogs. The time wore on. From outside, he says, they began to hear the short one weeping, asking questions in his language, but the tall one only cursed him, once then twice, and then ignored him.

So it was: they on the outside, waiting for the moon to fill, knowing: the trappers on the inside, in the pit, waiting but not knowing. Seven suns they were in there, feeding like hogs on broken bits of food flung through the smoke hole—for they remained bound, the rawhide shrinking on their wrists, and had to grovel for it. They fouled themselves and were gutsick on the scraps, he says, and the stench was so great that the women approaching the hole to taunt them held their noses and made squealing sounds. From outside, listening, his people heard words in the strange language: at first only the short one, calling the other Fink or Lance and sometimes Lancelot: then later, toward the close, the tall one too, calling the short one Tyree, though which of his two names this was no man could say, not even now, for they were Americans, a people whose names are sometimes indistinguishable, the last from the first, since they name not necessarily for the saints. At the end, however, they called to one another not by name but by growls, for the food was scant and hard to find on the dark earth floor; they fought for it like dogs, snapping their teeth, still being bound.

Then, lo, the moon would be full that night. Long before sundown the people were painted and ready, dressed as for the corn dance. The young ones wore only breech clouts and feathers, fierce with red and yellow bars of paint, but the older ones brought out blankets rancid with last year's grease and sweat. The cold had returned; the leaves were brown now, falling, and they crackled underfoot. It was yet above freezing, he says, and there was no wind, but the cold was steady and bitter and sharp and a thick mist came rolling off the river.

The trappers were taken from the pit as soon as the sun was gone. Their clothes were cut from their bodies and they were sluiced with hot water to cleanse them of their filth; they stood in only their boots and bonds, their hands purple and puffy because the rawhide had shrunk on their wrists, their skin first pink from the heat of the water, then pale gray, goose-fleshed, and their teeth chattered behind their bluing lips. Then was when they saw that the short one was covered with what appeared to be louse bites, small hard red welts like pimples. The time in the pit had changed them indeed, and not only in appearance. For now it was the tall one who kept glancing about, shifting his eyes this way and that, while the short one stood looking down over his belly at his boots; he did not care. Just as the tall one had used up his courage, so had the short one exhausted his cowardice. Then at a signal the guards took hold of their arms and they went toward the mound, stepping stiff-kneed. The old men with blankets over their shoulders walked alongside. The young men, wearing only feathers and breech clouts, leaped and shouted, their breaths making steam.

Atop the mound the chiefs were waiting, seated in a half circle with a bonfire burning behind them for light. They faced the stakes. One was a single pole with a rawhide thong up high; the other was two low poles with a third lashed as a crosspiece at the height of a man's waist. Then the trappers were brought. From the flat top of the mound, he says, they could see torches burning in the lower darkness, spangling the earth, countless as stars, for the people had come from three sleeps around; they stood holding torches, looking up to where the bonfire burned against the night. The tall trapper was tied to the single stake, arms overhead, hands crossed so high that only the toes of his boots touched the earth—the tallest man they had ever seen, taller than ever, now, with skin as pale in the firelight as the underbark of sycamores in spring. The short trapper stood between the two low stakes, his wrists lashed to the crossbar on each side of his waist. Both were breathing fast little jets of steam, partly from having climbed the mound but mostly from fear; for now, he says, they knew at least a part of what they had been wondering all that long time in the darkness of the pit.

The moon rose, swollen golden red, and now the dancing began, the young men stepping pigeon-toed, shuffling dust, and Otumatomba the rainmaker stood by the fire with his knife. When the dancing was done he came forward, extending the knife flat on the palms of both hands, and Loshumitubbe touched it. The drums began. Then Otumatomba came slowly toward the short one, who was held by four of the dancers, two at the knees and two at the shoulders, bent backward over the crosspole. He did not struggle or cry out; he looked down his chest, past the jut of his belly, watching the knife. What follows happened so fast, he says, that afterwards looking back it seemed to have been done in the flick of an eye.

Otumatomba placed the point of the knife, then suddenly leaned against the handle and drew it swiftly across, a long deep slash just under the last left rib. So quick the eye could barely follow, his hand went in. The knife fell and the hand came out with the heart. It was meaty and red, the size of a fist, with streaks of yellow fat showing through the skin-sack; vessels dangled, collapsed and dripping, except the one at the top, which was dingy white, the thickness of a thumb, leading back through the lips of the gash. Then (there was no signal, he says; they knew what to do, for Otumatomba had taught them) the men at the shoulders pushed forward, bringing the trapper upright off the bar, and for a moment he stood looking down at his heart, which Otumatomba held in front of his chest for him to see. It did not pulse; it flickered, the skin-sack catching highlights from the fire, and it smoked a bit in the night air. That was all. The short one fell, collapsing; he hung with his face just clear of the ground, his wrists still tied to the crosspole.

Hi! a brave, he heard one say among the chiefs.

But that was all; the rest were quiet as the rainmaker took up the knife again and turned toward the tall one, lashed on tiptoe to the stake. As he drew closer the trapper began to swing from side to side, bound overhead at the wrists and down at the ankles. When Otumatomba was very near, the tall white naked man began to shout at him in his language: No! No! swinging from side to side and shouting hoarsely, until the rainmaker, with a sudden, darting motion like the strike of a snake, shot out one hand and caught hold: whereupon the trapper stopped swinging and shouted still more shrilly, like women in the long-house at the death of a chief, in the final moment before the cutting began. While Otumatomba sawed with the knife, which seemed duller now and slippery with the blood of the other, the tall one was screaming, hysterical like a woman in labor, repeating a rising note: Ee! Eee! Then he stopped. He stopped quite suddenly. Otumatomba stepped back and tossed the trapper's manhood at his feet. The trapper looked down—more than pain, his face showed grief, bereavement—and now he began to whimper. Blood ran down his thighs, curving over the inward bulge of his knees, and filled his boots. He was a long time dying and he died badly, still crying for mercy when he was far beyond it.

Again the young men danced. The moon sailed higher, silver now, flooding the mound. In the distance the river glided slow, bright silver too, making its two great curves. Then it was over; the dead were left to the bone-pickers. The chiefs rose, filing down the mound, and he heard Loshumitubbe say to one beside him:

This will stop them. This will make an end.

Yea, the other told him. This will stop them.

But some there were—himself among them: so he says—who shook their heads, now it was done and they had seen, asking themselves in their hearts: Were they savages, barbarians, to come to this?

Here was a halt, the hour being noon, and after the midday meal and the siesta we returned to the house Royal: I the Governor, together with the aforesaid witnesses and scrivener: before whom the prisoner

Chisahahoma, in care of the guard, swore and subscribed and continued, making an end:

Sudden and terrible then came the curse on his people, the wrath of God. The moon was barely on the wane and they felt pain in their heads, their backs, their loins; their skin was hot and dry to the touch; dark spots appeared on their foreheads and scalps, among the roots of hair. The spots became hard-cored blisters; the burning cooled for a day and then returned, far worse, and the blisters (so he called them: meaning *pustules*) softened and there was a terrible itching. Some scratched so hard with their nails and fishbone combs that their faces and bodies were raw. Many died. First went Otumatomba the rain-maker, then Loshumitubbe chief of chiefs, he who had given the signal; men and women and children, so fast they died the bone-pickers had not time to scaffold them. They lay in the houses and in the street, self-mutilated, begging the god for sudden death, release from the fever and itching.

He himself was sick with the sickest, and thought to have died and wished for it; he too lay and hoped for death, but was spared with only this (passing his hand across his face) to show the journey he had gone. Then he lay recovering, the moon swelling once more toward the full. And he remembered the short trapper, the marks on his face and body when they brought him out of the pit, and he knew.

Then he was up, recovered though still weak, and was called before Issatiwamba, chief of chiefs now Loshumitubbe was dead. He too had been the journey; he too remembered the marks on the short trapper. The people still lay dying, the dead unscaffolded.

O chief, he said, and made his bow, and Issatiwamba said:

I have called; are you not the singer? This is the curse of the white man's god, and you must go a journey.

He left next morning, taking the trappers' canoe. Cold it was, approaching the turning of the year, with ice among the willows and overhead a sky the color of a dove's breast. He wore a bearskin and paddled fast to keep from freezing. The second day he reached the Walnut Hills, where the white man had a town, and went ashore. But there was no house for the white man's god; he was in the canoe, continuing downriver, before sunset. The fifth day he reached this place and came ashore, and here was the house of the white man's god and lo! the God himself as he had heard it told and sung, outstretched and sagging, nailed to the wall and wearing a crown of thorns and the wound in his side and pain in his face that distorted his mouth so you saw the edges of the teeth. And he stood looking, wrapped in the bear-skin.

Then came one in a robe of cloth, a man who spoke with words he could not understand. He made a sign to show he would speak, and the priest beckoned: Come, and he followed to the back of the house and through a door, and—lo again, a thing he had never seen be-fore—here was an Indian wearing trousers and a shirt, one of the flatheads of the South, who acted as interpreter.

The priest listened while he told it as Issatiwamba had instructed. The Indians had killed in the Indian way, incurring the wrath of the white man's god; now was he sent for the white men to kill in the white man's way, thus to appease the god and lay the plague. So he told it, as instructed. The flathead interpreted, and when it was done the priest beckoned as before: *Come,* and led the way through another door. He followed, expecting this to be the pit where he would wait. But lo, the priest put food before him: *Eat,* and he ate. Then he fol-lowed through yet another door, thinking now surely this would be the pit. But lo again, it was a small room with a cot and blankets, and the priest put his hands together, palm to palm, and laid his cheek against the back of one: *Sleep.* And he slept, still expecting the pit.

When he woke it was morning; he knew not where he was. The pit! he thought. Then he remembered and turned on his side, and the flathead stood in the doorway with a bucket in one hand, steaming, and soap and a cloth in the other. First he declined; it was winter, he said, no time to scrape away the crust. But the other said thus it must be, and when he had washed he led him to the room where he had eaten. He ate again, then followed the other to still a third room where the priest was waiting, and there again on the wall the god was hung, this time in ivory with the blood in bright red droplets like fruit of the holly. The three sat at table; the priest talked and the flathead interpreted, and all this time the god watched from the wall. Here began his conversion, he says, making yet again the sign of the Cross upon his person.

He heard of the Trinity, the creation, the Garden, the loss of inno-cence, and much else which he could not follow. When the priest later questioned him of what he had heard he found that he had not heard aright, for the priest had said there were three gods and one god; did that not make four? And the priest at first was angry: then he smiled. They had best go slow, he said, and began again, telling now of the Man-God, the redeemer, who died on the cross of sticks but would return. There was where he began to understand, for just as the Garden had been like Nanih Waiya, this was like the Corn God, who laid him down to rise again; perhaps they were cousins, the two gods. But the priest said no, not cousins, not cousins at all; and began again, in soft tones and with patience, not in anger. In time they needed the interpreter no more, for he believed and the words came to him; he understood; Christ Jesus had reached him, Whose strength was in His gentleness, Whose beginning was in His end. Winter was past, and spring came on, and summer, and he was shrived and christened. His name was John; John Postoak, for Postoak was the translation of his name.

Then, being converted, he called to mind the instructions of Issati-wamba; a duty was a duty, whether to tribe or to church. So he asked the priest, kneeling at confession: must he go to the authorities? For a time the priest said nothing, sitting in the box with the odor of incense coming off him, the smell of holiness, and he who now was called Postoak watching through the panel. Then he said, calling him now as always My Son, that was a matter to be decided within himself, between his heart and his head. And he said as before, Bless me, father: knowing. And the priest put forth his hand and blessed him, making the sign of the Cross above his head, for the priest knew well what would follow when he went before the authorities and told what he had told the day when the priest first found him in the bearskin, outside the church where Christ hung on the wall.

He went then to the sergeant of the guard, Delgado, and standing there told it in Spanish, what had been done on the mound and how and his share in the thing, and offered himself this second time, as instructed by Issatiwamba, not to lay the plague, however, but rather to lay the guilt in his own breast. Delgado heard him through, listening with outrage in his face, and when it was done gave orders in a voice that rang like brass. Then was he in the pit indeed, with iron at his wrists and ankles. He dwelt in darkness, how many days he knew not; the year moved into September, the hottest weather; and then came forth under guard to face ourselves, Governor and witnesses, in the formalities which ensued and here have been transcribed even as he spoke, including whatever barbarisms, all his own. So it was and here he stands, having told it this third time: God be his witness.

Q. If he had anything to add or take from this deposition, it having been read to him. Answered that he has nothing to add or take, and that what he has said is the truth under the obligation of the oath he took at the outset, which he affirms and certifies and says he is twenty-four years old, and he subscribes with me and the witnesses over the citation I certify:

Witnessed:	*he signs this*	John the Baptist
Joseph of Silva	Chisa- **X** -hahoma	of Elquezable
Frsco Amangual	HIS MARK	Lt Col Governor

DISPOSITION: BY THE GOVERNOR. In the said Garrison this September 27th 1797 without delay I, Mr John the Baptist of Elquezable, Lieutenant Colonel of Cavalry of the Royal Army, Provisional Governor of the Province of Mississippi, in view of finding the conclusion of the present proceedings, commanded that the original fifteen useful leaves be directed to the Lord Commanding General, Marshal of the Country, Sir Peter de Narva, that they may serve to inform him in reviewing my disposition (tendered subject to his agreeing in the name of His Most Christian Majesty) to wit:

Free him.

First: in that he has renounced his former worship which led him to participate in these atrocities, and intends now therefore (I am assured by the priest, Friar Joseph Manuel Gaetan) to serve as a missionary among his heathen people. Second: in that we are even now preparing to depart this barbarous land, being under orders to leave it to them of the North. And third, lastly: in that the victims were neither of our Nation nor our Faith.

For which I sign with my present scrivener:

J the B	*A Benito*
of El	*Courbiere.*

GEORGE GARRETT

# Feeling Good, Feeling Fine

A boy and a man in the park. Between them an old wooden bat, a battered and dirty baseball and one leather glove, well tended and cared for, oiled and supple, but old, too, its pocket as thin as paper.

The boy and the man are sweating in the late afternoon light. Lazy end of a long summer day. The park (no more than a rough grass field, really) is empty now except for the two of them. Somewhere not far away a car horn toots, a dog barks, a woman calls her children in for supper.

"Come on," the man shouts. "Knock it to me!"

The boy carefully, all concentration, tosses the ball up and swings the bat to loft it high above the man. Who, skinny and raggedy as a scarecrow, moves gracefully back and away and underneath the high fly ball. Spears it deftly with the glove. Then throws it high and easy back toward the boy. The ball rolls dead an easy reach from his feet. "Let's quit and go home," the boy calls.

The tall thin man shakes his head and moves back deeper.

"One more," he hollers. "Just one more."

Crack of the bat on the ball and this is the best one yet. A homerun ball high in the fading light, almost lost in the last blue of the sky. The man shading his eyes as he runs smoothly and swiftly back and back until he's there where he has to be to snag it. Snags it.

Then comes running in toward the boy, hugely grinning, a loping fielder who has made the final catch of an inning.

You might think the boy would be pleased to have swung his bat (the glove and the bat and the ball are his) that well and knocked the ball so high and far. But truth is the boy hates baseball. "It's my least favorite sport," he will tell anyone who asks. Anyone except the man running toward him, his uncle, his mother's brother, who has recently come to live with them after several years at the state hospital.

Uncle Jack, he's had a hard time of it. First time he went crazy, his wife ran off with their two daughters, the boy's cousins, to California or some place like that and disappeared for keeps. Boy doesn't know it, can't comprehend it even if he could imagine it, but he won't ever see that woman and his two cousins again. Uncle Jack is living with them for the time being, "until he has a chance to get things straightened out," the boy's father explains. When the boy complains about the hours spent—wasted as far as he's concerned—knocking fungoes and chasing flys and grounders with Uncle Jack, his father simply says: "Humor him, boy. He's good at it. Let him be."

He ain't that good, the boy sometimes thinks but doesn't say. Said it once, though, and his father corrected him.

"Listen, boy, he's rusty and he hasn't been well. But believe me, I'm here to tell you, he was some kind of a baseball player. A real pleasure to watch."

"Minor league," the boy said scornfully. Who can't imagine anyone settling for anything less than the top of the heap. If he liked baseball enough to want to play at it, he would be in the majors or nothing. He sure enough wouldn't be happy with some old photographs in an album and some frail, yellowing newspaper clippings.

And if he was a crazy old man back from the state hospital and had a nephew who was required to humor him, the boy would never pretend, let alone believe for one minute that he was getting himself back in shape so he could join the New York Yankees or the Washington

Senators or somebody like that. Shit, Uncle Jack couldn't even play for the Brooklyn Dodgers.

Uncle Jack now has the bat in one hand and the other arm around the boy's shoulders (the boy carries the glove and the ball) as the two of them slowly head for home in the twilight.

"You hit that last one just a helluva good lick," Uncle Jack says. "You could be a real hitter if you put your mind to it. It's all in the coordination and you have got that, all you could ever need."

Why, if he hates baseball, does the boy relish and rejoice in the man's words? Why, if his Uncle Jack is some kind of crazy person and is fooling himself and everybody else, too, about what a great ball-player he was and thinks he still is, why does the boy automatically accept and enjoy his uncle's judgment? Why, if his uncle is mostly embarrassment and trouble, someone to be ashamed of, does the boy at this very instant, altogether in spite of himself, wish more than anything that the tall, thin, raggedy, graceful man was and is everything he ought to be or could have been?

(Years and years later, when this boy is a grandfather himself, for reasons he won't understand then any more than he does now, he will tell his grandchildren, and anyone else who will bother to listen to him, all about his Uncle Jack who was, briefly briefly—but is not all beauty and great achievement as brief as the flare of a struck match?—a wonderful athlete, a baseball player much admired and envied by his peers, someone who, except for a piece or two of bad luck, would have been named and honored among the very best of them. Someone to be proud of. Someone who once tried to teach him how to play the game.)

They are close to home now. They have left the raw wide field behind and are coming under a dark canopy of shade. Houses with green crisp lawns, dark earth and, here and there, a sprinkler pulsing bright water. Can see the lights of the boy's house being switched on downstairs. Can hear briefly, before his father's voice calls out a crisp command, music playing loudly on the radio. That will be his sister or his little brother fooling around. Upstairs probably. They are almost close enough to see through the lighted windows of the dining room his mother and Hattie, the maid, who works late and long for them in this Great Depression, setting the supper table with flat silver, napkins and water glasses. For a little time, the short walk, more of a stroll into the gradual dark, he has been almost perfectly content. Weary, sweated out, but feeling good, feeling fine, soothed by his uncle's complimentary words. Suddenly confident that whatever he does from here and now to the end of his life will go well. Even more: that he will be able not only to enjoy this feeling of satisfaction, of joy, really, but will be able to share it with others less fortunate than himself.

What he cannot know, even as he and his uncle come across the lawn and into the house and shut the front door behind him, what he can't know and will not choose even to remember years and years later when he bitterly rakes the ashes of his life searching for even one remaining glowing coal, is what happens next.

At the table his father (who includes the whole family, even Hattie, in almost everything) will tell them about the long distance telephone call he received at his office this same afternoon from a doctor at the state hospital in Chattahoochie. The doctor has told him that there is a new kind of an operation on the brain that might, just might, cure Uncle Jack for good and all. No more coming and going, no more breakdowns and slow recoveries. It is a new thing. There can be no promises or guarantees, of course. And, as in any operation, there is always danger, there are always risks. But . . .

Everybody listens intently. (Except Hattie who elects to go back into the kitchen quietly.) Everybody listens. And then before Jack or anyone can say anything, his mother bursts into tears. Sobs at the table, trying to hide her face with her hands, her shoulders shaking.

Later that evening the boy will see his father, for the first and probably the only time, slap his mother full across her soft face, making her sob again and more as they quarrel about what may be the best thing for her brother to do. His uncle will settle the quarrel by freely and cheerfully choosing to return to the hospital to undergo this operation. And—the boy and man would warn them then and now, if there were some way, any way, if only he could—it went badly, as badly as can be, leaving his uncle no more than half alive, a vegetable, really, in that hospital for the rest of his life. The boy will live to be an old man, will go to war and live through it, will learn all the lessons—of love and death, of gain and loss, of pride and of regret—a long life can teach.

But none of this has happened yet. Man and boy have spent a long afternoon in the park together and, at the end of it, have come home. They come in the front door. Jack grabs his sister, the boy's mother, and gives her a bear hug, lifts her in the air. The boy goes to put the bat and the ball and the glove in the hall closet. Over his shoulder he hears his sister and brother coming down the stairs like a pair of wild ponies. Looking up, turning, he sees his father, smiling in shirtsleeves, coming out of the living room with the evening paper in his hands.

"Here they are," he says. "Here come our baseball players just in time for supper."

ALLAN GURGANUS

 Reassurance

For David Holding Eil (1981–)
and for Robert Langland Eil (1983–)

1.*

Death Of A Pennsylvania Soldier. Frank H. Irwin, company E, 93rd
Pennsylvania—died May 1, '65—My letter to his mother.

Dear madam: No doubt you and Frank's friends have heard the sad
fact of his death in hospital here, through his uncle, or the lady from
Baltimore, who took his things. (I have not seen them, only heard of
them visiting Frank.) I will write you a few lines—as a casual friend that
sat by his death-bed. Your son, corporal Frank H. Irwin, was wounded

* Section 1 quotes, unchanged and complete, Walt Whitman's letter titled "Death of a
Pennsylvania Soldier" from "Specimen Days"—first published in his *Complete Prose
Works* (Philadelphia, 1892), reprinted in *Whitman: The Library of America's Complete
Poetry and Collected Prose* (1982).

near fort Fisher, Virginia, March 25, 1865—the wound was in the left knee, pretty bad. He was sent up to Washington, was receiv'd in ward C, Armory-square hospital, March 28th—the wound became worse, and on the 4th of April the leg was amputated a little above the knee—the operation was perform'd by Dr. Bliss, one of the best surgeons in the army—he did the whole operation himself—there was a good deal of bad matter gather'd—the bullet was found in the knee. For a couple of weeks afterwards he was doing pretty well. I visited and sat by him frequently, as he was fond of having me. The last ten or twelve days of April, I saw that his case was critical. He previously had some fever, with cold spells. The last week in April he was much of the time flighty—but always mild and gentle. He died first of May. The actual cause of death was pyaemia, (the absorption of the matter in the system instead of its discharge). Frank, as far as I saw, had everything requisite in surgical treatment, nursing &c. He had watches much of the time. He was so good and well-behaved and affectionate, I myself liked him very much. I was in the habit of coming in afternoons and sitting by him, and soothing him, and he liked to have me—liked to put his arm out and lay his hand on my knee—would keep it so a long while. Toward the last he, was more restless and flighty at night—often fancied himself with his regiment—by his talk sometimes seem'd as if his feelings were hurt by being blamed by his officers for something he was entirely innocent of—said, "I never in my life was thought capable of such a thing, and never was." At other times he would fancy himself talking as it seem'd to children or such like, his relatives I suppose, and giving them good advice; would talk to them a long while. All the time he was out of his head not one single bad word or idea escaped him. It was remark'd that many a man's conversation in his senses was not half as good as Frank's delirium. He seem'd quite willing to die—he had become very weak and had suffer'd a good deal, and was perfectly resign'd, poor boy. I do not know his past life, but I feel as if it must have been good. At any rate what I saw of him here, under the most trying of circumstances, with a painful wound, and among strangers, I can say that he behaved so brave, so composed, and so sweet and affectionate, it could not be surpass'd. And now like many other noble and good men, after serving his country as a soldier, he has yielded up his young life at the very outset in her service. Such things are gloomy—yet there is a text, "God doeth all things well"—the meaning of which, after due time, appears to the soul.

I thought perhaps a few words, though from a stranger, about your son, from one who was with him at the last, might be worth while—for I loved the young man, though I but saw him immediately to lose him.

I am merely a friend visiting the hospitals occasionally to cheer the wounded and sick.

W.W.

2.

Dear Mother, It's Frank here, hoping a last time to reach you, and doubting I can but still I'm really going to try, ma'am. I want you to put your mind at rest about it all, Momma. That is why I am working hard to slip this through. You must really listen if this gets by the censors and everything, because I have limited time and fewer words than I'd like. I would dearly love to be there soon for breakfast and see that cussed little Wilkie come downstairs grumping like he always does till he's got a touch of coffee in him. I would even like to hear the Claxtons' roosters sounding off again. I remember Poppa, God rest him, saying as how other men kept hens for eggs but the Claxtons kept roosters for their noise and it was our ill luck to draw such fools as neighbors! The old man that wrote you of my end had the finest gray-white beard and finest-speaking voice I ever met with, finer even than parson Brookes we set such store by. The man who wrote you was here most days after lunch, even ones I now recall but parts of. He brought ward C our first lilacs in late April, great purple ones he stuck into a bedpan near my pillow. Their smell worked better on me than the laudanum that our Army chemists were so sadly out of. He read to us from Scripture and once, my hand resting on his safe-feeling leg, I asked him for a ditty and he said one out that sounded fine like Ecclesiastes but concerned our present war, my war. I told him it was good and asked him who had wrote it and he shrugged and smiled, he nodded along the double row of cots set in our tent here, like showing me that every wounded fellow'd had a hand in setting down the poem. He was so pleasing-looking and kind-spoken and affectionate, I myself liked him very much. Ice cream he brought us more than once—a bigger vat of it I've never seen, not even at the Bucks County Fair. Him and our lady nurses kept making funny jokes, bringing around the great melting buckets of it and the spoons and he himself shoveled a good bit of it into my gullet, grateful it felt all the way down. "Now for some brown." He gave me samples. "Now pink, but best for you is this, Frank. You've heard Mrs. Howe's line 'in the beauty of the lilies Christ was born across the sea'? This vanilla's that white, white as your arm here. Makes vanilla cool the deepest, my brave Pennsylvania youth." How I ate it. Cold can be good. If you hurt enough, cold can be so good. Momma? I do not love Lavinia like I forever said. I do not know how I got into being so mistruthful. Maybe it was how her poppa was Mayor and I liked the idea of pleasing you with our family's possible new station or how everybody spoke of Miss Lavinia's attainments and her skills at hostessing. It is my second cousin Emily I loved and love. She knew and knows, and it was just like Em to bide that. Em met whatever gaze I sent her with a quiet wisdom that shamed and flattered me, the both. Once at that Fourth of July picnic where the Claxtons' rowboat exploded from carrying more firecrackers than the *Merrimac* safely could, I noticed Emily near Doanes' Mill Creek gathering French lilacs for to decorate our picnic quilt later. You were bandaging Wilkie's foot where he stepped on a nail after you told him he must wear shoes among that level of fireworks but he didn't. I wandered down where Emily stood. She had a little silver pair of scissors in her skirt's pocket and I recall remarking how like our Em that was, how homely and prepared and how like you she was that way, Momma. She was clipping flowers when I drew up. I commenced shivering, that fearful of my feelings for her after everybody on earth seemed to think Lavinia had decided on me long-since. "Frank," Emily said. I spoke her name and when she heard how I said hers out, she stopped in trimming a heavy branch of white blooms (for, you know that place by the waterwheel where there are two bushes, one white, one purple, grown up side by side together and all mixed?). Emily's hands were still among the flowers when she looked back over her shoulder at me. Tears were in her eyes but not falling, just held in place and yet I saw the light on their water tremble with each pulse from her. It was then, Momma, I understood she knew my truest feelings, all.

"Why is it we're cousins and both poor?" I asked her. "Why could it not be just a little different so things'd fall into place for us more, why, Emily?" And she lifted one shoulder and turned her head aside. She half-fell into the sweet bushes then, white and green and purple, but caught herself and looked away from me. Em finally spoke but I half-heard with all the Roman candles going off and Wilkie bawling. She said quiet, looking out toward water through the beautiful branches, "We will always know, Frank, you and me will. Hearing as how you understand it, that already gives me so much, Frank. Oh, if you but guessed how it strengthens me just to say your name at night, Frank, Franklin Horatio Irwin, Jr., how I love to say it out, sir." Lavinia was calling that same name but different and I turned, fearful of being caught here by her, me unfaithful to the one that loved me if not strongest then loudest, public-like. "Excuse me, Cousin Emily," said I, and walked off and then soon after got mustered in, then snagged the minie that costs the leg then the rest of it, me, and no one knowing my real heart. Mother? I never even kissed her. Momma? Treat her right. Accord my cousin Emily such tender respects as befit the young widow of a man my age, for she is that to me, and not Lavinia that made such a show at the funeral and is ordering more styles of black crepe from a Boston catalogue even now, Momma. Have Emily to dinner often as you can afford it, and encourage her to look around at other boys, for there's not much sense in wasting two lives, mine and hers, for my own cowardly mistakes. That is one thing needs saying out.

I used to speak to my bearded visitor about brother Wilkie and all of you and I thought up things I'd tell my kid brother who has so bad a temper but is funny throughout. I'd want Wilkie to be brave and not do what the town said he should, like pay court on a girl who's snooty and bossy just because of who her kin is and their grand home. I would tell Wilkie to hide in a cave and not sign up like I did, with the bands and drums and the setting off of all fireworks not burned up in the Claxtons' calamity rowboat—but, boy, it sure did look pretty going down, didn't it, Momma? My doctor took some time and pains with me and, near the end, got like Lavinia in telling me how fine a looking young man I was. That never pleased me much since I didn't see it all that clear myself and had not personally earned it and so felt a little guilty on account, not that any of it matters now. The Lady from Baltimore combed my hair and said nice things and I am sorry that she never got the watch and the daguerrotypes to you. She is a confidence artist who makes tours of hospitals, promising to take boys' valuables home but never does and sells them in the shops. Still, at the time, I trusted her, her voice was so refined and hands real soft and brisk and I felt good for days after she left, believing Wilkie'd soon have Poppa's gold watch in hand, knowing it had been with me at the end.

Just before they shot me, Momma, I felt scared to where I considered, for one second, running. No one ever knew of this but I must tell you now because just thinking on my failing cost me many inward tribulations at the last. "I could jump out of this hole and run into that woods and hide and then take off forever." So the dreadful plan rushed forth, and then how I stifled it, choked practically. I never in my life was thought capable of even thinking such a thing, and here I'd said it to myself! Then, like as punishment, not six minutes after looking toward that peaceful-seeming woods, I moved to help another fellow from Bucks County (Ephraim's second cousin, the youngest Otis boy from out New Hope way) and felt what first seemed a earthquake that'd knocked the entire battle cockeyed but that narrowed to a nearby complaint known just as the remains of my left leg. It felt numb till twenty minutes later when I seriously noticed. It takes that kind of time sometimes to feel. It takes a delay between the ending and knowing what to say of that, which is why this reaches you six weeks after my kind male nurse's news, ma'am. I asked him once why he'd quit the newspaper business to come visit us, the gimps and bullet-catchers, us lost causes.

He leaned nearer and admitted a secret amusement: said he was, from among the thousands of Northern boys and Reb prisoners he'd seen, recasting Heaven. Infantry angels, curly-headed all. "And Frank," said he, "I don't like to tease you with the suspense but it's between you and two other fellows, a three-way heat for the Archangel Gabriel." I laughed, saying as how the others had my blessing for that job just yet. He kept close by me during the amputation part especially. They said that if the leg was taken away, then so would all my troubles go. And I trusted them, Momma. And everybody explained and was real courteous and made the person feel manly like the loss of the leg could be his choice and would I agree? "Yes," I said.

My doctor's name was Dr. Bliss and during the cutting of my leg, others kept busting into the tent, asking him stuff and telling him things and all calling him by name, Bliss, Bliss, Bliss, they said. It helped me to have that name and word drifting over the table where they worked on me so serious, and I thanked God neither you nor Emily would be walking in to see me spread out like that, so bare and held down helpless, like some boy. Afterwards, my friend the nurse trained me to pull the covers back, he taught me I must learn to look at it now. But I couldn't bear to yet. They'd tried but I had wept when asked to stare below at the lonely left knee. It'd been "left" all right! Walt (my nurse's name was Walt) he said we would do it together. He held my hand and counted then—one, two, three . . . I did so with him and it was like looking at what was there and what was not at once, just as my lost voice is finding you during this real dawn, ma'am. He told me to cheer up, that it could've been my right leg and only later did I see he meant that as a little joke and I worried I had let him down by not catching on in time. I have had bad thoughts, lustful thoughts and evil. I fear I am yet a vain person and always have been secretly, Momma. You see, I fretted how it'd be to live at home and go downtown on crutches and I knew Lavinia's plan would change with me a cripple. Lavinia would not like that. And even after everything, I didn't know if I could choose Emily, a seamstress after all, over so grand a place on Summit Avenue as the Mayor'd already promised Lavinia and me (it was the old Congers mansion, Momma).

It seems to me from here that your Frank has cared way too much for how others saw him. It was Poppa's dying early that made me want to do so much and seem so grown and that made me join up when you had your doubts, I know. You were ever strict with me but I really would've turned out all right in the end . . . if it hadn't been for this.

Momma, by late April, I could feel the bad stuff moving up from the leg's remains, like some type of chemical, a kind of night or little army set loose in me and taking all the early lights out, one by one, lamp by lamp, farm by farm, house by house it seemed. The light in my head, don't laugh, was the good crystal lantern at your oilclothed kitchen table. That was the final light I worried for—and knew, when that went, it all went. But, through chills and talking foolish some-times, I tried keeping that one going, tried keeping good parts sepa-rate, saved back whole. I felt like if I could but let you hear me one more time, it'd ease you some. Your sleeping so poorly since . . . that's just not like you, Ma, and grieves me here. Dying at my age is an em-barrassment, on top of everything else! It was just one shot in the knee, but how could I have stopped it when it started coming up the body toward the last light in the kitchen in the head? You told me not to enlist—you said, as our household's one breadwinner, I could stay home. But the braided uniform and the party that Lavinia promised tipped me over. Fevered, I imagined talking to Wilkie and all the younger cousins lined up on our front porch's seven steps, and me wagging my finger and striding to and fro in boots like our Lt.'s beautiful English leather boots, such as I never owned in life. I talked bold and I talked grand and imagined Emily was in the shady house with you, and beside you, listening, approving my sudden wisdom that'd come on me with the suffering, and on account of the intestine cramps, and after the worst convulsion Walt got me through, still that lead was coming up the thigh into my stomach then greeting and seizing the chest and then more in the throat and that was about all of it except for the great gray beard and those knowing eyes that seemed to say Yes Yes, Frank, even to my need to be done with it, the pain (the last white pain of it, I do not mind telling you, was truly something, Momma). I couldn't have held out much longer anyway, and the idea of choosing between my two loves, plus living on a crutch for life, it didn't set right with vain me.

This I am telling you should include that I hid the five-dollar gold piece I won for the History Prize at the Academy commencement up inside the hollowed left head-post of my bedstead. Get Wilkie to go upstairs with you and help lift the whole thing off the floor and out the coin will fall. Use it for you and Emily's clothes. Bonnets might be nice with it. Buy nothing but what's extra, that is how I want it spent. I should've put it in your hand before I left, but I planned to purchase my getting-home gifts out of that, and never thought I wouldn't. Selfish, keeping it squirreled back and without even guessing. But then maybe all people are vain. Maybe it's not just your Frank, right?

If you wonder at the color you are seeing now, Momma, the pink-red like our fine conch shell on the parlor's hearth, you are seeing the backs of your own eyelids, Momma. You will soon hear the Claxtons' many crowers set up their alarum yet again and will catch a clinking that is McBride's milk wagon pulled by Bess, who knows each house on old McBride's route. Your eyes are soon to open on your room's whitewash and July's yellow light in the dear place. You will wonder at this letter of a dream, ma'am and, waking, will look toward your bedside table and its often-unfolded letter from the gentleman who told you of my passing. His letter makes this one possible. For this is a letter toward your loving Franklin Horatio Irwin, Jr., not only from him. It is your voice finding ways to smoothe your mind. This is for letting you get on with what you have to tend, Momma. You've always known I felt Lavinia to be well-meaning but right silly, and that our sensible and deep Emily was truly meant as mine from her and my's childhoods onward. You've guessed where the coin is stowed, as you did ever know such things, but have held back on account of honoring the privacy even of me dead. Go fetch it later today, and later today spend it on luxuries you could not know otherwise. This is the rich echo that my bearded nurse's voice allows. It is mostly you. And when the pink-and-red opens, and morning's here already, take your time in dressing, go easy down the stairs, let Wilkie doze a little longer than he should and build the fire and start a real big breakfast. Maybe even use the last of Poppa's maple syrup we tapped that last winter he was well. Use it up and then get going on things, new things, hear? That is the wish of your loving eldest son, Frank. That is the wish of the love of your son Frank who is no deader than anything else that ever lived so hard and wanted so so much, Mother.

Something holy will stand before you soon, ma'am. Cleave to that. Forget me. Forget me by remembering me. Imagine what a boy like me would give now for but one more breakfast (ever my favorite meal—I love how it's most usually the same) and even Wilkie's crabbiness early, or the Claxtons' rooster house going off everywhichway like their rowboat did so loud. I know what you know, ma'am, and what you doubt, and so do you: but be at peace in this: Everything you suspect about your missing boy is true. So, honor your dear earned civilian life. Nights, sleep sounder. Be contained. In fifty seconds you will refind waking and the standing light. Right away you'll feel better, without knowing why or even caring much. You will seem to be filling, brimming with this secret rushing-in of comfort, ma'am. Maybe like some bucket accustomed to a mean purpose—say, a hospital slop pail—but one suddenly asked to offer wet life to lilacs unexpected here. Or maybe our dented well bucket out back, left daily under burning sun and daily polished by use and sandy winds, a bucket that's suddenly dropped far beneath even being beneath the ground and finally striking a stream below all usual streams and one so dark and sweet and ice-cream cold, our bucket sinks it is so full, Mother. Your eyes will open and what you'll bring to light, ma'am, is that fine clear over-sloshing vessel. Pulled back. Pulled back up to light. Be refreshed. Feel how my secrets and your own (I know a few of yours too, ma'am, oh yes I do) are pooling here, all mixed now, cool, and one.

I am not the ghost of your dead boy. I am mostly you. I am just your love for him, left stranded so unnaturally alive—a common enough miracle. And such fineness as now reaches you in your half-sleep is just the echo of your own best self. Which is very good.

Don't give all your credit to your dead. Fineness stays so steady in you, ma'am, and keeps him safe, keeps him lit continually. It's vain of Frank but he is now asking: could you, and Wilkie and Em, please hold his spot for him for just a little longer? Do. . . . And Mother? Know I rest. Know that I am in my place here. I feel much easement, Ma, in having heard you say this to yourself.

There, worst worrying's done. Here accepting it begins.

All right. Something holy now stands directly before you. How it startles, waiting so bright at the foot of your iron bedstead. Not to shy away from it. I will count to three and we will open on it, please. Then we'll go directly in, like, hand-in-hand, we're plunging. What waits is what's still yours, ma'am, which is ours.

—Such brightness, see? It is something very holy.

Mother? Everything will be in it.

It is a whole day.

—One two three, and light.

—Now, we move toward it.

—Mother? Wake!

BARRY HANNAH

Death and Joy

Anybody who paid him the slightest bit of attention, he thought, was an angel.

It was a way of seeing the world.

Imagine the later Tennessee Williams but a bit more bloated, a little balder, assless in green rayon pants, totally obscure. But Willifox howled from his obscurity by way of a braying, neighing laugh much like that reported of the stage master.

I never once asked Willifox if he was conscious of Williams, and did not think of their similarity until Willifox was gone a couple of years. Then I suddenly saw him alive again, straight out of a Williams play, there at the end of the bar, the wino librarian crushed by desire, sorrow and absurdity—and looking like Williams completely gone out to seeds. Willifox was a fag, too. Condemned and lost out here like a prop from a traveling theater troupe of the fifties. It had moved onto Shreveport and left him high and dry as a merry-go-round pony in the back lot of an AM station. I have forgotten to say he wore dense glasses, and stared through them bewildered under restless shreds of iron-gray hair. He parted it with a great gash on the right side.

During the years I knew him, he never changed bars. The bar was remodeled but he hung on it, same high stool at the south end. The last version was a wraparound fender of polyurethaned wood with a bandstand in the north of the building, a big hall. Named The Gun. Three in the afternoon, Willifox might be seen with a scrawny, bitter man who loved cats and worked the aisles of a small grocery, stamping cans with a Chicago snarl. But he would wax large and tender about cats and the bastards who might hurt them if he didn't step in. This, after several whiskies, and then he would begin tearing up about the strays he fed and the shyer ones he could not help.

This man is remarkable because he was the only man in close proximity to Willifox with whom he did not fall in love, although Willifox confided to me that Conrad, the bitter lover of cats, was certainly a saint. But Conrad's personal ugliness made a neighborly fence between them, and they chatted normally like two strangers on an airplane. Willifox was by no means handsome, but he rocked forward as if staring into a tube of love. When he moved his head from left to right, that tube might connect with anybody who had a civil word for him. In fact anybody who did not threaten to kick his ass. I briefly enjoyed, or was framed, by Willifox's love, but I will tell about this later. I am straight, but since Willifox died, no queer has made a gesture toward me and this worries me. I fear my charms have fled. I cannot find the long poem on index cards he wrote to me, but I am anxious to discover what my charms *were*. Poor devils, both of us.

I have no earlier pictures of Willifox. In the last twelve years of Willifox I suppose I was witnessing the wreckage of his charms as well.

He had become a shuffling lush who brayed from time to time over this or that tacky absurdity. For him, most of the world and its gestures were *tacky*, an old Southernism for bad style, especially among the pretentious. But I was in the college library, lost in the dark of some stacks because I'm not familiar with libraries, when Willifox grabbed me by the arm and dragged me to some door of light. We went out into a plot of grass with a tree in the middle of it. I had not realized I was on the ground floor and I never knew Willifox's real job in the library. It was a thankless rearguard task of some kind. The man was trembling, I could feel the hand on my shoulder. I barely knew him then. I wore my motorcycle leather and it was bright cool October, I recall. I was newly arrived to my old state and noting every wonder, almost every grass blade, especially from my Triumph Tiger, driven slowly on the country lanes. Look, just look and shut up! Willifox whispered.

In a notch of the pear tree stood a bird, cobalt blue, against the deeper cobalt of the afternoon sky with spangling white beards of cloud. It was a vision all right. Willifox had never removed his hand from my shoulder. I had heard he was one of those bewildered three-named Southern people from families aspiring to brilliance. Somewhere a sister had done well, but he was a bust, a shame amidst the brilliance of his line, yet stuck with the name Elkin Dixon Willifox.

Without shame, I tell you, the beauty of that bird, he said. I am not aware what breed, but on that limb against the sky, my God it's a thing as sweet as a prayer.

I looked at him, hair all shot up and his glasses tumbled down to the end of his nose. Why Elkin, you're a poet, I said.

I try, he said. The bird flew off like a shot of the firmament drawn back unto itself. I already had three whiskies down and such things struck me as a miracle too. But I was struck by Willifox's intensity more than the bird.

That was a bluebird, Elkin, I told him.

Naturalism is not my line, sonny.

Aw I heard you were a genius.

That's my sister. I'm only a joyful heart, a fool. You have blessed me with the title poet.

Well I heard that you wrote . . . poems.

Crawl out of my head try to suck the world.

What?

The things just crawl out of my head, don't know what you'd call them. Brain crawlies. Then he brayed, he neighed, loudly, as if having announced the terminal absurdity.

His boss once told me that Willifox did just enough to hold his job. He was very conscious of the fine line of ruin, and straggled to it. He was not rounded up in the infamous bathroom bust third floor in the library. On the internet this queer rendezvous was announced. This was too much for the university. Campus police put a stop to it, right in the middle of a spit-swap—two grad students, a professor, a preacher, an education official. Names in the paper, ruin. Willifox was not involved. I believe it might have killed him had he fallen into the net. Because he had already had his scandal, with the black boy.

In the saloon The Gun, in the restroom. His attempts were pathetic and unreciprocated, I guess. Maybe explosive, humiliating, groveling. Abject earth sucking. The grope, the squeal, the revelation of the boy. The owner of the bar told Willifox he could never return to the bar, never. This meant the collapse of his society and his heart. Willifox died and then he wailed, alone in his bunker of an apartment behind a brick house on the enormous slant of the town's biggest hill. The apartment just an afterthought of the house owner, really, a cave at the end of the driveway. He shook beside the telephone. He had no more destination, no oasis. The near friends, the angels, no more.

So he phoned the owner and bawled his case.

You cry and cry and then you die, Willifox told me.

He explained that The Gun was his entire society, his universe. How could he not be there.

So the owner relented, provided he was good. No groping, scaring the little ones or the big.

Willifox fell in love with the owner, a stout blond man in his thirties. When I was sitting drinking with him one afternoon Willifox told me he wished Mick the owner was his son. Mick stood behind the bar dully accepting Willifox's love, as he received the money of everybody. He had a high-pitched voice and was a man who'd kick a dog but barely acknowledged the world, only its math.

Without shame I tell you of my total infatuation, he said.

I noticed that he smoked a brand I had not seen since my adolescence. Belair, the menthol. As far as I knew, Willifox was their single remaining customer. A sporty Chevrolet of the fifties I once owned, the Belair. When I saw his smokes I thought about the turquoise and white '54 my pals and I went to Florida in. First life was to be had then. First girl, first smoke, and the first beer, a cold Country Club malt liquor that tasted like the Catholic religion. Here I was still working on it, and watching Willifox, who went mad in the navy in the fifties. Maybe he was arrested by the fifties, the figure in the Williams tragedy or even braying Williams himself. I discovered later that the navy paid for all his pills and therapy. He sat there, in love with yet again somebody else, with a small glass of red wine and a small glass of water with lemon in it. He was a rationally measured wino, or supposed he was, as each of us lushes imagined a set of rules that placed us apart.

The waitresses around us, attractive co-eds with nice legs, earrings and sandals, Willifox considered little seraphim. He teased them and they cackled like a bunch of nieces. Old Willifox was back in his bower, there with his piss-elegant wine and water, vowing to hold back the homo in him and grinning like a coon. A wag in town had called these screened waitresses goldfish, born to be seen gliding by in a bowl. I'll always remember the glee in Willifox's face when one of them paid attention to him. The guffaw, the choked gasp of laughter, then the bray.

In celebration of his rescinded banishment he bought a long green Pontiac of the seventies and was raving about it when I came in one afternoon nursing a hangover. I envied him, well drunk. The bitter little man to his left elbow spoke up.

You know what Pontiac stands for, he said into his Black Russian.

Stands for?

POOR OLD NIGGER THINKS IT'S A CADILLAC. Willifox froze in the face.

Dear Conrad, I'd rather remember you as a defender of cats than as a racist, he said. Willifox was truly saddened. I wanted to cheer him up, after a drink. I asked him to show me the car.

Motherfuckers mess with my cats I'll killum. Come on, motherfuckers, Conrad said, chastened.

Willifox's car was all right, sort of a widow's car, really. You could see a tiny-skulled old lady wrapping this thing around turns. He was beaming proud.

Within a month the car was dented and scraped like a staff car that had seen serious military action. There was a long black rent on the top of it, where he'd parked under something, I guess. At twilight, when Willifox left for home to avoid the frat boy crowd—too much desire or too much tacky, one—a small crowd had gathered on the porch of the bohemian café across the alley parking lot. They were there to watch Willifox depart from the crowded lot. He hit two or three cars, took off some brick from the bar structure and confidently rammed a telephone pole, backing up for space. One supposes he was anxious to get home and begin some honest drinking.

Then some months later he passed out in his car under a bridge over near Batesville, sleeping away until a cop found him and hauled him in for a nonmoving DUI, which Willifox thought was an impossible charge. He threatened suicide and bought a pack of bullets. It was the end, this jail, this disgrace, this distance from Oxford. The policeman promised to find him a gun. Willifox could not imagine how he had driven there into an alien county. But he revived and returned to his wine after a chat with his lawyer, with whom he fell in love.

He told me I must not destroy myself, and I loved him without shame, Willifox told me.

Then he found a new therapist, a woman he was totally enchanted with and minded like a dog. After a year he told me he was making real progress.

How's that? I asked out of an unspeakable hangover.

I've learned to clean up my room.

Mag . . . nificent. It was staggering what an infant he had become, but who wanted to take away his happiness?

I urged him to write more poems. I'd help him put a book together. It would be good for his pride, I thought. He looked very interested, but he was always distracted by love. He would be staring at some new barman, whose biography he had memorized and repeated in fragments. He seemed exhilarated even by the man's love life, the girls he dated and who was more nubile. How could he enjoy this, on such a level—the high school busybody? He was staring at a tall insolent oaf, crewcut and beady eyes, when I commented what a rude ass the man was.

Ah, he'd just rather be somewhere else, said Willifox.

The only person I ever heard him blast was another drunkard in sunglasses who called himself Fast Eddy, for his pool skills. The man, pale and middle-aged, lived on the money of his mother and her lands, and he even bragged about this. This fact may have been what drew Willifox's ire, more than his arrogant loudmouthing. He was a competing creature of the midafternoon hours, too, when there weren't many of us. Hilariously, as I look back, we each ordered our drinks with elaborate casualness, as if there were no rush at all. We even commented on their taste, like wine columnists. But Willifox truly resented Fast Eddy. He worked hard to get his drinking and social time in, coming to the library as early as six to get in his hours, on special dispensation. Like many drinkers, he felt he was an aristocrat and resented incursions into his leisure. With money, things would have been different. Earlier, he had taught high school in the delta. Now, there was the struggle to do just enough at the library not to get canned. Money, too, might have brought him more bed love, or its semblance, as it did Tennessee Williams. I never knew what Elkin Dixon Willifox's successes in love were, because I was not interested. Not much, I'd guess. He wanted it gravely, I know, because I had heard him remark on another queer about town, Oh Freddie, he only wants to hold hands. Willifox was no undecided fag.

Now cats, Fast Eddy announced one day, I love to take out a cat with my Boss double shotgun.

Conrad sat there next to the wall. You could see he was imploding and awash in rage, but he was too sick to even concoct a curse on the man, and he seemed even tinier, yellowed and creased with black around the eyes, mouth and brows. As in a Spitfire squadron, our crowd was falling. On death's orders, Conrad would stop drinking soon. The next week a photographer buddy went into a collapse right at the bar and was rushed off to emergency. In months to come, the Civil War buff would lose his voice box and almost his life. Raber the pool shark would come begging at my door for crack money at three A.M., forgetting that he owed me from loans before. Fast Eddy's tongue would turn black, the rest of him orange. The beloved Harleyite who rode with me and helped save my life would go down to lung cancer. The carpenter would be beaten within an inch of his skinny life for standing up for a black friend in a redneck bar up the hill.

I would not drink when I rode my motorcycle, since the consequences of riding drunk were immediately lethal. So I rode more and more with my pal, and was sobering up. I saw less of Willifox, by necessity, and even got into a superior pitying mode about him, because that is what new sobriety does to you, stupidly. Yet you have a wild pride in every day straight and it is hard not to become a beaming deacon.

I laughed along with the others while we listened to a tape a friend in the bohemian café had made of him, announcing an insight and then braying. I gathered on the porch with a cup of coffee in my hand, watching him crash out at twilight from the parking lot in what was left of his car. You could practically set your watch by the first bang.

But I always knew it was rotten to laugh. I was on and off the wagon, dragging about town to clear up my bounced checks. No position at all, and my work was all imagined, never put down, yet I yakked on like one of those blustering wrestlers with a microphone, soon to get his ass handed to him in public.

Once I was riding motorcycles out in the hilly country with my son when two deer came down a hill out of a pasture and leaped over us entirely, going on their way like white-tailed souls. This badly frightened me, as if they were some urgent event out of Revelation. I shook badly. Beyond the fact they could have killed either of us if they had struck us on the bikes, I felt that two souls of my acquaintances back in town had just fled. I hurried back to check on Willifox and a few others but they were okay. Two people did die in town that afternoon, but men not from our squadron.

At last came the spaghetti party, and this was two years down the road.

Willifox assured me that his spaghetti was legendary when he invited me and "just a few friends" to his apartment. When I arrived the tiny place was packed by tall boys and near men, some in National Guard fatigues, some in camouflage for no damned reason, as certain men in the South will be. New pickups were around the place, and a couple BMWs. The place was so small you could not get an impression of it as unkempt before Willifox's therapy revolution. Everybody stood and seemed lost. Hardly anybody knew who the others were, but they were waiting for the famous spaghetti. I presumed it was a large crop of whomever Willifox had had a crush on, but I knew that a couple of them, were they aware of this, would have stamped on Willifox's head. The spaghetti was finally achieved and we went to a great boiler on the stove like something out of the service. Willifox leaned and grinned around, a man of no posture at all, a refutation of *homo erectus* as a point in evolution. His hair was greased up and newly black, his potbelly forward like an involuntary thrust with a big initials buckle in the middle of it. His ass was nonexistent so his green pants hung straight down and rumpled off in the thighs. He had on new white bucks. For each man there was a special greeting and guffaw, then that sort of neigh of choked laughter. He never said How's it hanging or anything vulgar. It's more that he thought a comment like Hi Carl how's New Albany? deserved a riot of mirth and suppression.

Before I tasted the spaghetti I thought of Willifox in the navy. He was barely in it, in fact, only in OCS after graduating from college. Somewhere in Connecticut. When he went mad. The Korean War was over. Somebody told me he threatened suicide in order to save those he might kill. Another told me he was merely a chickenshit with precocious and farfetched battle hysteria. It was the postwar navy, for godsake. Pre-traumatic Stress Syndrome. I asked him about it and he said Oh Please. It was a hell of tacky, is all. All I wanted was the uniform and the sailors.

The afternoon you went mad, was it war—I began.

Oh stop studying war, son. I'd have sucked off both sides on the eve of Gettysburg, Union and Rebel. They wouldn't have dared have the thing then and some of their loved ones might've liked it better.

Willifox, you've got to do your poems. The world awaits. You've gotta. I was urging him on, maybe projecting from my own failure. I was sober and a famous motorcyclist to the sparrows but I was creating nothing, now for a long time.

So somewhere early in the spaghetti party Willifox, after a year's silence, handed me a stack of index cards big and thick, wrapped in a wide rubber band. Do Not Open Until It Looks Bad was printed on the outer card.

Enjoy, enjoy! Willifox knocked on a wine bottle with a fork and quieted the crowd, which had never had much to say. I have a little announcement later!

The spaghetti was ghastly, just a wad of starch in burnt chuck chunks and aggressive salty tomato curds. Who had ever told him this was a success? It was a tribute to either the kindness or irony of this town. A few men swore aloud, then muffled it. They had yet to figure out why the others were there, but all had been within range of the Willifox chortle and his tube of love. Something from outside shook him into this braying, and he could not help it. So much seemed a hoot, but then so much seemed like pure love.

A little rain started outside. Some crowded in from the driveway into an impossible situation, say the bottom of a troop ship, with tall bodies stood flat up to each other, the awful plate of spaghetti held grimly between us. It was way too warm.

Willifox supposed he was holding us in thrall with his spaghetti. I negotiated a big hole in my heap with a fork. The men were talking about girls, animals and the rain. Was I ever a social creature? Without the whiskey I was at a loss. When was I ever hungry for groups of others? Whiskey had been my friend. I mean literally it stood there laughing beside me, clued to every joke. Willifox here with his mind harem—despite the spaghetti I envied him, drunk for thirty years. A fool, handy for comparison. You were never quite the idiot he was, God bless him, neither fag nor drunk like him. He cheered you up. The man with no defenses either for love or life, lost in his dreadful spaghetti, misunderstanding. He got nothing and cried himself to sleep, and as a drunk he had a kind of saintly order. He was nearly a monk at the grand old profession. Then Willifox arose unsteadily on a kitchen chair and rapped the wine bottle again. Quiet went out and gathered.

The little announcement, my good friends, is that I have cancer. Throat cancer. But this is not a pity party. I have every confidence in my doctors. I just wanted to express my appreciation to all of you, my friends, that I love and who have given me such happiness in this little life. Eat on, my pals! And turn that music back up! I'm a reggae fool! No woman no cry. Nobody cry! It's only a new phase for yours truly!

Nobody loved Willifox enough to be stunned, I'm afraid. He was suffered as a right fool, Old Elkin, like that. The character over-friendly and concerned strangely about your happiness and love life. This is a sad testimony, but the only time I had deep true affection for him was when I was drinking. He might as well have been a two A.M. bargirl in that regard. Something swell before the lights went up.

Besides, men do not like spaghetti and cancer-announcement parties. There was no precedent for this at the Rod and Gun Club or back at the frat. Old Elkin, who thought so much was tacky, had joined the minions of tacky himself, there in his new white bucks and new black hair, raked back in desperation from his temples. Somehow, without there being a general movement, the crowd trickled away and vehicles roared to life outdoors. Some even seemed angry at this middle-aged man going all to pieces in public. They may have sensed, as I did, that it was a last bid for Willifox. That they should give love in wild pity.

I was left with three or four men who gave at least the appearance of concern, all of them who'd known Willifox longer than I had. Then

I myself got itchy and left, as if there were forever to discuss this matter.

Out in my big country house—rented—I took the rubber band off and began reading the poem, a single work dashed off with a real fountain pen. His previous poems I thought truly exceptional and I expected a long narrative chronicle of his life, perhaps a small-town fag epic. But the poem, endless in squares of verse on the index cards written front and back, was a love poem to me, his beseecher. For asking him to carry on with his poems I had become the object of his great desire. My brown eyes, my sailor's gait, my motorcycle leathers, my "untamed smile," my "steel friendship" for him. I quit reading. I did not have the heart he thought I had, and the physical stuff embarrassed me.

I have read that Tennessee Williams, in the back row in attendance of his own *Streetcar Named Desire*, howled with laughter when Blanche expressed the famous line "I have always depended upon the kindness of strangers," a line that thousands have found very poignant. You wonder whether the line embarrassed him, that he expected to be laughed at for it, it was so bare? Or was he conscious of what a common whore he was inside, despite high comment in his work. Or is the hysterical word *kindness*? Did he realize that more often you would be kicked and used by others who would remain permanent strangers in this world? Yet later Williams defined lovers as those who use each other, what else? That night I felt unkind and strange and put away the cards somewhere, as though they were pornography. It was then I knew, however, that Willifox was not pretending about the cancer.

He came out of the hospital one day to dry out before the anesthesia and the surgery. He visited friends of mine, shaken and white in withdrawal from liquor, and expressed the same merry confidence in his doctors. He had, of course, fallen in love with his chief surgeon, a man he had seen very briefly in a conference. He visited a while and my friends were very glad he did, because they never saw him again. He went back into the hospital the next day after a phone call of trembling cheer, as if he was returning to a hot love rendezvous.

A story went around that the doctors killed him. An accident during anesthesia when Willifox went into dt's right on the table. If there was nothing to the story, why did we hear it? My namesake uncle, another alcoholic, was mistreated similarly during the dt's and died in a hospital back in the fifties. We all had suspicions but what did it matter? Throat cancer. Overfriendly wino. Terminal alcoholic. Unproductive to society. Played all his cards anyway.

The fifties, the fifties, about which I warm overly. Willifox never left them. The new white bucks, the lounge singer's new black backswept hair, Korea, Marilyn, Eisenhower, fountain cokes and wire chairs, Tennessee Williams, Marlon, the librarian with A Secret Agony.

Why did I write this? I am not that guilty about Willifox. There is not much more I could have been or done, driven toward him in booze companionship, driven away from him in righteous sobriety. The man wrote an enormous love poem to me, didn't he? All my charms listed out there for God to see. Where is it, for godsake? What *was* I? Me and Willifox, both minor dreams of the great lyrical Tennessee Williams at his best?

Willifox should have been there in the American Embassy in Paris with us, receiving an award for his poems like Allen Ginsberg did, five years after Willifox's death. I had seen and heard Ginsberg read his poems here in Oxford. Concerning his later poetry I had also called him a fool. Still, I honored him for his big "Howl" of the fifties. It might have been my first literary influence. I promptly began dressing like a beatnik after having read it, and was mocked in my high school for it. In Oxford young college men who did not dig the scene heard Ginsberg state his desire for companionship in his long stay here. They asked, Well, a redhead, a brunette or a blonde, Mister Ginsberg? None of that, he told them. How about a black boy? They were stunned, but there is progress here at the school. They did not drag him to the city limits and stomp him. I had seen him smoking very long cigarettes in Oxford, where he took pictures with his camera constantly, even one of me. In Paris I told him I noticed he had stopped smoking and asked him if he felt better for it. He told me No, but the doctors say it's necessary for my heart. He seemed touched that I had asked about his health and took my hand in a very natural way and walked with me out to the courtyard, near the security men who had tried to take away his camera. But Allen had fought and won about this matter. Now he took a picture of the security men themselves. I am a professional, he told them. Then he took my hand again, and I swear I felt blessed. This act may not have been possible anywhere but Paris. I was like his nephew, at ease with the grand eminence, *mon oncle*, fool and seer. Soon afterward, in New York, Allen died, attended by great love. A thing Willifox missed. Another thing.

I believe everything would be true and right if Willifox had taken the prize there, had held out his hand, and I had taken it, walking with him out to the courtyard. Maybe that was all he wanted. Same as when he walked me out to show me the bluebird in the tree, like a prayer.

WILLIAM HOFFMAN

The Secret Garden

I am a flower—sometimes a tea rose, occasionally a purple iris, often a long-stem tiger lily.

Mostly we discovered her moods by what she played on the piano. She'd carry a vase of freshly cut yellow asters and a glass ashtray to the Baldwin in our music room. Typically she napped and lighted a cigarette before walking down the wine-carpeted steps. She remained careful of her cigarettes despite seeming to be always a little off course, gently bumping tables and wainscoting or tripping over Oriental rugs. Often we noticed faint blue bruises on elbows and forearms used as fenders.

Though able, she performed no classical selections. She preferred the romantic ballads like "Smoke Gets in Your Eyes" and "Deep Purple," tunes popular during the era before World War II. She still visited Pastor's, Richmond's antiquated music store where clerks wore ties and starched smocks, the listening booths were dusted daily, and a person could buy a golden harp whose strings children loved to sneak to and snag a lingering twang.

I, her son, watched. We all did—my grandmother, my sister, and our maid Viola, who crossed town each morning on the bus. Viola and Mother smoked together in the kitchen. Viola's blackness became powdered when she rose holding the flour sifter from the wooden barrel kept beneath a trapdoor of the long stainless-steel counter to roll out her biscuit dough.

Mother no longer drove. If the weather were wet or cold, she called a taxi. She liked to walk, especially spring and summer. She gazed at flowers and plantings along the brick street. Frequently she brought bouquets from colored women who sold them on the corner of Strawberry and Grace. Whenever she left our stone Victorian house, she wore a large garden-party hat as well as gloves, hose, and heels. She'd been sent to a horsy Warrenton girls' school run by a severe French headmistress who drilled into her charges that a lady unless properly attired never permitted herself to be touched by light of day.

Mother dyed her hair black and wore it longer than the current fashion. She was conscious of her posture, yet her body became askew like a person who feels the ground under him tilt or meets a dip in the road. Perhaps in her mind memory was a fissure that had to be stepped around. We in various rooms listened to her play—my grandmother upstairs, Viola in the kitchen, my sister and I wherever we happened to be.

If it were one of Mother's better days, she'd play everything allegro, hitting notes correctly from the first try. She liked to sing, her voice girlish, though she often stopped in the middle of phrases to reach for cigarettes. Her favorite brand was unfiltered Lucky Strikes.

When the music's tempo slowed and became confused, we looked at each other through walls. She might touch her temple and transform "Blue Orchids" into a wandering dirge. If we peeked through gaps of the mahogany sliding doors that had brass handles, she didn't appear unhappy or distressed, yet her fingers fumbled, causing dissonances she apparently didn't hear. Her voice changed, no longer innocently girl-like but more the throaty chanteuse, husky with lots of vibrato.

We waited for packages. She carried many home. Delivery trucks arrived, a few at first, then some days half a dozen—from department stores, gift shops, bakeries. At Sears she ordered a set of tools she had no use for we could divine. She did keep the canaries she purchased for her bedroom—the same in which she'd grown up, it still maidenly, though smelling of Luckies. Recently pastels drawn by my sister of flowers from our garden had been framed and hung on walls: sweet william, Shasta daisies, red roses and peonies.

"I've made up a new list," my sister said, she three years older than I and an art teacher at Hollins. Slim and blonde, her actions quick and precise, she didn't favor Mother, who was dark-eyed, flowing, languorous. She couldn't draw a line, while my sister as a child had been able to take a piece of yellow chalk and scratch horses, giraffes, and elephants on the concrete driveway. Now my sister had a particularly fine hand with pond scenes, the willows drooping boughs into greenish waters and leaving shadowed furrows.

The list she spoke of lay in the drawer of a small cherry table by our house's front entrance. The table held a rectangular silver tray used in days when people still presented calling cards, my grandmother's day, who sat most of the time in her upstairs den. She suffered rheumatoid arthritis and positioned her chairs by windows so she could look down to the lawn, the birdbath, the garden, the street. She needed a cane to move about. Whenever my mother left the house, my grandmother leaned to the window and peered as if searching for a long-sought shore.

Grandmother too had been a pretty woman. A closeted album held snapshots of her during a European tour. Flanked by costumed guards holding halberds, she stood before the Tower of London, gloved fingers at her throat, a hand steadying a great round yellow hat. Her hair then had been coppery. Now it was thin and gray, almost a skullcap. Her pale blue eyes were still good, and she liked to read newspapers, including the Wall Street *Journal*. She'd gotten in the habit through my grandfather, who'd been a partner in a Richmond investment house that dealt primarily in trading municipal bonds.

"How many today?" Grandmother asked. She wore stylish clothes and rings on crooked, hurting fingers. Through the window Grandmother had looked to the street to see my mother returning from downtown carrying parcels. Once when I entered the den so softly Grandmother didn't hear, I'd found her weeping quietly, crippled fingers touched to her powdered brow. Becoming aware of me, she straightened and said nothing but turned away.

"Only three," I answered. I'd already entered deliveries on the list.

"Ten days more or less," Grandmother said. "Perhaps two weeks."

My sister and I returned packages, those my mother hadn't already given as gifts. She loved giving. We'd wait till she was out and slip into her bedroom to remove them. My sister drove Grandmother's Lincoln downtown. That mission no longer embarrassed her. Store clerks knew and made no fuss about credit exchanges. Kindly people after the southern fashion, they were fond of my mother, smiled at her, sent cards on her birthday.

My sister alerted Dr. Richard Winston. He'd danced with Mother during his courting days. He told me he'd never seen a lovelier woman. She'd been standing, he told us, in a field of daffodils, the sun beaming on her and acres of blinding yellow blooms. He said it was as if she'd grown among them, been one of the flowers, out of the earth, her face itself a blossom, bees buzzing around her, the sun golden on her laughing face.

I've always loved gardens. Times I've knelt among forget-me-nots, collected their fragrance, felt we've sprung from the same black loam. I've been fed upon by bees. I've lain in soothing grass and become part of it. I welcomed ants, who crossed my breasts. I placed them gently upon the ivy-covered sundial. My bare arms wave in the sultry wind like weeping willow boughs. I am the vine, the rose, the nectar.

"Rachel, no!" they call to me.

Even later they scold, after they've no right, seizing me from the succulence of daphne, the hummingbird's visit. Always calling. I stop my ears. I drip my fingers onto piano keys and ride bursts of color. Voices forever nibbling. I make a garden of quarter notes. I climb music as if it's a rose trellis reaching skyward.

"You are indeed something," Richard Winston says, he too lying in the sun, a pliant male flower on a white blanket, he perhaps Monk's Cap. I spread my petals and see him feed from me. His skin is slightly salty, and I love salt. I don't understand how salt harms growing things. Mother pours it to kill grass edging the walks, but Richard's salt is sugar on my tongue.

"You may not," my father tells me, his refrain. He's tall, courtly, his face long, and he wears a Phi Beta Kappa key across his vest. As a child I reach to it when he dangles it over my eyes. I grasp too tightly and tear loose a black button. He pushes at the fabric as if it will join and heal itself.

"You're dismissed," Mademoiselle says to me, a lady of burnished ivory, spectacles, a gray shirtwaist closed at the collar, her raisin-like eyes rarely blinking. Her dun hair has been set so hard it might chip. "Climbing from a window!"

Flowers sheening in sunlight. There are always gardens. Up and down every street, on windowsills, in narrow alleyways. If you look carefully when people gather, they are also blooms. Women give off nectar to the bees. It is so obviously a part of nature you wonder why everyone doesn't see we are all gardens.

I cover my eyes. Winter strikes and ice cracks. I hate the redness of eyelids. I do not like blood. Screams, shouting, the sounds of hate. I have argued I possess rights. I am an adult. They examine me. People forever have their hands on me.

When the deep purple falls, Over sleepy garden walls . . . is the best time. I know deep purple. I am Spanish iris. My body hardly touches sheets till blazing yellow butterflies light on me. Music starts in my breasts and lives in my fingers, though I sit at no piano. Even in darkness I feel sunshine as if I'm an opening poppy. You must not! they say.

No. No. No. What does a garden understand about no? I love rain. I grow in rain. I luxuriate. I lie eyes open and offer my tongue to the darling drops. I become a living tree. I imagine fruit growing along my arms. I am a pear, a plum, a Georgia peach. Men feed off me.

But always the winter, the ice, the red shrieking wind which rends the gardens, dashes them into swirling night. Words are often wind. Pleas and threats. The first rule is never trust any wind.

I build a high wall around my perfect little garden. It is deep within me where wind cannot enter, my private place. Only a riot of blooms, the bees, the music. We twine as the deep purple falls.

They don't know what I've learned about my mother Rachel. More than my brother, like all boys smart and dumb. I realized early I was more devious. I once explained that the reason we have rain is that clouds weep for the pain we cause God. He looked at the sky and cried. Nobody could fool me that way.

So many times my mother touched a finger to her temple, the tiny new moon hidden by the curl of her dyed hair. Grandmother never told us. My brother and I'd lived with her since a time she won't speak of. I asked, and Grandmother in the glow of her Tiffany lamp stared as if my voice hadn't reached her.

What and who were we? Unlike my good little brother, I questioned. Grandmother told us the war had killed my father. Where was his grave? I asked. I'd picked mums to lay by his headstone. He was, Grandmother said, a naval commander whose submarine plunged to the sea's bottom and never rose. He rested in an unreachable dark canyon of the Pacific.

Yet where were his pictures? Why was there no photograph around the house or in the album? We are not people who put stock in pictures, Grandmother said. I'll ask Mother, I said. You must never cause her pain, Grandmother said, feet drawing together and hands tightening on her chair arms. But I do. I found vacant patches on album pages. I sat beside Mother as she played "Blue Orchids."

"Did they try to find the submarine?" I asked. Her hands fell from keys to her lap. Her dark eyes became moist and luminous. Mother? I asked. She lifted a pink dahlia from the Chinese vase and offered it to me on her palm. That night Grandmother phoned Dr. Winston.

My cousin Wendy and I attended Camp Sail each summer, the green cottages located on bluffs above the Rappahannock. She was prettier but I the stronger swimmer and won the racing trophy. I knocked her off the dock and ducked her till wailing and choking she told me what she'd heard whispered from her mother. I held her under, and she became limp in the tidal flow. That night she called her parents to come fetch and drive her home.

I barely remember moving to Grandmother's, a rainy day which had a chauffeur named Hubert carrying in baggage. Mother wasn't with us. She came and left, came and left. I began to sense a rhythm to it. Grandmother provided the money. Once a quarter an elderly man from the bank sat with her in the parlor to go over finances. Grandfather, a faceless shadow from my child's mind, had left her rich.

During my fourteenth year Grandmother sent me away to school, not the fashionable place my mother went, but St. Helen's in South Carolina. I knew none of the girls. I asked why I didn't go where Mother had gone. Grandmother told me that Mademoiselle had died and the school's standards had slipped.

I learned the terrible things from Alfred, a second cousin once removed. We hated each other. He had red hair and a prissy mouth. When canoeing on the lake, he used his paddle to splash my new sunsuit. I stuck a yellow-eyed puff adder in his bed. He screamed like a girl. For what he told me his father spanked him hard, but I heard the words. I found out.

I could very nearly set my watch by the regularity of their calls. We had a procedure, a routine to deceive, if in truth that's what we did. I thought of Rachel browsing among the arbor, blue juice on her scarlet lips. Bees attempted to drink from them. She wore black hair to her hips, and burst grapes had stained her white pinafore.

I dated her before med school, that wonderful Christmas of my senior year at Hampden-Sydney when invitations gathered along the mantel. She was the first girl to bare her breasts to me. She unbuttoned a ruffled blouse, jerked up her brassiere, and took my head between her palms. She laughed when I proclaimed my love for her.

"You love Rachel's ripe apples," she said and became shockingly ardent.

I rarely saw her after I entered the university. I phoned several times, but she was usually on trips with her mother—to the Homestead, Italy, west to New Mexico and a dude ranch. I saw a photograph of them in the society section of the Richmond *Times-Dispatch*. They wore sombreros and sat astride sad-looking burros. Cactuses bloomed around them.

I made a last date with her during a steamy summer break. I believed then she was considering me, thinking of casting her net for me as my mother put it, the future doctor who would earn an income allowing Rachel to continue living the graceful life. So mistaken I was. She had no understanding of how to use people. She simply gave herself to those she liked.

We drove to the bay where I'd borrowed the use of my uncle's Cal 30 sloop. No wind crossed the water, and we weltered becalmed in the lower Chesapeake. Rachel lounged under shade of the listlessly flapping mainsail, her long, tan body oiled and enticing, water beading her skin, her then chestnut hair shiny wet from a dip.

"I hate clothes," she said and stretched toward the sun. "I hate being bound. Clothes are a sham. They are trickery. Would you love me naked?"

"I'd love you anyway anyhow," I told her and meant it.

"Poor Richard," she said. "I cause him such terrible yearnings."

And she removed her black-and-red striped bathing suit, a slow sexual ballet, and we settled to the blanket on top the cabin, all the while the sail swinging and snapping above us, bay water splashing against the white hull. She was soon married, and I now believed that last afternoon a gift to me, her way of saying farewell and thanks for my admiration, presenting me the best of what she had, and what she had more than anything was the gift of love.

I never done nothing to cause it. I had my job gunning the backhoe when we laid the new water mains down the old brick street lined with three-story mansions. Dog days, the August sun blood red and out to blister the working man. Hot dazzle reflected in sweat along my brown arms.

Those awninged houses made me think of fussy old women who sniffed at you when you was dirty. I walked to a corner pile of stone big as church to fill my water jug, knocked at the back door, and asked permission to use a yard spigot.

The yard had a birdbath, a pond with goldfish, and a million white lilies. Water dripped from the mouth of a green iron frog. She was sunning herself among the lilies, and when I walked past I didn't know she was lying there till she sat up and stared. She reached for the top of her two-piece bathing suit and covered her breasts. Her dark eyes ate me up.

"Take all the water you want," she said. "We have our own deep well. Wait. You've hurt yourself!"

It wont no hurt, just a scratch from a lug wrench which slipped while I was tightening the blade. She come toward me, this tall lady who set on a yellow straw hat. She laid fingers on my arm. I never felt volts travel so hot from a woman.

"Anytime you need water," she said, and those fingers with red-painted nails slid along my skin, leaving rows in my sweat. "I know what it is to be thirsty."

I filled my jug and got out of there. Sometimes when I was operating the backhoe, she'd step out on the house porch and stand holding her hands behind her back. A black maid cared for a couple of kids. As we worked down the street, I never believed I'd see her again close till the Friday evening when we quit work. As I swatted gnats, flies, and skeeters and climbed into my pickup, the Chrysler drove up beside me and stopped. A light clicked on when she opened the door.

"Just as you are," she said. We parked on a bluff overlooking the James. She licked my sweat and called me earthy. I'd been among women, but none like her. I was a big man, strong, yet she wore me down.

She took to driving to my rented room south of the river, always at night. In a crazy way I guess I kind of loved her till her father come charging in the door. She screamed, and he just fell out on the floor without me hitting him. Blood shot from his nose and mouth. They threw me in jail, and I had to prove I never touched him. The old lady's lawyer brought money for me to leave town. I come down to Carolina, hell yes, where I got me a good woman and a boy. But I remember Rachel laying her fingers on my arm. I've never been able to figure things out, yet I know it was a loving act.

She said love can't be contained. "Can foxglove or hibiscus?" she asked. I told her anything can be contained except death and even that held in abeyance a while. I fled. I became certain of nothing. Who did I see when I looked at the children? She didn't act guilty. There was no shame. Rueful, yes, slyly saddened, but no remorse that led to repentance. I had a name, a position in the community, and she treated me as if those attainments were negligible.

She caused me to doubt my manliness. I secretly arranged an appointment with a Charlottesville doctor.

"She asks more than I can give," I told him.

She seemed always to be eyeing me. I was a normal male. Tests proved that. She devoured me with her dark eyes. Nights I'd wake to find her staring at me and waiting. A terrible thing to be under the constant gaze of sexual judgment.

I never understood Rachel. I think she loved love, or what she took it to be. When I discovered she'd been with Bobo Gaines, my old roommate from Duke, at a Jekyll Island hotel, I didn't confront him but her.

"He was so nice," she said. She pulled strands of hair before her face and stroked them with a long-handled silver brush. "He'd just come from the ocean, water dripping from him, a leaf of sea lettuce on his tan shoulder. I found it difficult not to let him take my hand."

"Your hand?" I asked. "If you want to save this marriage, it has to stop."

"Bobo looks so dashing in his hunt attire," she said. "No man in boots has better legs."

It did not stop. She was the wayward one, yet I experienced the guilt. I felt despair more than anger. How could such beauty be so wanton? When toward the end I became frantic, she gazed at me from those bottomless nocturnal eyes, shook her head, and lifted a palm as if to indicate she was helpless.

"We are all flowers, and they are beautiful children," she said. "Who serves best, the bloom or the bee?"

Her mother came after her and arranged the divorce. I remained in Raleigh, remarried, and became the father of a daughter I can be sure of. Why should I continue to carry guilt?

God keeps score and never forgets. We do not escape. I saw that article of His justice when the perfidious part of me gave way only once in my life—a scratching at the door of my London hotel by the sleek, passionate Italian tenor while Henry shot grouse in Scotland. I believed I'd buried the lie deep till I witnessed Rachel's openness, her ardor, the innocent giving of herself. She loved every cur dog who strayed into the neighborhood. She never passed a panhandler she didn't wish to open her little purse for. She dug a cemetery at the rear of the garden where she laid to rest a sparrow that flew into a parlor window. She had a heart too soon made glad.

Joseph, the teenage boy from south of the river, his skin undoubtedly darkened by a strain of Negro blood. Summers he rode his bicycle to the house and cut the lawn. I missed her. When I quietly opened the door of the white shed where garden implements and the mowers were kept, a flash of flesh broke shadows. Their bodies slanted across stacked bags of bone meal used to nourish my box bushes.

I slashed Joseph with a trowel. Blood seeping among his fingers, he ran never to return. Rachel rushed crying to her room. I followed and found her pressed back among fragrant dresses of her closet.

"Was he inside you?" I demanded. "Dr. Shokley will tell."

I drove the Packard. Dr. Shokley had been our family physician since I was a girl, a benign, lumbering man whose skin was like fresh cream. His white hair straggled over the rear of his jacket collar.

"She's been penetrated," he told me, his voice little more than a whisper. "After such a short interval, a douche should suffice."

The douche did not. Rachel had to be sent to Chattanooga where my sister Emily kept her till the thing was done. Henry, my good and trusting husband who had no eye for suspicion or the delving of secrets, became half crazed. He didn't go to his office, and it was the only time during our marriage I saw him falling-down drunk.

Yet when Rachel returned, she was as lovely as ever, if anything more beautiful, stunning for a girl so young. She'd been in the house less than thirty minutes before boys rang our bell. I sent them away. Father Alex, our pastor, counseled her. She simply smiled at him. God punishes us for our sins by letting us see their ugliness in those we hold dearer than life.

Henry and I hoped to save her from herself. Rachel attended private schools which provided discipline. She never traveled alone and was allowed to be escorted only by boys whose families we approved of. Still, as she grew older, we couldn't keep her caged. Gaps of time existed she wouldn't account for. When she came in late, she didn't answer our questions or heed our rebukes. She passed by us and glided up the steps to her room. We'd hear her singing to her canaries.

We wanted only a safe marriage for her, a loving protective husband, and when Charles Fontaine of Raleigh proposed, we believed our prayers answered. It wasn't she didn't love Charles. She loved everybody. She didn't know where to stop—as if there were no differences among people.

Then the night of terror Henry surprised her in the arms of that brute of a laborer. I had no choice. After the funeral, arrangements were made. I hated God for His using beauty to inflict the greatest punishments of all.

*　　*　　*

People are so foolish. I wipe the curl of hair from my temple and watch my fingers lower to the keys like a gentle spring rain. Often my fingers seem separate from me, to live their own lives—tiny people going about their business. They make the notes, little workers creating melodies for me. I have nothing to do with them, and music rises to form bouquets of amazing colors.

Colors are music, the scent of lilacs, and music is a wall, though sometimes howls intrude like wild dogs in the night. She watches me. She is upstairs in her chair but sees down through walls. My children eye me. They listen. When I kiss them, they stand obediently and try not to show their wish to draw away.

Yet many have desired my kisses. I gave them away on grassy terraces, weltering boats, and darkened rooms above the Atlantic. I remember looking over a quivering muscled shoulder and seeing gulls soar at dawn. Dazzling white, they rode air currents and cried freedom. I sailed with them on the ocean wind.

I have been used. I am a tea rose, a purple iris, and often a long-stem tiger lily. I scare men. I see fright flare in their eyes. I try to explain the nature and completeness of my gift to them, but they do not want completeness. They expect possession as if I could disassemble myself, present them an arm, a leg, a breast. Occasionally my petals fall.

Mother has always watched. If I sunbathe in the garden, she peers from shadows behind the window. She does not allow me my own breath. Yet many times I've eluded her, drifted from the house like smoke in the night. My father too spied on me. When I attended dances, he followed in the Packard. I weep for my father and all flowers that have withered and died. Many, many flowers. I have been chiefly a flower. It is the great truth I've perceived.

I dressed in my summer dinner jacket and drove to the house, my medical bag in the trunk of the Buick. I hadn't understood during her mother's first visit to my office, the chauffeur waiting at the front curb in a No Parking area.

"It's time again," she'd said, her brittle body curved to the ebony cane. "Did not Dr. Shokley inform you?"

Dr. Shokley lay in his grave. He'd died while sitting in his backyard workshop repairing an antique clock. I'd inherited his medical practice. Such was our understanding when I'd agreed to become his associate. After she left I checked files. There were two sets—one on the ground floor, the other in a locked basement area. Dr. Shokley had left keys for me. I found them while going through his desk drawers. The embellished penmanship on the envelope read: Be above all discreet and forgiving.

I studied Rachel's medical history. At a time people believed her to be on a European tour, she'd been a patient in a Philadelphia clinic. The first time I examined her and fingered the rigid curl off her temple, there waited the scar hardly larger than a caraway seed. My hand flinched as if I'd touched fire. The operation which had seemed to offer so much promise in those years now judged a horror seized upon in desperation. Then a second act of surgery which ended life's renewal.

At the house ancient, uniformed Viola opened the door. I sat in the dusky parlor, its dimness hardly penetrated by light from the teardrop chandelier, till Rachel descended the steps, this time wearing a black silk gown and pearls. She would've appeared regal except she listed slightly and an arm nudged the carved oak railing. I offered my hand. She took it, righted herself, and kissed my cheek in lingering fashion. I pinned to the shoulder of her dress the orchid I'd brought. Her lipstick had not been precisely applied. We sat on the blue divan to smoke and drink manhattans Viola served from a silver tray.

Her son and daughter approached to say good-bye. They spoke words and kissed her, but they'd be relieved when she left the house. Rachel gazed at them as if they were articles in a shop window. Viola opened the door for us. She and the children stood on the stone porch. As we walked to my car, I carried a covered canary and knew that if I looked back at the upstairs window Rachel's mother would be watching.

During the trip to Baltimore, Rachel smoked Luckies and chattered. Headlights reminded her of fireflies. She liked to remember the year she'd been a member of the Water Maidens, a swimming team at the Warrenton girls' school whose members formed floral patterns in the gym's turquoise pool. Her fingers moved as if a keyboard lay across her lap. She might become excited, suddenly cry or attempt to kiss my mouth. When her agitated hands fluttered, I'd capture and grip them till they quieted.

Entering between the gates, she straightened, touched her hair, and smiled at floodlit flowers planted inside the concrete circle before the partially darkened main building where she was known, treated, and cared for.

"Coralbells," she said.

MADISON JONES

 # Sim Denny

The death of Earl Banks had consequences that went beyond the near-riot it caused and the bitter feeling that lingered for a long time in Okaloosa's black community. One of the people affected, in a different way, was Sim Denny.

Sim Denny was a Negro with skin about the color of an eggplant. He was a tall man though stooped a little now, after sixty-six years of which at least fifty had been years of hard work. It was not just the years that had bent him, though. Partly it was a shortness of breath that had come on him: it seemed he could breathe easier when he bent over a little. His heart, he reckoned, and did not inquire any further. He just went a bit slower at his job of cement finisher and occasionally thought about hiring a helper to take some of the load off of him. He had used to employ two helpers. But that was before his wife died, six years ago, and before everything got so different. Since then working, and being, alone had got to be a habit. It was a hard habit to break, even when finally his lonesomeness began to frighten him.

Sim had never been very talkative but there had not been any reason except that he was quiet by nature. When there started to be another reason to keep quiet he hardly even minded, at first. He went on with his cement finishing, working almost always for white people, proud when he pleased them and made them acknowledge his mastery, the finish like glass he could put on a cement surface. He went on showing respect, even when he did not feel it, saying Yas Sah to them—Yas Sah this and Yas Sah that. And he went on making three or four visits a year, for old time's sake, to the home of Mr. Will Cottrell over there in the hill section where the class white folks lived. In those days Sim did not mind a bit breaking his accustomed quiet to give a piece of his mind to offending black people. "What you want go to school with them for?" he would say. "Ain't black folks good enough for you?" Or, "You behave yoself, they treat you awright." And that first march, about the schools, had made him sneer. "Crazy niggers. Making trouble for ev'ybody."

That was how it went, back then. Sim was the aggressor and half the people he confronted like this were silent in ways that meant they agreed with him. Soon, though, there were not so many. In time there were almost none at all, or none who would admit it. That was when his remarks began to be answered not with silences anymore but with open scorn and ridicule. There were some people who now called him, right to his face, Uncle Tom or Rastus or White Man's Nigger. Even his own daughter Maybelle sometimes did, though this was mostly because of her husband.

They lived in Sim's house, in the Creektown district of Okaloosa. It was a nice house, small but of clean sound white-painted frame, on a street where now the rest of the houses resembled beehives made of red brick. In back of the house was a little outbuilding where Sim had used to keep his tools but where, nowadays, he spent most of his time when he was at home, sleeping on a cot he had put there. There were two big shade trees, a black oak and a chinaberry, and between the house and the street a decent stretch of yard that Sim, until lately, had always insisted be kept swept bare. Just like a nigger. That was what Maybelle had said to him, more than once, quoting her husband Herman. From the very first Sim had been more than half afraid of Herman.

It was not so much a physical fear, though there was some of that.

Herman had bad light eyes and an ugly razor scar like a worm on his neck. He was not big, he was just too quick. He moved around like a nervous cat, especially when he was angry, and he seemed to be always angry, seething. But Sim might have lived with this. What made him really afraid was something else about Herman. He could see it reflected—more than a reflection—in his own daughter, who had gone off to Birmingham one kind of a girl and come back another kind, pretty near as much of a stranger as that one she brought with her. Right here was the trouble, though. All of a sudden it was like Sim was the stranger, in his own house. Maybelle said things to him, hushed him up. Herman with those bad light eyes just looked at him. Then there started to be meetings in Sim's house, people he had known since they were children who looked at him now almost the way Herman did, as if Sim was something between a joke and a threat. Things he heard said in his own house gave the same kind of hitch to his breathing that hard work did sometimes. By now Sim had all but stopped saying the kind of things he used to say.

He moved out, into the toolhouse. "It make a fine room," he said to Maybelle. "Mo private. Won't be no bother to you."

"You don't have to." Maybelle's underlip was out, purple-looking, and her voice was flat. "This here yo house."

It did not seem like it. "It's awright," he said. "Make a fine room."

"We be out of here fo long." She kept on mopping the floor, with long hard thrusts of the mop. "Soon's Herman make them white people at the mill pay him mo money."

Once Sim would have said, "It's plenty good jobs for maids you could get." Now he said, "It's awright. You welcome here."

It was all right in the toolhouse, with his bed and cabinet and chairs and his wife's picture on the board wall. Except at breakfast and supper he rarely had to see Herman at all and he could not hear the voices when the meetings took place in the house. It seemed like his thoughts went better too, as if they had got almost free of spying eyes. He could drop back unseen to his childhood days on old Mr. Will Cottrell's farm, to young Mr. Will and himself, naked as a pair of snakes, diving off the sycamore tree into the blue creek pool. And the billy goat Sam they used to bait, making him hit the fence like a cannonball. Riding on top of the cotton wagons, deep in cotton, on gold late October afternoons. Mr. Will. Months since Sim had gone to visit, to sit on the back stoop or in the kitchen with him and call up those old things and talk about these new times and shake their heads and have a drink together. Lean Mr. Will now, rheumy in his eyes. And months had gone by. This thought was like a heavy weight riding on Sim's chest.

There was another weight riding on him, one that was more constant and growing heavier week by week. There were times when he felt like somebody in enemy country, a spy who people knew was a spy and who, since he was not a very dangerous one, they simply let be. At the start of that big mess about the schools, when the black people made that first march up to City Hall, Sim had watched from the sidewalk and sneered and said things to the people around him. When almost a year later the second march happened he watched it too, but in silence now, the sneer locked up in his breast. Standing mute on the sidewalk with a little space between him and the others, he watched, knowing many or most of the marchers, the sullen black faces passing by in ranks, and watched their mouths stretch open when they started to sing like they were walking into a church about how they were going to overcome. Overcome. He shook his head. It was a gesture nobody noticed. He went home feeling lonely.

That was the same week when Sim decided he would not go to church anymore, not until they stopped all that and got back to the Bible. He stuck to it. Sunday mornings he slept and read his Bible and let his mind drop back, dreaming. He began to work harder at his job, even if it did make his breath come short, and down on his knees stroking wide with his float he put finishes on cement floors that a person could see his face in. Then winter came on, a wet winter with skies dripping all the time and the earth a slush to walk on and there was not much work for him. Most of the day he was in his little room out back and when he did not turn on his lamp the light was like a desolate leaden-colored pall. That was when Sim started to be afraid.

His dreams seemed to be the cause. He was now in the habit of lying on his bed and, between sleeping and waking, letting his mind drop back to the old time, the childhood time. But so often now something would happen that he could not control. Suddenly, back there in the middle of one of those bright memories, he would look around and not be able to find Mr. Will, no matter how hard he looked—or anybody else either. He would be, maybe, out in the big pasture behind the house and, looking around for Mr. Will, discover also that the house was gone and the land was not green anymore and the sky gave no light except this desolate leaden one. It was a winter place, without any motion or voices or any landmark to guide him out of it.

Sim thought it would be better when spring came and sunlight and hard work again. But the bad weather kept on into April and then, when May came, that first strangling happened. The event did not seem at first to mean anything special for Sim. An old white lady strangled in her home on the other side of town: Mrs. Rosa Callahan. Sim had known the family long ago. He silently shook his head. Such a time. But there was more to it than he had foreseen. Within a few days there was a tale, a rumor going around. Sim was late to hear it. People, even Maybelle, did not tell him things anymore and because Herman had been absent for a couple of days there had been no talk at the supper table for Herman to listen in on. So the rumor was already at full flower on the night Sim first heard Herman talking in his bitterest voice to Maybelle about it.

"Nigger hair. Yeah. They knows nigger hair when they sees it . . . ev'y time. Yeah."

Afraid to ask, afraid of drawing Herman's anger, Sim had to listen a while before he could get it straight. Hair. They had found it under one of the dead lady's fingernails: black hair, nigger hair. So it was a black man that had done it to her. Bent over his plate Sim kept on making his hand lift the food to his mouth.

"So a nigger done it. That's all they need, a little black hair. If it's bad, a nigger done it."

Without looking Sim could see those light eyes on fire. He could actually see, obliquely, Herman's knotted brown hand holding the dinner folk as if for a weapon, making it shimmer under the bright light bulb.

"Got to get 'em one, now. They be down here to get 'em one. Anybody do fine. Might be me."

Bowed, Sim kept working his jaw. Then he felt the eyes and suddenly could not swallow what he had chewed.

"Won't be you, Uncle. You got white folks. They takes care of *their* niggers."

"Lay off him," Maybelle said, but not with much force.

Sim managed to swallow the food but he could not meet the eyes, the anger coming straight at him.

"He one of their pets. He ain't got no worries."

"Ain't nobody's pet," Sim said gruffly.

"Lay off him, Herman," Maybelle said.

Herman withdrew his gaze, let it pass carelessly across Maybelle's face and settle on his half-eaten plate of food. He speared a carrot with the fork. "All the same, I wouldn't feel easy if Uncle thought *I* was the one done it."

Sim drew a breath, drew hard to fill his lungs. "Ain't nobody's pet. I'm a black man same as you."

Herman bit off the carrot. Chewing he said, "On the outside, awright. But just only yo hide, is all." Still chewing he got up from the table and went into the living room and then out the front door, letting the screen bang shut.

"Eat yo supper now, Daddy."

He could not eat. He pretended to, hiding the crisis of breath that had come on him, until it was possible to escape.

The next Sunday, after more than six months, Sim went to church. Somebody was there already sitting in the place up front that used to be always saved for him and he had to sit near the back close under the white-painted wall where hung the picture of Jesus making the waters be still. It was like Sim was not noticed, had not even been missed. His nods and his smiles drew nothing but the slightest kind of answers and he sat there under the picture feeling like somebody invisible, too still to be noticed. When the singing swelled he tried to join in but his breath was short. It seemed like the River Jordan was rolling over his head. When Brother Dick in the pulpit got going, lacing the Pharisees and the Sadducees and the white people all at once, with his voice coming like waves cresting and breaking and his strong young spade-like hands shaping out the rhythm of it; when the groans and the Amens started and the heads began to pitch and sway as if a big wind was blowing through the church; then Sim felt like somebody struck dumb and stiff and cold, unable even to stir in his pew. He kept trying, as if it was a tight shell of ice he had to break, to shatter. Finally he could move his head and then his lips and could shape the word Amen and utter it. The word came out wrong, off-key, missing the beat of things—like a tune he had failed to catch. He did not risk another try. He nodded his head, moved his lips, and hoped it would be enough for the eyes around him.

That was Sim's first effort to get back in and in a way the result frightened him more than any of his dreams had. This setback only drove him the harder, though. He not only kept on going to church, he also began to make efforts in other directions. For one thing he hired a boy, Tod Nells, to help him with his cement finishing. For another he changed his manner with white people. Or he tried to, for he only succeeded in part: his old nigger courtesy would too often come back on him, defeating the impression he meant to give. Still there were unexpected things he said and expected things he did not say that put a look of surprise on the white faces. It was pain for him, but with Tod behind him he stood it. Also he was not so scrupulous about his work now. In fact, on purpose he would sometimes leave a whorl or a nick in a cement floor and then turn sullen if there was a complaint. Shoddy work was pain too, though. He had moments in his room when it felt as if those whorls and nicks were graven on his soul.

It seemed when it was black people Sim talked to that he could not say those things rightly. Always there was that note like a cracked bell, ringing false. It was not only too plain to him, it also made people's eyes look at him with second sight. His one and only try with Herman, a remark about "Whitey" he had overheard somewhere, brought that look and more besides into Herman's face. "Look out now, Uncle," he said, showing his yellow teeth. "What yo white folks gon think about that kind of talk?" Sim learned not to say those things except when he had to and then he studied about each one, figured how to say it. Most of the time he settled for just agreeing with what he heard said, nodding, and poking his lip out.

They did not believe him, though. It did not seem to matter how often he went to church or how many people he nodded his agreement with or how painfully rude he made himself act with white people sometimes. Because it was an act. You had to be what you pretended or people saw through it, heard it in your voice. To say a thing right you had to be it. And this meant you had to give up things. Like Mr. Will, thinking about him. Like letting your mind drop back, too. Now Sim tried not to think about those old things anymore. And finally he got another idea. But that was not till September, after that fifth white woman got strangled and the police killed poor old deaf and dumb Earl Banks for it.

The night after that happened there was a big meeting outside the Baptist Church, with people crowded in the churchyard and the whole street too, singing, and Brother Dick and Hershel Rawls on the church steps shouting and praying and waving their arms. Some gangs of black boys went uptown on Cotton Street and broke windows and yelled at the police and got, a lot of them, put in jail. The day after that there was a march, to City Hall, and a meeting on the steps between the mayor and Hershel Rawls. In those days Creektown was like a place on fire, except there were not any flames or smoke. The nights were noisy, broken with sudden outcries and cars going by faster than usual and people talking in the streets. Nobody talked about anything else. And Sim was afraid.

It was, when he could think clearly about it, not a fear that any personal violence might be done to him. And yet to make himself come out of his little room in the backyard was all Sim's strength could manage. It was as if outside there were howling winds with fierce eddies that would seize and twist his body and cruelly wrench his limbs out of their sockets. He lay on his bed straining for breath. And yet he went out. He was at the meeting at the church that night. The next day with everybody else he marched to City Hall and stood there in the crowd, standing so far back that he could see nothing except, now and then, the bald head of the mayor and the agitated black one of Hershel Rawls. Of what they were saying, of their voices even, he could not hear anything. What were they saying, talking about? Suddenly, like a dream coming on, he could not even imagine what, any more than he could think why he and all this listening murmurous crowd of black people were standing here in the town square in the harsh sun of early September. But that moment grew from dream to nightmare, in which it seemed to him that he stood here alone of all this crowd in helpless ignorance, among all these black heads filled with a knowledge he could not even conceive of and that he would have given everything he had in the world to share. The sweat ran down his body, his breath came hard. His head was as light as an empty shell set on top of his neck.

But out of that terrified and confused moment Sim got his idea. He had a savings account at the bank that came to over fourteen hundred dollars. He had been building it for a good many years, putting in a little bit almost every month, and once it got past a thousand it began to be a considerable thing in his mind. He read his statements every month and thought about the money lying there in one big pile that nobody but him could lay a hand on. He had no idea of spending it, ever, he meant to leave it. There was a sort of awe in the thought of a man, a colored man anyway, having that much money to leave behind him when he died. The thought he had in bed that night after the march was still more awesome: it left him stunned. By morning, though, he had made up his mind to it and he was uptown waiting outside the door of the bank at least an hour before opening time.

That was such a day. Leaving the bank with that sealed envelope full of green money clutched tight in his hand he walked as he had used to walk thirty years ago—straight-up, long-stepping, with easy breaths of the morning air swelling, gorging his chest. Walked better in fact, as if he had grown taller and need not look any way but down into the black faces he greeted along the way. Up Cotton Street and across, ignoring traffic, down Willow Street to Bean and into Creektown he never once broke his stride or felt one lapse of this new power trilling in his blood. Children watched him as if they knew, could see it, and so, now, did the men and the women he passed by. He slowed his steps to savor it. Even so he got there too soon and, to let it build, he paused for a minute or two outside the door. It was a rectangular brick building, once a grocery, and a sign on the wall said: OKALOOSA IMPROVEMENT ASSOCIATION.

It did not go as Sim expected, all complete in one triumphant stroke. Hershel Rawls was not there. A secretary in the small front office, in front of a shut door with a glass pane you could not see through, told him to try again in an hour. He would not state his business. He went outside and paced the street and never for long let his eyes wander from the front of that building. He was not at all crestfallen, not yet. The envelope full of green money went on ticking away like something alive between his tight thumb and fingers. An hour would make it better, the greater for being put off. The astonished smile, the welcome, on Hershel Rawls' stern face.

Sim was not to see it, though. Every hour when like clockwork he entered the building again he was met with just such another disappointment. One time, when he went in right at noon, he had thought it was about to happen for sure, because the woman told him Hershel Rawls was back there, in conference, behind that pane of glass you could not see through. But he never came out. There must have been a back door and Hershel Rawls came and went by it. At five o'clock when the whistle blew and Sim walked out of the building for the eighth and last time he felt almost as if the whole thing had been spoiled. He had not wanted to do what he finally did. It was that woman's impatience, wanting to know his business, and her face nearly as light as a white woman's. She got it out of him finally and got the envelope out of his hand. He stopped her from dropping it into a box that was there. "You give hit to him, yoself. You tell him who. You tell him Sim Denny."

She said she would, not to worry, and gave him a smile that reassured him a little.

"He got a surprise coming. When you gon give hit to him?"

She said maybe even tonight, if she saw him. Then she said, "And I know he'll be wanting to get in touch with you, to thank you."

That was most of the comfort Sim took home with him that evening. Hershel Rawls would get in touch with him, to thank him. He would send for him, or maybe even come by the house, come out back to Sim's room. And anyhow there would be that smile when he opened Sim's envelope. This thought kept coming back and growing in Sim's mind, shading out his long day's disappointment. By suppertime it had raised him almost to the pitch of this morning's elation.

He was too full to eat but he ate a little, waiting for his moment. He would have liked, to launch him, some little break in the silence over the table. But it did not come, forbidden by Herman's sullen face, his look as if it was anger alone that drove him at his food. Tonight, though, this was not enough, not for Sim. He said, "Old Hershel Rawls got him a surprise coming."

"What you talkin bout?" Maybelle said. Herman went on eating.

"When he op'm that *envelope* I left for him." Sim looked straight ahead of him at the green plaster wall.

"What *envelope*? What you talkin bout?"

"That'n I left for him." He paused. "Got foteen hundert and twenty-seb'm dollar in it."

Even Herman stopped eating. Maybelle said, "Of *yo* money?"

"Ev'y penny."

It took Maybelle a moment, with her mouth open, to digest the fact. "You done gone crazy?"

"For the Move*ment*," Sim said. "Hershel Rawls be in touch with me." He put a bite of something in his mouth, started chewing. His head felt light with triumph.

"You gone plumb ravin crazy," Maybelle said.

"Naw." This was Herman. His bad light eyes were looking at Maybelle. "He just think he can buy his self black." Now he was looking at Sim. "Ain't that right, Uncle?"

At first somehow this shot was more confusing than painful to Sim. All he could think to say was, "I ain't 'Uncle.' "

Herman made a small derisive noise with his tongue. "Come on, Uncle. What you care bout the Move*ment?* Yo white folks is what you care bout." Herman suddenly put his head back. "Hey, wait a minute." He got up and stepped through the living room door and came back immediately with a letter. "From yo white folks, Uncle." He placed it on the table beside Sim's plate.

It was hard to see but Sim could see this much—in print up in the left-hand corner. William Cottrell. And Sim's own name in the middle, shakily written with ink. He could do nothing but stare at the letter.

"Better open it. He might need you to come shine his shoes."

"Don't shine no shoes," Sim faintly said.

"Lay off him, Herman," Maybelle said.

Herman went on standing there. He said, "I'll thow it away for you, Uncle, if you don't want to read it."

Now Sim lifted his eyes, slowly bringing Herman into focus.

"Want me to thow it away for you?"

"Lay off him."

"It don't matter," Sim murmured. "Be awright."

"Okay, Uncle," Herman said and picked up the letter and flipped it into the trash box by the stove. "So long Mr. Will." Then with a toss of his head he left the kitchen.

"Finish yo supper, Daddy."

Sim just managed to eat a little more. He would not think about it. He would not wonder what it said inside, in that shaky handwriting, and he would not let his mind drop back. If a dream tricked him in the night he would wake up and think about the next day and Hershel

Rawls being in touch with him. But he had to walk a long time in the streets before he was tired enough to go to bed.

The next day was Friday but Sim did not go to work, he waited. He waited on the front porch, in the swing, watching every car approach and keep on past his house. The mailman did not even stop at his box and all day long the telephone was silent. At nearly four o'clock he set out walking. He walked to the Association office and after a little pause outside went straight in, straight up to the desk and the woman who had skin like a white woman. She gave him the smile that some-how had been more comfort to him yesterday and said Yes, Mr. Rawls would have it by now, because she had put it in the safe last night. That was not what she had said she would do. "How he gon know who hit come from?" Sim said. That smile again. Because she had written it on the envelope, in big letters: Mr. Sam Denny. "Hit's Sim," Sim said. "*Sim* Denny." She was sorry, she would fix that. And Mr. Rawls would be in touch with him. Behind her that door with the pane of glass you could not see through looked as if it might have been nailed shut.

It did not happen the next day either but the day after that would be Sunday. By Saturday night he had got it in his head that Sunday would be the day. It would be at church, maybe, and people would know and maybe, just maybe, when the time came for announce-ments Brother Dick would speak it out from the pulpit. Then Sunday and meeting in the morning and evening both went by and it did not happen. He went back to work on Monday.

Something did happen on Monday night but it was not at all what Sim was waiting for. It was in the newspaper that Maybelle showed him. "Yo white folks done died, Daddy." He stared at it for a couple of minutes at least, though he never got past understanding that it had happened last night at the hospital. At the hospital. It was like his mind had got stuck on this fact—this and the thought that he never had been to a hospital and never would go to one. He kept thinking this, just this one thing, on until he finally went to sleep that night.

Such as it was, what Sim had been waiting for came to him on Wednesday, after a long day in which he had put on a cement floor a surface like a pool of water that mirrored a clouded sky. It was a letter and Hershel Rawls' name was signed. ". . . your generous gift . . . men like you . . ." it said. He showed it to Maybelle, who only shook her head and gave a sigh. He did not show it or even mention it to Herman. He put it in his pocket. When he got to his room after supper he read the letter again and put it in his cabinet drawer. Then, conscious how his body ached, he lay down on his bed without undressing and went to sleep.

The next afternoon while Sim was down on his knees drawing his float with long sweeping strokes across the wet cement his breath stopped on him. He had to fight to get it back. It came with pain and then he lost it again. This kept on until Tod Nells, alarmed, led him off to the car and drove him home. Sim was better by then. He made Tod go away and went around the house to his room and got on his bed.

Maybelle appeared half an hour later (Tod had found her at a neighbor's down the street) and wanted Sim to go to the hospital. He said he wasn't going to no hospital, that he was all right now, but Maybelle called them anyway. They came and took him, over his protests, by force really, and carried him on a stretcher into an elevator and up and into one of those windowless dim-yellow hospital rooms.

Sim died on the night of the next day. They had thought he was much better, out of the woods now, and just an hour before he died said it would be all right for him to have a visitor or two, if he wanted. A little later Brother Dick appeared and the nurse went into Sim's room ahead of him. Sim was lying on his back with his face turned the other way, toward the wall. He seemed not to hear the nurse the first time she spoke to him. "Mr. Denny, it's Brother Dick," she repeated. "He's come to visit you."

Still there was silence for a few more seconds. "Mr. Denny." The nurse could see that his eyes were open.

"Tell him go way." Nothing but his lips moved.

The nurse was surprised and made another brief try. She got the same answer, spoken exactly as before, and she had to go out and send Brother Dick away with a little bit of a lie.

Half an hour later the nurse was in Sim's room again, to check on him. He was still lying with his face to the wall. She heard him say faintly again, "Tell him go way."

"He left a long time ago, Mr. Denny."

"He out there. Got a letter fo me. Don't want to see no white folks." There was a pause. "Don't want to see no kind of folks."

He said nothing else, would not answer the nurse, and about twenty minutes later she found him dead.

MICHAEL KNIGHT

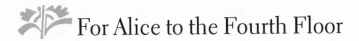 For Alice to the Fourth Floor

Alice emptied her purse—hair brush, pepper spray, cigarettes, matches, birth control pills, mace, phone bill, power bill, Visa bill, leg weights, gum, lipstick, stun gun, movie stubs, horoscope, breath mints, wallet, playing cards, sixty-one cents—not once but twice searching for her keys. The second time she left a nickel on the sidewalk, and Custer picked it up and gave it back, and she dropped it in her purse without speaking. Christmas was only nine days away. Tinsel angels shimmered on lampposts, and parking meters were hooded with Free Holiday Parking bags. Alice was drunk. They had buzzed every apartment, but it was past midnight, and no one would let them in.

"It's because of the serial killers," Alice said. "If they knew it was me . . . Did you know that more people were murdered in Richmond than any other city last year? Per capita, I mean."

"I saw it in the paper," Custer said.

"There are three serial killers at large right this minute. There's the guy who goes after lonely old ladies and such—The Pearl Necklace Killer—and the one who tricks women on the highway and pretends they have something wrong with their car, and then the one who—who—I can't remember what his whachamacallit is—"

"His M.O.," Custer said.

"Right," Alice said, "but I know it has something to do with women. All these crazies loose in the city. People have to be careful."

Rows of brownstones lined both sides of the street, checkered with lighted windows. They created a perfect funnel for the wind and Custer hunched in the entryway of Alice's building, his coat shrugged up around his chin. On the sidewalk, Alice stamped her foot, whether out of frustration or against the cold Custer didn't know. The air had sobered him some, but he was still tight, getting sleepy now, and he wondered how long before he could make a gentlemanly exit. "Come up on the steps," he said. "The wind's not bad up here. We'll think of something," but Alice flounced onto the curb and rummaged in her purse like she had remembered a secret compartment.

"This happens every time," she said. "I meet someone nice and he asks me to dinner and I lose my keys or something and everything goes to hell."

Custer watched her retrieve a cigarette from her handbag and poke it between her lips, watched her shake the breeze-wild hair out of her face. She struck a match and the wind snatched it out. Second match, same result. He shoved his hands into his pockets. He would let her help herself. When the third match failed, she plucked the cigarette out of her mouth, whipped it into the street and he watched it cartwheel under a parked sedan.

"I mean who wants a fat girl with a kid?" she said. "Nobody, that's who. Perverts and creeps and A-holes with exactly zero prospects."

She wasn't bad looking, Custer thought, round-cheeked and blue-eyed, hardly a dozen pounds past pretty. The simple thing would be to hike over to Monument Avenue and hail a cab and invite her to his house. He knew exactly how it would go: he would kiss her, maybe run his fingers along her stockinged thigh or palm her breast on the outside of her sweater. She would or would not sleep with him. It didn't make a difference.

Now, he sat beside Alice on the sidewalk and took the purse from her lap.

"He's a delivery man," Custer said.

"Who is?"

"The other serial killer," he said. "I just remembered. He has a van. He pretends to be a flower guy so women will let him in."

"You're right," Alice said. "That is exactly right."

Custer found her matches and cigarettes and situated one in his mouth and drew his head into his collar like some shy turtle. Then he untucked his shirt and reached his hands in from bottom. Sheltered, he struck a match and puffed on the cigarette until it was going good. When he passed it to Alice, he noticed that her hands were trembling.

She said, "You looked like my humidifier just then. The smoke coming out of your neck. I have a humidifier for my son."

"How old is he?" Custer said.

"Two," she said. "My mother's keeping him. She could bring us a spare key, I guess, but I can't think where there's a phone around here."

A low-slung Cadillac with tinted windows sharked past, music pounding in its wake. The bass resonated in Custer's chest like heartbeat. He helped Alice to her feet and steered her into the alcove out of the wind.

She said, "You're not going to ask me out again, are you?"

She gazed at him with sad eyes and he said, "Alice, listen, let's focus on getting you inside. Your hands are freezing."

"I'm sorry," she said. "I've had too much to drink. I turn into such a whiner when I've had too much to drink."

"We've had a nice time," he said. "Dinner was good. The company was good. Let's get you home and we'll see about—"

Alice began banging suddenly on the door, and Custer saw a figure moving beyond the leaded glass. He yelled and Alice yelled, but whoever it was faded down the long hallway like an apparition. Power lines snapped in the wind. Alice slumped against the bricks, drew her knees up and angled smoke from the corner of her mouth.

"We shouldn't have let the cab go," she said.

"I wouldn't have let the cab go if I'd known you lost your keys," he said. He sucked in a breath and covered his forehead with his hand. "I'm sorry," he said. "I'm sorry, Alice. I didn't mean to snap."

"You're mad," she said.

"I'm not mad," he said. "I promise. I'm just cold."

But it was too late. Her face was already crumpling, her lips pulling back horribly from her teeth, her eyes squinting shut, her shoulders jumping.

"Don't cry, Alice. It's not your fault. It's one of those things that happens sometimes. I've lost my keys so many times I practically have to safety pin them to my underpants. It's not a big deal, Alice, really."

He knelt beside her, waited for her to cry herself out. He hoped the apparition would return. What sort of person, he thought, leaves two people stranded outside on a night like tonight? And so close to Christmas, when everybody should be feeling more charitable toward their fellow men. Alice snuffled and shook. She wiped her face on his lapel.

"It's because of the serial killers," she said into his tie. "They would have let us in if not for the stupid serial killers."

"I know," Custer said.

He raised her chin with his finger. Her eyes looked bigger and bluer amid the smear of mascara on her cheeks. At some point, her cigarette had broken against his shoulder and Alice brushed the ashes from his coat.

"What sort of name is Custer?" she said.

He gave her his standard reply. "It's an old Indian name," he said and she laughed, stepping on his punch line. "It means very, very stupid white man."

Two blocks away the street began its mile long slope to the river, and when Custer hung his head into the wind, hoping that, by some holiday miracle, a locksmith or a police car might be passing nonchalantly by, he could see parked cars tapering into the distance and the optimistic, illusory shimmer of city life. But, at this hour, no one worth knowing was still out and about. Alice hauled herself up by his shirttail, tottering slightly on her heels.

"You're a nice guy," she said.

"No," he said. "Not really."

"That's not true," she said. "You're skinny and tall. I'm a mess, but you stayed with me out here in the freezing cold." She huddled against him and pressed her hand flat against his chest. "You bought me a nice dinner and you were funny. Did I already say you kept me company in the freezing cold?"

"Something like that," he said.

Her eyes were still teary, still swimming. Her lips were moist. It was so cold he could barely smell her perfume, just the vaguely metallic smell of winter. She threw her arms around his neck and sagged into his embrace. When she kissed him, he tasted apples and cigarettes.

"Okay," he said. "Okay."

Her breath was humid on his neck. Her nose was cold. He wondered how he always managed to get himself into this sort of fix. The moment for a civilized retreat had, as usual, come and gone without attracting his attention.

He held her shoulders and said, "Let's don't. Let's just concentrate on getting inside for now. Okay, Alice? Is there another way in?"

Alice leaned against the door, let the crown of her head knock against the pane.

"I always try too hard," she said.

"That's not it," he said. "Listen, I think the best thing is for me—listen, Alice—our best bet is for me to walk up to Monument and try to hail a cab. Then—"

"You can't leave me," she said, clutching his coat sleeve with both hands. Her eyes were huge with panic. "The serial killers," she said. "You can't leave me here alone. I have a son."

"Easy now," Custer said. "We'll relax for a minute and get this sorted out. Do you want a smoke? Let me see your purse."

Custer felt wiry with frustration. He lit a cigarette for Alice and found a breath mint for himself, and they stood side by side and eyed the building across the street. There was only one bright window that he could see, five stories up, color flicking against the glass. He pointed and said, "Christmas tree lights, I think. The blinking kind."

"I hope they haven't fallen asleep," she said, her voice shy. "That's a real fire hazard."

He nodded and she dragged. Her teeth chattered quietly. Custer's watch had stopped two weeks ago—he was only wearing it for show—and he wondered what time it was, tried to recall how much Alice had had to drink. Maybe six or seven glasses of wine, which didn't sound like all that much, but you never knew with women. He studied her now, the pale scoop of flesh beneath her chin, her lively eyebrows. She didn't mean for this to happen.

"They think it's a gene," he said. "These scientists have isolated what they call the Evil Gene. They studied the brains of dead serial killers. It's just like for blond hair or left-handedness. It's sad when you think about it. I mean, that being crazy is the same as having brown eyes or whatever."

Alice's was looking waxy in the yellow light. She said, "Is it possible to have the gene and not be evil?"

"I don't know," he said. "I wouldn't guess."

At that precise moment, Alice jerked her elbows behind her like chicken wings and hunched her back and vomited on his shoes. Custer made a face. He skipped sideways and kept his eyes on the window across the street. He couldn't look at her, but he knew she was on her hands and knees. In six days, he would leave Richmond on an airplane to spend Christmas in Alabama with his brother and his brother's wife and kids. He'd done his holiday shopping months ago in eager anticipation. Presents enough to fill a pair of duffel bags, he thought. Beloved Uncle Custer from Virginia, he thought. His brother's wife was nice looking and kind. She reminded Custer of their mother in a completely wholesome way. His brother had three kids, the boy and the twin girls. They were good kids. But here he was now, aching cold, watching Alice blot a strand of saliva from her lips.

"We're gonna die out here," Alice said.

She was breathing hard, her body shaking epileptically.

He said, "We're not going to die, Alice. Pull yourself together. I'm sorry, I don't carry a handkerchief."

"That didn't happen," she said. "I'm a mother. Mothers don't vomit on people's shoes."

"They're old shoes," he said.

He stood by while she pushed herself up. She seemed a little better, unsteady but lucid, her demeanor less maudlin. She rubbed her hands together, tossed her hair over her shoulders.

"Hell," she said.

"Alice," he said, "I want you to concentrate. Is there another way into your building? If not, I'm going to walk up to Monument and hail a cab. This is getting ridiculous. No serial killers are going to come and get you."

Absently, she said, "The sliding doors on the balcony are unlocked."

"Good," he said. "Show me."

She gripped her coat around her and wobbled down the sidewalk a few steps, then aimed her finger at the side of the building.

She said, "Fourth floor. The one with the plastic chairs."

Hers was an old building, turn of the century, designed in such a way that it vaguely resembled a Victorian manor. Each apartment above the first floor had a small balcony with an iron railing. The ground floor apartments were built with elaborate street level windows and painted rain gutters. It can't be more than thirty or forty feet, Custer thought, how hard could it be really? He was washed with a peculiar sensation that he had lived this night before. He had already climbed Alice's building and delivered her safely from the cold and rescued her from the clutches of wily serial killers. He was in a hurry to put this night out of its misery, of course, but what he felt was more than impatience. He had a distinct sense that he was in the midst of something preordained.

"Okay," he said.

"Don't even think about it," Alice said. "You can't be serious. You're half drunk."

She grabbed his hand, but Custer shook her loose. The wind tugged at his overcoat.

"When I'm half drunk," he said, "I'm twice the man."

The way to do it, he figured, was to shimmy up the rain gutter, then step over to the ledge above the window. From there, he might be able to reach the second story balcony and pull himself up. And that's exactly what he did. It was like watching himself in a movie, inching his hands up the tin pipe, catching the supports with the soles of his feet. It was the simplest thing in the world to take the long step over to the concrete ledge. He flattened his body against the bricks. Above him the sky was milky with clouds, the clouds faint gold with reflected light. He didn't stop long enough to think, just felt along the wall until he found purchase on the balcony with his left hand, then his right, and he was climbing again before he knew it, swinging his legs fluidly over the railing like he had scaled at least one tall building every day of his life.

"Holy crap," Alice said.

"Hey," Custer said. "Damn."

He stared at his hands—palms dusted white from the rain gutter, fingers irritated red—like he was surprised to find them on his wrists.

Blood ticked electrically in his veins. Below him, Alice lit a cigarette and, when she exhaled, he couldn't tell where the smoke ended and her breath began. He took off his coat and tie, tossed them down. The wind caught his tie and Alice had to dance after it a few steps.

"Okay," he said again.

"I mean it," Alice said. "You be careful. Nobody has ever done anything like this for me before."

He held his breath and eased himself onto the crossbar, bent double, one hand over his head like a rodeo cowboy, the other touching the bar between his shoes. The railing wobbled beneath his weight. Alice was saying something but her voice sounded miles and miles away. He gathered himself and lunged, and in the fraction of a second that he was rising toward the next balcony—just after his feet left the railing and just before his fingers closed around the iron bars—that strange, premonitory confidence evaporated and he was drunk and cold and lonely and more afraid than he had ever been. His eyes were shut tight, and he knew, without question, that he was going to fall. He thought of his brother way down in Alabama and his brother's wife and his brother's kids and how sad they would all be to hear of his demise. At least Alice would bear witness, he thought. Alice would remember what he did. Seconds passed. Like waking from a profound sleep, it occurred to Custer that he was not, in fact, falling. His hands had nabbed the railing, his legs were twitching like monkey tails. He peeled his eyes open and he could hear again. "Oh Lord," Alice was saying. "Oh Custer, oh Lord. I swear I'll never lose my keys again." He threw his left leg up and wedged his foot between the bars. He wormed his hands a little higher and a little higher still. He hauled his knee up and suddenly he was safe, over the rail, his feet planted firmly on the balcony, and he stood there, air skidding in and out of his lungs, for what seemed like a very long time.

Alice said, "This is all my fault."

"I'm all right," Custer said. "I'm okay now."

"Don't move another inch," she said. "You stay right where you are. Don't you dare lift a finger toward that balcony." She walked in a nervous circle, dragging Custer's coat behind her on the sidewalk. She slapped her arms against her side and said, "I will never touch another drop of alcohol. I swear I will carry more keys than any person could ever lose."

Custer had let himself forget that this was only the third floor. The very idea of climbing made him light-headed. His bones went watery. His stomach rose balloon-like in his throat.

"I can't do it," he said.

"Don't worry. I'll think of something," Alice said. She seemed wholly sober now, her brow bunched in thought, her foot tapping rhythmically. She laid her hand over her heart in what struck Custer as a pretty gesture. "I can't believe you made it," she said. "That was probably the best thing I've ever seen."

Right then, a light came on behind him, and Custer spun to see the curtain sliding back, a man's terrified face peering out at him. Without speaking or breathing or thinking, he mounted the rail and launched himself for the fourth floor, caught a post and heaved himself over, leaving the man hopping around and grasping at the air where Custer had been. He belly flopped and pressed his face against the deck.

He heard Alice say, "Go back to sleep, Mr. Caldwell. It's just me."

"That wasn't you on my balcony," the man said.

Alice said, "No, sir. It's a friend of mine. We're locked out."

"I know," he said. "I heard you buzzing. He broke my plant."

Custer saw it then, a poinsettia in a red clay pot, spread across the sidewalk on a spray of soil. He hadn't realized that he knocked it over. Mr. Caldwell mumbled something about being reimbursed and closed the door behind him. Alice shook her head, incredulous, and waved and Custer went inside alone. The apartment was dark. He sagged against the sliding door, waited for his eyes to adjust. His fingers felt stripped and raw. His shoulders were vibrating beneath his skin. A red light flickered near the door, followed by a buzz and, for an instant, the entire room was lit by that tiny bulb, couches and lamp shades and candlesticks silhouetted by the glow. A tricycle beneath the breakfast table, a darkened Christmas tree in one corner, a coat rack draped with scarves and empty winter jackets. In the quiet that followed, Custer heard another sound—a rustle of fabric, a whispered voice—and he was sure someone was in the apartment with him. The refrigerator purred evenly. The sink dripped. He said, "Hello," because wouldn't that have been just his luck to find a serial killer waiting all along. "Hello," he said. The odor of cigarette smoke brought his head around, but it was only a trace of Alice having been here before. The buzzer sounded a second time. Custer crossed the room, dodging furniture, that momentary vision of her apartment fixed in his head. Something happened tonight, he thought, but, for the longest time, he wouldn't be able to put his finger on what it was. Custer pressed the button. He held it until he heard Alice's footsteps echoing in the hall.

WILLIAM HENRY LEWIS

 # Germinating

for Taylor Lynne

There was that time, that series of years, fifteen through seventeen, that passed in such a manner that it felt like one long, evolutionary drag of a time-ignorant year. I had been lucky then, or so I thought, through the time of thirteen and fourteen. Puberty had been kind. Not many pimples, no cracked voice, no incredibly frog-like legs. It seemed as if the flow of events in my family, the family itself, or the death of what youth lived in it, willed me to be older without much thought or feeling of the passage.

There was no anxiety, no interaction with girls, or should I have called them *women?* I can't remember what my mother called them. Maybe *ladies?* I felt nothing. For or against. To or from. They were just there, my father had me believe, like paintings, like distance, like my mother, or my great aunt, Lauralinda, and her territorial smile.

Nothing very eventful or strikingly different occurred until the year that was seventeen came along. There wasn't a new car to be excited about, or even a driver's license, but sometime during a series of hot, dusty, columbine days in early June there was that family reunion in Denver.

Some memories of my childhood are more vivid than others, either vaulting into or escaping from the white space of daydreams and the ghosts of rules I affirm or deny as having followed, gone against or forgotten. I envision scores and columns of relatives in some of my daydreams, so many of them are now left behind in the trapped time of that reunion; others remain clearly distinct and alive, and a small few flit in and out of my head like standard-bearers to the army of my most elusive memories.

What I often remember first is the dust and visible heat of City Park and the weight of mile-high air on some of the older relatives who sat under large oaks, trying to fan themselves free of their breathlessness and discomfort. I remember relatives grouped by common names and similar smiles, but I also remember never noticing so many different shades of brown skin in one place. I remember there being too many people, too large of a mass for me to receive any one part of them to mark with lasting clarity beyond that day. Then I remember that they are my family.

The folks migrated to that park in Denver much the same way they had moved North and West drifting from the Post-Reconstruction, traveling with a sense of promise and unhurried urgency. They came slowly to Denver, as old people do: on trains, not planes, driving reliable Chryslers and Chevys and riding in back seats with pillows and magazines to ease the wear of the long trek.

I was sitting on a concrete bench watching my relatives who were holding paper plates of cold chicken and looking for someone to embrace. My father sat next to me and told me what it was like to be them: old and still outliving the rest from year to year. A whole group, a whole parkful, an entire family, missing somebody to hold. I gave this some thought, but I was also doing my best to look indignant for having been forced to be there. My father's words rolled off me, and soon I was into my chicken, greasing my cheeks.

"Just like every child your age: sit and eat, tend to yourself. . . . That better be the best chicken you ever ate, boy." The voice, from behind me, cut into my ears, and I lowered my plate to my lap. I turned around and rose.

"Ohhh, hello, Auntie Lin—I mean, Lauralinda." I hugged her small body. "I was so glad that you decided to come. I didn't think you would."

My great aunt, Lauralinda, who hated to be called Auntie Lin, stiffened slightly in my grasp and then broke free. She tried to appear as if she were looking for something in her purse. Her purse was very large. I thought to myself that it might be funny to ask her if it were meant to carry everything she had brought with her from California. But I looked at the rich, serious tone of her light brown face and knew that she wouldn't laugh.

In the shade of low branches, her posture avoided an easy guess of her age. She showed years, but I couldn't tell how many. My grandmother used to tell me that her sister liked to stand in the shade because it showed off the tone of her light caramel-rich skin without the haze to give it a yellowish appearance.

I stood there wondering what to say. Her face wore an expression that made me feel that she was about to say something, but she just looked at me. I was too young to realize it then, but I think that she had a way of making you speak to her first. A real "lady" would never speak first. I stood there, not knowing that it was meant for me to say something.

"Well, Lin, hah, have you tried the potato salad?" My father started in. "Ole Gail has done it up good again!" He ate while he spoke, alternating food with words and pocketing chunks of potato in his cheeks to enunciate what she craned to hear. "And how 'bout that chicken? Damn!"

I noticed that Aunt Lin had no plate to hold and she wrung her hands. She looked like she didn't want to be holding anything.

My father continued to eat, not paying attention to whether she answered or not.

"Hey Dad," I said, "I need some more Kool-Aid. You going over to the drinks?"

"Noooo sir! Chicken's too damn good! You got young legs, boy, get it yourself!"

We three stood there for a long moment, my father still eating, Aunt Lin and I watching him eat, both of us understanding the situation.

She didn't say anything. She looked at my father and he stopped eating. I figured that she must have practiced a long time to get that expression, and it must have been one that I was raised to recognize, because it made me want to leave. Then again, maybe it wasn't really that look, but instead my own uneasiness. I only knew the weight of her stare.

With a quiet voice made audible by the shakiness of it, she leaned to my father and gestured with her hand, "Roland, go get some beer."

And as if a lever had been pulled, my father went off in search of the beer cooler. I watched him walk away, thinking how out of place he looked at this reunion: bright blue seersucker and red bow tie. He always had an appearance of forced change about him that led people to say, *well, my, Roland, you have changed . . . hair cut? lost weight?* Last year it was yellow pants and a green double-knit shirt.

Aunt Lin was looking straight ahead, her hand still half raised in the gesture that had sent my father off. She was looking at something far away in the rippling haze of heat beyond the shade of the oak trees.

"Your father . . ." She reached for something in her purse, "he isn't a bright man. Is he?" Her concern for wrecking whatever conception I had of my father was secondary to whatever was in the leather-looking vinyl bag that she carried like a baby. From her purse she pulled out a large lace handkerchief. The handkerchief was fine, perfect, and yet this moment was uneasy to me. The air, the mass of relatives, my father, Aunt Lin's strange pale-green hat, which I'd just noticed. I only had a feeling that I should say something. We looked funny, both silent, both still standing.

"Yeah . . . I mean, yes, Dad is sorta weird at times." Something better than that.

She caught my eyes before I could look away. "Weird? I didn't say *weird*, child." She flashed the cloth. " 'Not bright' is what I was meaning. *Dim-witted.* Understand?"

"Just s'pose it's that beer, Auntie. With that tie he does look kinda simple, though," I said it quickly and made an attempt for my neglected chicken.

"Son, some people *look* simple and some just *are*." She seemed satisfied with herself and began to fold the kerchief into a neat triangle. She dabbed the cloth roughly around her lips, unknowingly removing bits of flaking makeup.

"Sit down," she told me.

And we sat. At that age, I had begun to figure out the importance of conversations that I would have with adults by the tone of their voice when they told me to sit. Usually my mother was best at directing me; her powers of implication were phenomenal. It didn't take more than a very simple, quiet, *let's sit for a while.* Or sometimes it was just a look, like in a social setting where she could not rely on my ability to understand her spoken implications; she knew that look would land me. Something about *that* look. It was damn powerful. I can remember my father driving home drunk from an Orioles game explaining to me that it was important for women to have that look. He breathed it out in a half mumble and never explained why, but the thought intrigued me. After my father had set me off on that thinking, I considered myself an expert at tracking that look down. I was certain that my sister had grasped the notion of it by the time she was three, and I figured that my only defense was the ability to recognize it.

I looked at Aunt Lin for a long while. It was different with her; no implications. I remember she once said that *ladies* could be indirect when it was absolutely necessary, but otherwise it was frivolous; ladies who get what they want are direct. She studied the channels of fabric in her handkerchief. Very direct.

"You really shouldn't stare at old people," she said.

"Just noticing your hat." I told her it looked nice.

"Shouldn't lie either."

"Sorry."

"Shouldn't have to apologize all the time."

"Sor—Okay." We sat there for some time. I was watching my Uncle Jimmy from Milwaukee try to explain the rules of horseshoe-throwing to some second cousins when I heard my aunt sigh deeply. It was a breath that sounded more like fatigue than boredom. She took off her hat, set it in her lap, and began to poke at it with the hairpin that had held it there. Amazing. The youth of her hair. Her face. She looked at me with a curve to her mouth, and I thought she must have smiled like that when she was a child.

"It's an ugly hat." She looked to the horseshoe game. "I didn't have to worry about looking my best here. And besides—"

"Isn't that the hat that Ginny gave you?"

She turned to me quickly at the mention of my other great aunt. "Yes."

Her sister, Ginny, had always been too flashy for Lauralinda's taste. Ginny carried clutches. Lauralinda had a purse. And she only wore a light foundation makeup to highlight her light brown skin. Ginny had proudly brandished red lips throughout her life.

I started to say sorry. While she watched the game, I looked at her hair, knotted up neatly, perfectly. It was too shiny, as if it were not her own. I could not help staring at it; I had never seen her without a hat outside of her house. All these years, hidden under hats and in the dim light of her home in San Diego, her hair had not aged. Barely any color was gone.

At that time, when privacy and mystery were everything to a boy my age, it seemed to me that the deep brown on her head was her best kept secret. I felt deeply satisfied in that.

"I wonder where your father has got off to." She began working to put her hat back on. She was just filling dead space, a true lady holding up her part of a conversation; I felt that she didn't really want an answer. I didn't want to reply.

She was still struggling with the hairpin. All I could do was watch her. *Shouldn't stare at old folks.* I reached to help, but she pulled away and quickly jabbed the pin into the hat on her head so that it stuck at an odd angle, like an antenna. I wanted to laugh. It was obvious that it was not as perfect as she would have wanted, but she had done it herself, without help. She didn't need to look for the mirror in her purse.

Across from us, the horseshoe folks had taken a break to grab a new batch of ribs off the grill. Someone yelled about getting some more pictures. Someone else hooted about getting more beer. They were good folks. They wore their best leisure clothes. Hugged each other. They laughed with their teeth showing.

Aunt Lin still faced the horseshoe poles. Her hands rubbed her thighs.

"You don't understand what's going on here, do you, child?" She watched the wind sweep the grass. She just sat there, waiting for me.

"Well, I don't know. There's a lot of people here I've never seen. I don't know them."

She sighed and clutched her purse.

"Good. That's . . . . . . good." She turned to me and her face looked weakened. I thought she might cry, but she put the handkerchief to use and covered her face; somehow it prevented tears.

"That's very good in a way," she breathed. "It's really not worth it. You're too young to know it, but these folks really don't matter. It seems like you can hug them all now, get to know them for a few days, but soon they'll leave. They'll be gone."

"Well, we can't always be together, Auntie," I laughed. "That'd have to be an awful big house if—"

"No." There was a slight wheeze in her voice, but then strength. "No. They will leave you."

"Auntie?"

"This is the last one of these damn things I'm coming to. It's not worth it. Spent a whole life getting away from these crazy people. And now you come back and they don't understand what's going on. Trifling Negroes. They're worthless. They just leave you. And it doesn't even matter; they never had any class anyhow." There was sweat at her temples, and she looked off towards some of the older relatives sitting near the drink table. "Soon they'll all be gone. Take your pictures now; only way they'll ever look like *somebody*."

For a moment I lost the sense of where I was. All of those relatives seemed to be floating through the park, blending into and separating from one another, and the visions of those who were dead lurched out of a past that my parents had pressed on me. I could envision the mass of my family at some point dispersing and slipping from me as I grew older, carried away on silent waves. I imagined myself on some expanse of water, watching them drift to different bodies of land. There was Aunt Lin, sitting on a beach at sunrise, much like the beaches my grandmother had told me about, where they used to go as girls and look for seashells. I envisioned Aunt Lin sitting on that beach holding her arms to her body as if their frailty might make them fall off. She had her face held high, not smiling, but also not frowning, not appearing to want much of anything more than what she had right then. She was looking into the sun. She was the only one on that beach.

"I don't like pictures all that much, Auntie," I said, feeling a need to breathe.

"Well you better start!" She seemed surprised at me, and I couldn't meet her gaze. Her voice came out clear and definite. "You'll come to care about them. You have to. You won't even want to; you'll reject them, but you can't get away from them."

I was hearing her, but I was also forming and editing a picture in my head of my mother, father, sister and me as the only passengers on some cruise ship just off the shore of the daydream beach where my aunt was. I wasn't sure where we were going. It felt like a long way away, though. And I couldn't swim.

"You don't like your mother, do you?"

"No, I do . . . I—"

"Or your father. It's all right. I figured you were lonely; that's why I came over. Not good to hate so much and be so lonely. Not yet, child."

We sat and stared at parallel horizons, each with our own focal point, but both out past the shade of the trees, the overflowing trash cans, the sand boxes of the horseshoe pits and even further, beyond even the near flawless green of the golf course. If we had been on a pier, we might have been looking at the same harbor entrance for different boats to arrive.

"You don't like *me* much, do you?" She didn't look at me.

"I—I don't know, Auntie."

"You better not. You're better off that way." She gave out another life-tired sigh. "Besides, you kids these days don't know how to treat a lady. Stare too much." And then she giggled like she had let out another secret.

I looked over to where most of the relatives were lining up to get ribs. I barely knew any of them. One man, my third cousin Clifford, was trying to take pictures, but he was standing against the sun, and the relatives were reluctant to get their photos taken. Finally, he took a few poor shots to satisfy himself that he could take them whenever he wanted, and put his camera down. I had the feeling that Aunt Lin was watching me watch cousin Clifford. I turned and met her eyes looking at me. Many things hit my head right then: the quality of anger that lies hidden between the known and the unknown, people who were cared for dearly, too much, not enough. Relatives lost and found. Drifting and forgotten. Alone.

And the thought of my aunt's hair, unraveled, in the dark, far away in San Diego, spread on some clean sheet for no one to see, not my grandmother nor even her other sister, Ginny, now dead. And the photographs that would come from this strange family reunion. Re-membrances through eyes such as Clifford's. We looked at each other a long time, my Aunt Lauralinda and I. Shouldn't stare at old folks. I smiled. I tried to imagine the picture that we might make together.

"That really *is* a nice hat you've got, Auntie."

She eyed me, looking as if she meant to break the confidence of my compliment. I thought she might tell me to leave. But then her face softened, a hint of that young girl's secret smile.

She looked away for a moment and then back. Her fingers were working the leather straps of her purse in the absence of something to hold. Maybe we both felt like hugging each other right then.

I got up slowly, not worrying about saying "sorry." I went off to get Aunt Lauralinda a plate of chicken, thinking how when I got back I would ask her about hunting for seashells on the beach at sunrise, and she would take all afternoon to tell me. I would listen quietly, not bored nor bitter, sitting there with her, smiling.

JILL McCORKLE

 Life Prerecorded

When I quit smoking I dreamed of cigarettes. And when I was awake, cigarettes seemed omnipresent. They were everywhere: dangling from lips, burning in ashtrays. I felt the thin cylinder between my fingers, heard my words shrouded in fog, listened for the zip of a lighter, the scritch scratch of a match. I could smell cigarettes from blocks away. Surrounded by hordes of people in the subway, I knew exactly who smoked and who didn't. I moved close to those who did, envying the habit, the rustle of cellophane in their purses and shirt pockets. I wanted to suck the stale tobacco from the fabric of their clothes.

I begged a cigarette from a complete stranger, a man with dreadlocks who carried a brightly colored duffel (I didn't *look* pregnant after all) and ducked into a dirty public restroom, stood in a nasty stall that had no door and read still nastier graffiti while inhaling and exhaling. And as I got down close to the brown filter (a much harsher brand than the one I'd abandoned), I kept hearing my doctor say how he could tell which women smoked by the appearance of the placenta and I could almost feel the poison I had just taken in settling like silt onto that little cluster of cells safely hidden from the world by skin, underwear, jeans, sweater, heavy down coat.

The nurse who took my little cup of urine and poured it into a vial—another sample lined up with all the others waiting to go to the lab—didn't know how to arrange her face when giving results. A wedding ring is no guarantee. Age is no guarantee. It was easier for her to tele-phone, easier to deliver the news without a face, only monotone sylla-bles: *your test is positive*, confirming everybody's home stick tests just like the one I had already tried twice. I found myself reassuring *her*. That's wonderful, I said, and I could hear her lengthy sigh at the other end, like a balloon let loose into the air. She faced a waiting room full of the others: the young girl with mascara stained cheeks, Clearasil and homework assignments in her synthetic leather purse, the one with some boy's ring and promise strung around her neck, the one who had no earthly idea how it could have happened.

The dreams started early, odd little snippets. I was at a table with friends, in a lively colorful cafe with hot pepper lights and I felt so jolly, robust and jolly, and when the cute young waiter, his hair slicked back like a flamenco dancer, came whirling by I asked for an-other fruit juice concoction like the one I'd just finished. Delicious stuff. I ate the cherries and sucked the pineapples. I discreetly picked my teeth with the frilly little parasol. *Fruit juice?* he asks. *Fruit juice?* and the music stops, all heads turn to my table, to me, my abdomen clearly visible under a skintight top like I have never owned in reality. *Lady you just sucked down your fourth double tequilla sunrise.* What? *Lady, you look discombobulated* he says with a shocked face and that word, *discombobulated*, with all its loud harsh syllables seems to rico-chet around the room. I get stuck on the word, my head bobbling, reeling, about to fall off. The images came to me, woke me, the black-ened placenta slipping onto a clean hospital floor, the wide-spaced stare of fetal alcohol syndrome. That one was a recurring dream, right up there with the one where the bathtub is steaming and bubbly and this beautifully shining naked baby shoots from your hands like a bar of soap into the well of an empty tub or out an open window. There's the one where you leave it on the hood of the car and speed off down the highway, and the one where you accidentally pierce the fontanel, that soft spot, with something as innocent as the wrong end of a rattail comb.

There were times in those early weeks when I couldn't help but smoke. How bad could one cigarette really be? How bad could one little paper tube be compared with nervous energy and honest-to-God craving? I walked blocks to a strange, distant neighborhood with a drugstore where no one recognized me, to buy a carton and then I hid them in the apartment, here a pack, there a pack, so it seemed like they weren't even really there at all. Early mornings, I stood in my nightgown and watched from our fifth floor window until my husband disappeared around the corner. I climbed out on the fire escape with matches and an ashtray. The knowledge that I *was* going to smoke allowed me to slow down, take my time, angle myself so that I had a good view, red brick buildings and sidewalks rising up Beacon Hill. Then I puffed furiously, the late November wind making me shiver as people down below scurried past in their down coats and scarves and hats. I watched our neighbor walking toward Charles Street, his steps slow, as methodical as the metallic click of his prosthetic heart valve.

Our neighbor. As we were moving in, we had been told by the single woman below us—the one who wore faux zebra spandex minis and catered to at least five Persians I could see lounging in her bay—to avoid *the old man* at all costs, to look the other way. He'll talk your head off, she whispered and then rushed off to her job at a small gallery on Newbury Street. She never once asked what I did, somehow having gotten stuck in the groove of my husband's job (he's an actuary). Like many people who aren't sure what one *is*, she simply stopped talking and left.

I met our *old man* neighbor that same day while the mover was still bringing our things. It was only late August but already felt and looked like what I knew as the beginning of autumn in the south; there was a breeze off the Charles River and with it the sharp, water smell that I grew to appreciate, even to welcome, as home. The light seemed sharper, whiter, the shadows longer. It was a surprise to find that I *loved* this city, the street, the building. I thought about all of this sitting on those old concrete front steps, smoking one cigarette right after another—right out in public—and watching our belongings come off the truck.

It was while I was watching my Great-Aunt Patricia's pie crust table angled and turned through the door that Joseph Sever stopped to introduce himself and then (as the other neighbor had predicted) proceeded to talk. He told me how he used to smoke, how he smoked Lucky Strikes, started during the war, liked them so much he kept right on. He said if he hadn't had such a good reason—his life—to quit, that he'd still be smoking three packs a day and enjoying every puff. But of course that was before his wife of forty years, Gwendolyn, died, before the heart valve, before his temples atrophied. He had been an accountant right there in the downtown area and he described those April evenings when he worked so late, lighting cigarettes without even thinking, sometimes finding two lit and burning in the ashtray as if he had an invisible partner.

He asked (it was clear he'd give consideration to any possible answer) how I spent my time. When he stopped speaking and there was a lull in the hoisting and heaving of the movers, I could hear his valve, a metallic click as it swung closed to prevent his blood from rushing back to its source. I told him that I worked as a copy editor for one of the publishers in town and with that entry, he started in talking about books, his favorites from as long as he could remember: *Look Homeward, Angel* as a young man new to the city, and then *Anna Karenina* and *For Whom the Bell Tolls*, all of Hardy and Conrad, a little Jack London. "I'm a bit of a literary dabbler," he said. "I have written some perfectly horrible poetry myself." He liked T. S. Eliot and he liked Yeats. He liked to pause and quote a line or two with some drama, always stopping, it seemed, just as his breath gave out, at which point he tipped his latest L. L. Bean hat and bowed.

I came to learn that he purchased a new hat each season: the panama in the summer, the wool huntsman cap in the winter. I imagined a closet filled with hats, stacks and stacks like in that book, *Caps for Sale*, a favorite book read in my memory in the voice of Captain Kangaroo. It turned out that at the end of each season, he continued to do what his wife had called *purging*. He gathered up everything he could live without and took it to the Salvation Army bin down on Cambridge Street. "Everything except books," he qualified, "and of course the cats." He and Gwendolyn had always had cats, sometimes one, usually two. During his fifty years in the building, he had had fifteen different cats and could name them in one fluid motion, their names rhyming and rolling as each received an apositive: the friskiest of them all, the one with a terrible urinary problem, the one Gwendolyn never got over, the one who ate a rubber ball. He said that I should come visit his apartment and see what fifty years of books will look like. "This will be your future," he said as he slowly mounted the stairs. "There are rows behind rows of books, in closets and in one very special kitchen cabinet. Gwenny always used *Heart of Darkness* to balance the lamp that wobbles by our bed." He paused on the landing before taking his flight to the second floor, the big brass-plated door propped open by the movers. "I keep it there. The lamp is a hellish thing, old and shorted out, but I keep it there."

I kept dreaming I was having a kitten. I looked at the faceless doctor and said, "Oh thank God she didn't have her claws out." I told him that yes she was really cute, but that I was kind of disappointed. I really wanted a baby. At which point he laughed, just slapped his knee and laughed in a way that marked the absurdity of it all. *Imagine wanting a child.* Then I dreamed that I *couldn't* have a child, there was no child, and I went to a special clinic seeking help. I rode the T, changing trains twice; I took a boat and a bus and a taxi. The building was no bigger than the little drugstore around the corner and women of all ages and sizes and shapes were pressing up to the counter behind which stood a woman in white guarding the shelves of test tubes. "Ah, yes, Mrs. Porter," she said and nodded when it was my turn. "We have your child." Suddenly all the other women were gone and I was being carefully handed a small glass tube. I held it up to the light and inside it I saw a beautiful little girl no bigger than Thumbelina, who I remembered from my childhood fairy tale book. She had dark brown hair that waved onto her shoulders, and big blue eyes that I was absolutely certain I saw wink and blink in affection.

"Freeze-dried," the woman said. "Same process as coffee. Just go home and add a little water, you'll see." The woman looked like someone I knew, a former teacher, the mother of a classmate, I couldn't quite place the face. "Be very careful with her, now," she added and handed me a special cardboard tube much like what you'd use to mail a stool specimen or a radon test. Carefully, I kissed the precious glass tube and slipped her into the sturdy container and then into the special zippered section of my purse. I put that into a brightly colored duffel and looped the strap over my head for extra security. In the dream I had dreadlocks and a joint hidden in my bra.

"Oh by the way." I was almost out the door when I remembered the important questions I had planned to ask, all of the things that my husband and I had discussed before my long journey to this place. "Her medical history." The room was buzzing with grappling grabbing women again and I was being shoved out of the way. "Please. I really have to know all that you know about her." The woman seized my arm and pulled me behind the counter and back behind the heavily rowed shelves. She leaned close and whispered. Now I knew that I had never seen her before in my life. I would have remembered, the shiny broad forehead, the missing teeth. "You must never reveal what I'm about to say. If you do people will want your baby. They will never let her alone." She leaned closer, her mouth covering and warming my ear as I strained to hear. "Her mama was Marilyn Monroe," she said. "And her daddy," she paused, looked around nervously. "JFK." I felt stunned, disheartened. Why couldn't my baby just be the product of Flo Taylor and Ed Smith from Podunk, Wisconsin? I didn't think to ask why they were giving *me* such a burden. *Is it all random or have I been singled out, especially chosen?* My worries turned to mental health issues, substance abuse genes, square jawlines, and prominent teeth. But then all because I was wondering about the rich and famous, I found myself thinking about good looks and talent and Southern roots. I dreamt I said, "Do you have one from Elvis?"

At three months, that magical time when you supposedly cross the threshold from morning sickness to a sudden burst of energy, the uterus slightly larger than an orange, we decided to take a vacation. The reason was clear. It was freezing in Boston not to mention the fact that everywhere we turned people were saying to us, *Your life is about to change, it will never ever be the same.* Like birthdays, weddings, funerals, it seemed important to mark this transition, to continuously remind ourselves that something was in fact happening. We chose the Virgin Islands as a way of feeling we had gone very far and yet not left the country. I just didn't feel I could be pregnant *and* in another country.

The first day of our trip was like a perfect dream. I lazed in the sun, calypso music playing down the beach, the warm clear water as blue as the sky. I listened to the birds and the steel drums while I ran through lists of names in my mind—names of relatives long deceased. The voice of the man who was trying to interest my husband in a time share wove in and out of my thoughts. He'd sat himself down in his shorts and Hawaiian shirt, canvas shoes with laces untied, smelling like Hawaiian Tropic and some kind of musky aftershave and asked my husband if teenage girls were better looking than ever before these days or was it just him? I heard him tell my husband that he preferred younger women, always had. "Like that one, Mmmmmmmm, Mmmmmmmm," he said, his words oozing in such a way I half expected to see them like black oily leeches crawling off his tongue. I opened one eye to his gleeming white teeth just in time to follow his look to a string bikini, oiled brown thighs too young for cellulite. I wanted to sit up and tell him that of course he *liked 'em young,* that any grown up woman with any sense whatsoever wouldn't touch him. But the warmth of the sun and the distant drums, the hunch that even the very young woman who had just passed would not give this two bit Peter Pan salesman the time of day seemed satisfaction enough. That and the fact that I had lifted his almost empty pack of Marlboros and hidden them deep in my beach bag. I listened to him pat his pockets and look all around. Let him have a little nicotine fit, get a grip on the libido. I devised a plan: I would get up in the middle of the night and tiptoe out onto our balcony. I would huddle off to one side and blow my smoke with the wind just as I had done through screened windows of a locked bathroom as a teenager. A little mouthwash, deodorant, hairspray, cologne. If no one saw me, if I didn't confess, it was like it never happened.

The next morning I woke to the sensation of wetness, the gray numb of sleep suddenly startled by recognition as I hurried to switch on the fluorescent light in the bathroom. It was real; I was bleeding. Slowly, carefully, I called out to my husband and lay on the cool tile floor. I felt detached, like I was in someone else's room, on someone else's vacation. I imagined a honeymoon couple, whirling and dancing, drunk and giddy, collapsing on the bed while the stark sunlight and still blue sea lay beyond the sliding glass doors. Same place, same room, same toilet, different life. I lay there and questioned everything.

Why did I buy the crib so early? Why did I smoke that Marlboro Man cigarette? I lay there wishing that we were home. I wanted the cracked broken black tiles of our own bathroom; I wanted our neighbor sitting with me on the front stoop, the smell of the Charles River, our pots without handles and the rickety three-legged couch I complained about every time I sat on it; I wanted normalcy. I said, *Let's Make a Deal.* Let me win this round and I will never ever again smoke. I will go on great missions and try not to gossip. But more than anything I solemnly swear to never again smoke.

It seemed to take forever, phone calls, a slow walk, the idle chatter and words of sympathy and well wishes from the time share man, his gaze taking in the freshly raked beach. There was a boat ride, and then an ambulance that really was a station wagon with a light on top. There was an emergency room and then a closed door, a hall where pregnant women perched like hood ornaments on cheap aluminum stretchers, some crying out in labor, their wings spread in pain. They had no ultrasound; they had no answers. I was thinking about the used car lot that was across the street from my grandmother's house when I was growing up. I thought about the little plastic flags strung across that lot and the way they whipped in the wind. *It's a Good Deal* the sign said and whenever anyone commented on it, my grandmother simply leveled her eyes at the person with a solemn stare as if to say you better work hard to *make* it a good deal. Woman by woman, I rolled past. They looked lifeless; used and worn and tired.

I spent a week sitting in bed or on a chaise on the balcony, the room littered with room service trays; the hotel had limited choices: conch chowder, conch fritters, conch omelet, conch conch. I could hear my husband down below, in my absence forced to hear more time share news, to have young supple bodies pointed out for his perusal, while I clicked a channel changer round and round hoping that all of a sudden I would find more than one station. Over and over they advertised a parade that had taken place the week before, people in bird suits, feathers and bells, marching. I lay in the bed and watched little yellow sugarbirds fly up to suck the jelly packets I placed outside, the breakfast tray discarded on the dresser. The Kings Day Parade. The Kings Day Parade. It was a bad Twilight Zone. It was like the world had stopped suddenly and thrown everything askew.

*   *   *

Everyone has a story. Perfect strangers come up and tell me the most horrible story they've ever heard about pregnancy and childbirth. They will say, I shouldn't be telling this to *you* and then proceed without ever pausing to draw a breath. You hear about the woman who miscarried after the three month mark and about the woman who knew at seven months that her baby was dead but was asked to carry it into labor all the same. "Oh sure," people will say. "It's common to bleed like that. Happens all the time. No real explanation." Que sera sera. A miscarriage is just one that was never meant to be, you know, a genetic *mistake*. If you lose this one you can always have another. But look at it this way, you haven't lost it yet! *It ain't over til it's over. The fat lady ain't done singing.*

The river is within us, the sea is all about us. Joseph Sever's voice quavered out the line as he leaned closer to me, all the while looking at my abdomen now two months beyond the Twilight Zone scare. He insisted that I read aloud, anything I was reading, anything my husband was reading. We should be reading aloud all the time now. He had read an article about it, the words, the sounds traveling through the layers of clothes and skin, thick hard muscle to those miniature ears, lanugo-coated limbs gently swishing and bathing. "Who knows what's for real," Joseph said as he tipped his hat and once again reached for my grocery bag piled high with cigarette substitutes like licorice whips and Chunky Monkey ice cream, greasy Slim Jim sausage sticks, the taste for which I thought I'd outgrown. "We know nothing of this world, this great universe," he paused, hazel eyes squinting in thought as he waited for me to nod. "Take God for example," he said and laughed softly, "and which came first, knowledge or man's *need* for knowledge?" I motioned him on with his errand, his own marketing trip. It was our daily struggle, trying to help one another on the icy brick sidewalks. We argued who was more in need: an old man with a bad heart or a pregnant woman who would not believe that everything was really okay until she gave birth to, saw, held, heard a healthy infant.

I dreamed of my grandmother. She was naked and alone in a rubble of upturned graves. I squatted and cradled her in my arms, so happy to find her alive after all, forget the damp orange clay and what seemed like miniature ancient ruins. Forget the pale shrouded family members wandering aimlessly in search of loved ones. (Was this Judgment Day?) And then I dreamed myself sleeping, my husband on his side, his face a comfort. My own head was inclined toward him. I wore the very gown I wore in reality and within the dream I woke to a chill, a cool draft that filled the room and I sat, startled, and turned on the lamp by the bed where stuck to its base was a little yellow post-it note with the words *I came to see if you believe* written in a small deliberate hand. Yes, yes, I believe. I believe. I woke myself with this affirmation. I woke to discover that my husband was already up and in the shower and that I wasn't entirely sure to what or to whom I had given this great affirmation of faith. I woke to the tiny buzzsaw, vibrating uterus, a pressed bladder, the dim gray light of day.

Early that summer—week 28, the time designated for a baby to be "legally viable"—Joseph and I went to see the swans being brought to the Public Garden pond. It was warm and we walked slowly, taking our time to point out to one another lovely panes of amethyst glass, the little catty-corner building that looks just like the drawing in *Make Way for Ducklings*, the bar that was the model for *Cheers*, crowds of people waiting in line to get inside and buy tee shirts.

Joseph talked about how Gwendolyn always saved old bread to scatter for the birds. We sat on a bench in the shadiest spot we could find, the ground in front of us littered with soggy bread that the overfed fat ducks were ignoring. I told him about the Peabody Hotel in Memphis and how as a child I had been taken there to see the ducks marching from their penthouse to the elevator and down and across the lobby to the pool. I told how I had looked around that lobby and marveled at the people staying there, this fine hotel with its rugs and chandeliers and fountains. I was with a church group, one in a busload of kids stopping here and there to sing for other congregations. It was supposed to be an honor (not to mention an educational experience) to get to go on that trip, but I spent the whole time reading Richie Rich comic books and wishing myself home. It was the summer before Martin Luther King was shot. It was when Elvis still walked the rooms of Graceland in the wee hours of the morning. It was when my sister was practicing to be a junior high cheerleader and my grandmother was still walking the rows of her garden.

With the arrival of the swans (they had been staying across the street at the Ritz), Joseph cleared his throat and began reciting. *Upon the brimming water among the stones are nine and fifty swans.* He paused and laughed, and added, "Or what about two swans?" But with Yeats's "wild swans" he had once again opened his favorite topic which led eventually, as the crowd began to thin—baby strollers pushed away, ambulatory children led away to visit the bronze ducklings in a row, couples spread picnic blankets—to Eliot and one of his all-time favorites, "Journey of the Magi," which led him to "The Gift of the Magi" and then into his own Christmas story, one I'd heard on several other occasions. *Christmas with Gwendolyn.* The picture of Gwendolyn I always conjured to my mind had the look of a Gibson Girl even though I knew that she wore her straight gray hair cut close with bangs and that the waist of her dark wool coat hit high around her short thick middle. He kept a photograph on top of his dresser: Joseph and Gwendolyn in 1945, standing on a busy sidewalk, each cradling a shopping bag, his face filled out in a way I'd never see.

"It was just the two of us," he began as he often did, pausing with the unspoken question—one I never asked—about whether or not they had ever wanted a child. His close attention to my own growth, his comments on my coloring and my hair, seemed answer enough. He described their Christmas Eve, the rushing home from work in the midafternoon to find the other waiting on the stoop—her with a black wool scarf wrapped around her head and tied beneath her chin, him with a gray fedora he felt certain she was about to replace that very night. He said that when he looked back it seemed like it always snowed right on cue. *Let there be snow.* Inside their windows fogged with cold dampness, the lights they strung glowing as they pulled old boxes from the closets, tied red velvet around the cats' necks. They waited until dark and then they walked down to the waterfront, the freezing wind forcing them to walk huddled up like Siamese twins. They listened, ready to stop with the sound of any carolers, any church bells, paused and looked up into windows to see the lights and children and greenery. *The city was never more beautiful.*

They ate in a small dark restaurant at a table by the window. First they ordered bourbons (hers with a lot of water) and then they spent the first hour just talking over the year behind them. Oh, there were those years when the plans went awry, when one or the other was upset about this or that, work or a sick family member; there was that year when, for reasons he didn't feel it necessary to discuss, they were farther apart than they had ever been, complete strangers coming and going for a period of three months. They feared that they would lose each other. That there would be no forgiveness. He said this part quietly, nodded a slight nod as if to say *you must understand what I'm saying*. "That was the worst Christmas," he said quietly. "Really the only bad Christmas." He laughed then and looked at my abdomen, gestured to it as if speaking to the child. "Trust me. We were better people once it was all over. We made it." We watched the swans circling, necks arched proudly as they didn't even acknowledge the various breads and cracker crumbs tossed out onto the water. "In my mind the Christmas, *the* Christmas is the way I've described it. Our dinner talking over us. Our life and our future."

On all of those Christmas Eves it seemed they were the only people out. Others had rushed home to family gatherings but neither of them had relatives close by. They were alone with each other. The best part of it all was that they always got the very best tree left at the Faneuil Hall lot for just three dollars. (It had gotten up to ten by the time Gwendolyn died.) Then they dragged the tree home and decorated with common little items, things they already had. Paper chains cut from glossy magazine pages, tinfoil stars, spools of thread, her jewelry, his neckties, fishing gear, chess pieces tied off in twine. "We had a glorious time," he said. "Brandy and poetry and her crazy ornaments until the sun, that cold winter light, came through the window."

This Public Garden day, with the temperature at at least eighty as we made our way back down Charles Street, we once again argued over who was in the worst shape, a thin old man with a prosthetic heart valve or a pregnant woman so far beyond her normal weight she thought she'd never wear shoes other than the rubber clogs from Woolworths. *A hard time we had of it*, he said in short gasps as we began our climb up the dark stairs to our apartments.

I dreamed my husband and I went to a party. We were greeted at the door by the mother of an old friend of mine, a childhood friend I had not seen in years. In real life I knew that the mother had recently died of leukemia and in the dream I knew this truth. And I knew that it was not my friend's mother who greeted us but a three-dimensional image of her. Somewhere in this room there was a silent projector.

My husband said how wonderful she was. He said, *no wonder you love to be over at their house all the time*. (I had not seen the house in twenty years.) I could not bring myself to tell him the truth, that we could pass our hands straight through her body; that there was absolutely nothing there.

The dream jumped the way they do and the party was over; we were almost at the car when I remembered that I had left my coat behind. I raced back only to find an empty room (had the others there been projections as well?) and on the wall was her image, stilled. They were projecting an image I'd forgotten. It wasn't the way she looked racing up the gold-carpeted stairs of her house, demanding that we explain the cigarette burn in my friend's brand new windbreaker, or the one she wore a year later when she handed me my first sanitary napkin and elastic belt, or the one she wore the day the moving van arrived to take them to California. Rather, the expression I saw, frozen there on the wall of the dream was one more subtle and fleeting; it was the one she wore most of the time.

My friend and I are in the backseat of her Country Squire. We are taking turns inking the initials of the boys we love (high school boys we've never met) in cryptic fashion on each other's Blue Horse notebooks. In the wayback, her brother and his friend are bouncing up and down until her mother casts a quick glance in the rearview mirror. "Settle down, boys," she yells, a forced furrow in her brow. They obey, at least while the light is red, and she goes back to her humming. And this is the moment: the second glance in the rearview mirror, the look after she yells, when her face relaxes into a half smile. On the radio is "We'll Sing in the Sunshine" and she sings along, her voice a little nasal, twangy with confidence. And that's what I see on the wall, over and over, that look, and in that look, I see Indian Summer, the fashionable ponchos my friend and I had shed balled up at our feet, the flat terrain of our hometown passing us by.

I had back labor. We took a taxi across town to the hospital, me stretched and riding as upright as I could manage, my face pressing into the soiled gray ceiling of the cab, smelling the traces of smoke that lingered in the upholstery. The cab was smoke free, or so the driver said when my husband hailed him; at the time I was squatting in front of our building, my face against the concrete steps. Just the day before, Joseph had been in that very spot waiting for the cab that took him to the very same hospital for a brief stay, a series of routine tests. In the hospital, we were still neighbors, though wings and floors apart, and I wanted to get a message to him but at the moment I felt discombobulated and all tied up. *Would I like narcotics? Why yes, thank you very much.* I said that I'd also appreciate a needle in my spine just as soon as they could round up an anesthesiologist. *Epidural, please.* The words rolled right off my tongue; I had forgotten everything I knew about breathing.

My friend and I were eleven years old and in love with Tommy James and the Shondelles. "Crystal Blue Persuasion" was playing on her little hi-fi on the floor when we heard her mother coming up the stairs.

"Where did you girls get cigarettes?" She flung open the door to my friend's room and stood there, hands on her hips, frosted hair shagged short on top and long on the neck.

"Junior's Texaco," my friend whispered meekly. There was no need to paint the picture, the two of us riding double on her banana seat bike, me pedaling furiously while she held onto my waist, her legs held stiffly out from the spokes. We were on the service road of the interstate. The glittering black asphalt was still steaming from a recent rain.

Labor went on forever. A monitor was strapped to my belly for contractions, another to the baby's head for its pulse. I was telling jokes and calling my sister long distance by then. I was watching a contraction rise like an earthquake reading, the needle going wild to register my unfelt pain. I was ready to push when I realized that I'd been talking for hours and that the doctor had never left my side. Then I realized that all was not well, that my husband was too quiet. I had come this far—no cigarette had come close to my mouth—and yet, there was a problem. The baby's heart rate dropped, a heart so small I couldn't even imagine. It was a simple procedure, this C-section, but it had to be done quickly, now, this instant. They knew what to do; they had all of the right equipment to slice through the layers of skin and muscle, to pluck from my body a fully formed baby.

*   *   *

My friend's mother reached into her bathroom cabinet and handed me a sanitary napkin and a little elastic belt. I had seen them before. I had practiced wearing one at home; I had envied those girls who had already turned the monumental corner. She said that she understood if I felt I needed to go home but she really hoped that I'd stay the night as we had planned. I stood barefooted on the cool tile floor of her bathroom, my eyes still red from chlorine, my hair bleached and like straw from the local pool. I watched the toilet paper and the fancy little embroidered guest towels sway with the blast of central air conditioning. She sat on the end of her bed, the first queen size I ever saw, and talked while I nodded embarrassedly. Here was the moment I had been waiting for, the threshold, and I felt gawky and foolish and uncomfortable. But I stayed and we went to Teen Night at the community pool, where we played ping pong and sat on the hard wooden benches that lined the chain link fenced area. I felt like I was sitting on a garden hose but maintained my position for fear that the outline would be seen through my shorts. I kept thinking about my friend's mother on the foot of that bed, ankles crossed, a flash of pale pink polish on her toenails. A million years later when I heard about a girl several years older who faked sick to stay home from school and then slept with her boyfriend in her parents' house, this was the bedroom I pictured even though they had long since moved to California. I saw the bed, the chenille spread pulled up tight, pillows rolled and pressed against the scratched headboard. I saw the brown tiles of her bathroom floor, smelled the blast of central air and the lingering chlorine. My friend's sixth grade school picture was on the dresser in a heavy gold frame. At the height of first love, Saturday nights in parked cars or on the busted couch of somebody's forsaken gameroom, the friction of adolescent passion driving me forward, I thought of that picture; the bed, the coolness, the distant glance, all insecurities and reservations temporarily brushed aside.

The day after my daughter was born, I woke to great relief which was quickly followed by a fit of anger, a cold seizing of what might have been or might not have been. Fifty years ago and maybe my child and I would have been the names with slight ages on tombstones. Many times I had gone with my mother and grandmother to tend my grandfather's grave; they weeded and planted, brushed the pine needles from his marble footmarker. My grandmother pushed a whirring handmower up and down the hill of his plot. I never knew him, her husband, my mother's father, my grandfather, but I imagined him stretched out there beneath the dirt; I saw a young man in a World War I uniform even though I know he lived to be a very different man, a much older, frailer man with wiry gray hair. On a nearby grave there was a tiny stone lamb and dates that equalled nothing, the baby born and died on the same day, the mother dead just one day later. The more I looked over the mossy slabs, the more I found. "Oh honey," my grandmother said and squeezed my hand. "It *is* sad." So many of them must have died for such simple simple reasons.

I asked that the stitches in my abdomen be eternally blessed; I praised modern medicine, saluted and sang. I called everyone I knew or had heard about who had, in so many words, squatted out in the woods like an animal, gnawed tree bark and umbilical cord, stoically delivered in absolute isolation. "You idiot. You goddamned selfish idiot," I raged and hung up before they knew who I was. In some places I am thought to have an accent.

Hurricane Andrew took the hotel in the Virgin Islands and all of the nearby time shares. I keep thinking of the place as if it still exists. I do the same with Joseph Sever. We moved a year after my daughter was born and when we left, an August day much like the one of our arrival, he was out on the stoop wearing his panama straw and reading the Boston *Globe*.

The week before the move, we had finally done all of those things that visitors do: the bus tour, the battleship, the Old North Church. I spent a whole afternoon at the top of the Prudential building, my daughter tucked away in the little sack I wore strapped to my chest, as I fed quarter after quarter into the viewfinders. In a random glance toward Beacon Hill I spotted the steeple of the church on our street, and from there it was easy to swing back and find our building, to travel up the red brick to the roofline. I found our bay window, the plant on the sill; I half expected to see myself enter the room, my abdomen round and hard and waiting. I had that same odd feeling that I get from time to time, the feeling that maybe I *can* pick up the phone and call my childhood friend or my grandmother at those memorized numbers long disconnected. That I can find a clean path into my childhood where I might race my bike, down the street and into the yard, the wheels spinning and clicking—a triangle cut from an aluminum pie pan clothespinned to a spoke. That I *can* run inside and find my parents thirty years younger, younger then than I am now, as they talk over some event that will soon be lost to that hour. I moved the lens just one hundredth of an inch and there was Joseph's living room, the outline of what might have been a cat.

We exchanged greetings over the next couple of years—Christmas cards, postcards. The last card to arrive was addressed to my daughter, an Easter card, one of those you open and confetti comes out. I hate those drop what you're doing and go get the dustbuster cards and yet there I was, my daughter delighted by the sparkled shapes while I imagined him there on Charles Street in one of the fancy card stores, thumbing through racks in search of the right one. The news that he died came from another neighbor in the building, and even then, seeing it all in print, it didn't seem quite real. I couldn't imagine the orphaned cats being given away or the years' worth of warped books pulled from the kitchen cupboard, the dilapidated bedside lamp left on the curb in a heap of garbage bags along with *The Heart of Darkness* and all the makings of a thrown-together Christmas. Instead I saw, see, him out on the stoop or down at the corner grocery picking his fruit from a table out front, his breath visible and keeping time with the click of his heart.

My friend and I went to the cemetery to smoke cigarettes. She pedaled the bike that time. Her legs weren't as strong as mine so we wobbled and nearly fell on the small dirt paths. It was a new cemetery, the kind where there are no raised stones, only flat slates of marble at the foot of each grave. The flowers, whether artificial or real, look as if they have sprung up from the graves. People in our town liked the smooth new look and the serene white statue of Jesus in the center. But as I inhaled and exhaled, narrowed my eyes like I'd seen smokers do, I told my friend that I preferred the place my grandfather was buried. I liked the huge trees perfect for tire swings and clubhouses except they were in a cemetery. I liked the moss and the dates before I was born. Here, the people started dying in the sixties and it all seemed too close. I told my friend how my Dad could palm a lit Camel nonfilter and hide it in his pants, how he had once done that in high school when the principal walked by. I had heard the story many times, and I had seen enough old photos to picture him there, his hair combed back high off his forehead—a pompadour—as he leaned, tall and thin, against the brick wall of the gymnasium. I turned my cigarette inward, heat near my hand, to demonstrate. My friend did the same, the fabric of her jacket singeing when she tried to slide her hand into her pocket. We smoked and smoked until our heads felt light and then we chewed three pieces each of Teaberry gum and rubbed our hands in the yellow clay of a grave recently dug. Everywhere else there was perfect green grass, rolled out like a carpet, flowers sprouting up from the dead.

I think of that place every autumn when I kneel to plant bulbs, when I sprinkle a teaspoon of bone meal into each hole as my grandmother advised. And at Christmas I pull up Joseph's scene, the walk to buy the tree, the brandy and makeshift adornments. I give Gwendolyn Gibson Girl hair and a rhinestone cigarette holder. I give her the face of my friend's mother. "How old will you be when I'm one hundred?" my daughter asks, enunciating in a way I will never master and I say "one hundred and thirty one." I catch myself looking at her in absolute amazement, that she is here and the time is now. A faster sperm and she wouldn't be here; there would be another child or no child at all. No day beyond that moment would be exactly as I know it now. It might not be a bad life, just a different one. What we don't know is enormous. "I want you to live forever," she tells me. "I want a guinea pig and a Fantastic Flower kit. I want long wavy hair and I want to be like Jesus and have people pray to the god of me forever." I tell her that I would like nothing better, that it's every young mother's dream.

Sometimes I think of the woman, cheered by the long-awaited phone call that she is pregnant. The nurse on the other end is relieved. Everyone is overjoyed. She goes upstairs to take a nap and never wakes, an ectopic hemorrhage. Would the fanatics in the street argue that the life within, this bundle of cells unintelligible to the human eye, killed *her*, these people who rummage the back alley dumpsters of emergency rooms to find some hideous example of sin in a jar, these people who take someone else's worldly loss and turn it into a freak show? I can barely keep my car on the road when I see them gathered in protest, their hideous pictures waving in the air. "Why don't you *get* a life?" I want to yell. "Go after handguns. Go after R. J. Reynolds." *nothing worse than killing own child*

I dreamed of my grandmother; I lifted her as she had once lifted me, my feet potty black from her garden, through the damp dirt-floored shed where she stored her jars of tomatoes and peaches, floating jewels, pickled and preserved. In the dream I watched people wandering, stones overturned, granite lambs tilted on the heaving mounds of cracked earth. Was this Judgment Day? "I don't know what all the fuss is about," she said and I was there holding her, pulling her closer, corn and tobacco fields beyond the upturned graves, holding her and whispering the song she made up years before, a lullaby sung to the tune of an unknown hymn, *you're my baby, you're my baby, you're my baby, yes you are.*

When I was fifteen, I spent many afternoons cruising the streets of my hometown with a friend who drove a baby blue Mustang. It was a car to be envied and we were like queens, the radio blasting the top forty, our suntanned arms hung out the window to flick our cigarettes. I was a bona fide smoker then, a pack of Salems in the zippered part of my vinyl purse, fifty cents in my pocket in case I ran out. Sometimes we drove way out of the city limits, out where we were surrounded by flat fields and little woodframed houses, churchyards overgrown, the rush of the brisk country air drowning out the music of the radio. Those rides gave me such a rush, tingling scalp and racing heart; I felt powerful like I could look out over those fields to the end of the world.

Now I find my daughter all dressed up in front of a mirror. She is almost five and is wearing a faux leopard poncho and a little pillbox hat with netting over her face. Her high heels are silver-sequined and wobbling to one side. She has a pencil held between two fingers and with her other hand on her hip, takes a deep drag from the imaginary cigarette. She tilts her head back, purses her lips and blows at her image, eyes closed while she says, "I must be running now, my dear." She turns quickly and stops when she sees me there, her shoes leaving marks as if she had suddenly put on brakes. "Oh hello," she says in the same affected tone. "I'm pretending it's long long ago. Back when cigarettes were good for you." With that she takes another puff and blows her smoke my way and I lean close to breathe it all in. I breathe in as much as I can take for now.

LEWIS NORDAN

 Tombstone

In an odd coincidence, because it just so happened that the day I'm going to tell you about was my late son Robin's birthday, I found a manila envelope in the day's mail that struck me as odd. I laid the other mail aside and took a look at it and said, "What the hell—?" and tore open the seal and discovered that a friend down South whom I hadn't heard from in years had sent me, just because it was so odd and it made him think of me for some reason, a black-and-white photograph of a graveyard in Mississippi where some of the grave markers were hand made. It had been fourteen years since my son died and the guy who sent the package would have had no way of knowing about his death, and certainly not that today was his birthday, so this was a true coincidence.

I was living up in Pittsburgh by this time—my wife Annie and I lived in the Squirrel Hill section of the city in a fine old Tudor style home that was always needing some damn thing done to it, pointing the bricks, replacing the slate on the roof, lining the old chimneys with stainless steel sleeves—and generally feeling pretty well satisfied that my grief was by now mostly only a memory and that full repairs had been made to my grief-damaged marriage. So it came as a complete surprise to find myself looking at this photograph and suddenly thinking of Susan, a woman I had had an affair with all those years ago when the grief was fresh and nothing could relieve it at all and I would have done anything to black out the reality of my unbearable pain, even betray the wife I loved.

This memory of Susan came back to me with such power that I could almost believe she was standing there in the room beside me, the smell of patchouli hanging like a cloud in the atmosphere, and the pathos of her sad eyes and big feet. It's odd the things memory holds. I stood there looking at the photograph of the cemetery. I felt a little light-headed. I regularized my breathing. I could hear Annie knocking about in the kitchen. I felt guilty suddenly, overwhelmingly guilty and guarded, secretive, as if all the betrayals of the past were still fresh and the pain new and that all our forgiveness and new promises had never happened. All this from looking at the photograph of a cemetery.

Annie is my second wife, not Robin's mother. She didn't even know Robin at the time his body was found. This was one of the things that came between us, I'd have to say, his having no personal reality to her. Annie only knew Robin as the violence that left our new marriage in a shambles and crushed all our dreams to dust. She hated him for all our lost hope, and I hated her for hating him. Or so it might have seemed from some of the fights we had back then.

Robin gassed himself with a hose from his exhaust pipe, out in the Mississippi big woods. He was seventeen, had only had his driver's license for a year. I almost did the same thing a hundred times afterwards, gassed myself I mean, with a green garden hose I bought at the Shadyside Hardware Boutique. I know, it's ridiculous, a hardware boutique, especially as a place to buy an instrument of potential suicide, and the prices are outrageous, but the store is so convenient, and they have anything you can think of. The place is owned by an older couple, two gay guys who look like Tweedle Dee and Tweedle Dum. I don't know, the place appeals to me for some reason. Anyway, I believed that if I followed Robin in death—well, actually I'm not sure what I believed. Mainly I was simply out of my mind with pain.

Robin had been depressed, he wouldn't take his medication—that's really all I know about why he did this terrible thing. His body wasn't found for two weeks, so you know, things were as bad as they could get. He was identified with dental records. The police photographs of his car showed it to be covered with flies. For a long time I blamed myself, the divorce, you know, every harsh word I had ever said, guilt of all kinds. The truth is, nobody can ever really explain a child's suicide, it's a terrible mystery, terrible.

So anyway, Annie was in the kitchen, and I was standing at the mail table. The house was fragrant with warm cooking odors, dill and garlic and I don't know what else, sweet onions and bay maybe. A fire was crackling in the fireplace. I'm trying to set this domestic scene to show what a normal day it was before the photograph showed up in the mail. No family is ever really normal, I realize, and especially not after a child's suicide, even fourteen years afterwards, no matter how much therapy you get, how well you seem on the outside to be doing. After a child commits suicide you finally figure out that no one is safe, anything can happen, that we're all alone in the world. You forget this from time to time, you have to in order to keep going, but it's always there.

The fact that Annie was in the kitchen at all would seem odd if you knew Annie. Annie's not much of a cook, let me just say that right away, straight out. I'm not talking behind her back, she knows she's no cook, she would tell you the same thing herself, she's proud of it, it's a badge of honor that she can't cook. I've always fixed the meals for the family, so I'm the one who gets cookbooks and aprons and special pots and small appliances for gifts. I had to draw the line at a chef's cap one Christmas. I'm no gourmet, I'm just saying I'm the cook. I mean, it's misleading to report that Annie was in the kitchen and the house was fragrant with a pumpkin soup bubbling in the oven in its own rich dark-orange pumpkin shell, the garlic and bay and dill and the other rich aromas perfuming the house, as I was going through the mail that day. It's misleading because this particular domesticity is just another one of the day's coincidences. Any other day of the year Annie wouldn't have been found anywhere near a kitchen.

Maybe twice a year Annie cooked a special dish for this "support group" she belonged to, and it just so happened that, along with the other coincidences, this was her month to host the group. She got the recipe out of the Moosewood Cookbook, which she claimed was the only cookbook she could read. It's a little too heavy on tofu recipes for my taste. Her friends, the support group, were coming over for their monthly get-together that night. I was supposed to get lost, make myself scarce, so Annie could have the house to herself. I thought I might hit a movie, walk around the mall, whatever. I can't say I really understood what a support group did, but Annie seemed to enjoy the meetings, so what the hell.

It was November, and so winter was not far away, the hardwoods were gray and bare, the last of the apples had rotted under the tree out back, the last of the leaf blowers was whooshing away, down the block, and the air had a nip in it. I had laid a fire in the fireplace, as I said—aged hickory logs we buy from an outfit in Pittsburgh—nice guys, who stack the stuff out back under the shed and hang around chatting about getting into graduate school in forestry, or whatever—and fat pine kindling that I ordered from L. L. Bean in a handsome shipping tin and burlap bag. So anyway the fire was crackling away and the soup was bubbling, and it suddenly occurred to me that this image of marital perfection was something Annie and I had been putting together for a long time, maybe in the hope of canceling the hex that Robin's suicide had placed on our dreams, maybe in the hope of living long enough to fit into it and feel comfortable there, and true. It suddenly occurred to me that we might have been kidding ourselves for a long time.

I kept standing by the mail table in the library—we actually have a room we call "the library," if you can believe that, with built-in bookshelves to the ceiling—looking at the photograph I had just unwrapped from its packaging and thinking about Susan, this skinny, stringy-haired, big-footed, knobby-kneed, patchouli-smelling hippie girl I had the affair with all those years ago. Where in the world was she, I wondered. She had moved to Eugene, Oregon, I thought I remembered, where now she still lived, I supposed, a thirty-six-year-old retro-hippie of the great northwest. God, could she really be in her mid-thirties, and had I really been so selfish as to seduce her with my overweening grief?

The photograph, though. I won't get fancy and try to describe the composition of the photo, the arc of light and dark, the leafless scrub trees that frame the little cemetery, the rightward swing of the eye across the field. I feel silly saying even this much. I don't really know the vocabulary of photography well enough to feel confident to say anything at all in this area. I'll just say what is obvious: this was a graveyard of the poor—four graves on barren ground.

The grave marker farthest back in the frame was a proper store-bought monument—it must have required sacrifice to buy, a small granite or marble cross with a name and date chiseled expertly into the stone. Another marker, homemade obviously, seemed to be a dark slab of thick, possibly varnished wood with the name John Taylor and a small cross and small heart crudely carved above the man's name, then painted white to contrast with the darker wood. Tiny crosses and two dates, one on either corner of the marker, look a little like home-made tattoos on the arm of some rough looking guy in a truck stop. Those guys break my heart, really, those truckers: a heart, a cross, carved into their flesh with God knows what instrument and doused in blue ink.

What I'm trying to get around to describing, though, is the tomb-stone at the center of the photograph. I mean this tombstone was really something. It seemed to be made of concrete, and weirdly shaped to look like the man whose grave it marked. I'd hate to walk up on this baby in the dark, I can tell you; it would scare the bejeebers out of you. I was just standing there in the library, books all around me, the fire crackling in the fireplace, the pumpkin soup adding its rich texture to the house. Annie was in the kitchen, and I was looking at this photograph of a homemade tombstone. And thinking of Susan, for no apparent reason. It was an odd moment, to say the least.

The tombstone was basically just a big rectangular slab of concrete standing in the middle of this scraggly-ass cemetery. It had the dead man's name (Evan Stewart) and the dates of his birth and death etched into it. Somebody had drawn these details in with a stick when the cement was wet. It looked like a sidewalk some kid had scratched his initials into. A crude, concrete tombstone, that's what it was, but the power this picture held over me was frightening. The thing had a head, the tombstone, I mean. A head had somehow been fashioned from the slab, when the cement was wet, and now this head rose from the shoulders of the thing, the statue, monument, whatever it was. And that was not all. Concrete angel wings stuck up from the "shoulders" of the monument on either side of the head, white-painted and etched with lines—to represent feathers, I'd say. This thing was strange, I'm telling you. The statue's closed eyes and its broad nose and other features had been etched into the cement, also when it was wet, I'm guessing, and a short beard had even been painted onto the face with black paint. I'm not doing justice to this description. I just had never seen a grave marker that brought the image of a dead person in a grave so immediately to mind.

My first instinct, for some unknown reason, was to hide the photograph from Annie. Maybe I believed that by looking at it she too would be reminded of Susan and of my betrayals and all our tamped-down pain and know that somewhere inside me still resided sufficient agony and fear to drive me to such desperate measures again, to lies and betrayals and dangerous secrets. I don't know, maybe this sounds overly dramatic. All I mean to say is, I felt suddenly secretive and unwilling to share anything at all with anyone else, least of all Annie. Suddenly the pain of Robin's death came over me with such force that I believed I would die, and that Susan was the only person in the world to whom I could safely speak the truth of my heart.

Annie called from the kitchen, "Was that the mail?"

I heard the oven door creak open as she checked the soup. I hesitated. I said, "Yes."

"You sound strange. Are you okay?"

I walked into the kitchen and found Annie wearing one of my aprons. I had never seen her in an apron before. For a moment, seeing her there brushing a strand of hair from her face with the back of her hand, then holding open the oven door to peek at the pumpkin shell, almost broke my heart with what we had lost and suffered and how Annie, in this one image anyway, seemed suddenly reborn as innocence, plain and simple.

I said, "This photograph came in the mail." I held it out and she took it from my hand and looked at it uncomprehendingly. I said, "It made me think of Susan, for some reason."

She looked at the photograph for a long time, and then she looked up at me.

She said, "Did Susan send you this?"

"No," I said. "No, of course not."

She looked at the photograph again, and then again at me. She said, "You haven't heard anything, have you?"

"Heard anything?"

"Is Susan—" I looked at my wife and realized she was crying, almost crying, tearful. What she said next took me completely by surprise. "Susan didn't die, did she?"

"Jesus, honey," I said. "No. I mean, Susan?"

"Oh God," she said. She dropped the photograph onto the floor and held me suddenly, crying now, all-out crying, until my neck and shoulder were wet with her tears. When she could talk, she said, "I was so frightened. God. I thought she had died."

I bent down and picked up the photograph from the floor and held it for both of us to see. I said, "It's just a photograph. It's a graveyard in Mississippi. Those are homemade tombstones."

Annie cried some more, then took off the white apron and blew her nose into it and handed it to me, and went into the library and sat in front of the fire. I followed her into the room.

I said, "Are you okay?"

She said, "I feel as if you should call her, be sure she's all right, you know?"

I said, "Call Susan?"

She said, "I was so frightened when I thought she was dead."

I sat down then as well, and we didn't say anything, only stared into the fire.

She said, "I've still got that one appointment." She meant she had to go to her office for an hour or so, though it was already almost dark.

I was smoothing the snotty apron across my lap, slowly, as we talked.

She said, "I don't know what got into me. Those tears. God."

I kept on smoothing the apron across my knees.

She said, "She's been with us so many years. She's a part of me. Susan, I mean. I was afraid I had lost her."

Annie looked up at me and smiled a wan, apologetic smile. She looked back down at her hands.

I was in over my head. I knew this. Suddenly I understood exactly what a support group was for. I knew I needed something that neither Annie nor Susan nor any woman on earth could give me. I needed support of some kind, and I had no idea where to turn. I was afraid

Annie would notice this and understand that she had outgrown me. I had not felt so alone since the early days after Robin's death.

Annie looked at her watch then and stood up and kissed me goodbye. She went to the kitchen and turned the oven to Low. She was headed to her office on Ellsworth to meet with her last client of the day. I followed her to the door, still carrying the apron, and watched her make her way down the slate walk, pulling on her light coat as she went.

When she was gone I knew I could not stay alone. I felt agitated and hopeless. I paced. I tried to watch TV. I called information for Susan's number out in Oregon, but hung up before an operator answered. I left the house, still carrying the photograph in my hand. I knew where I was going, though I did not know why.

Most of the Shadyside businesses were already closed, though Starbucks was busy, and so was Schiller's Pharmacy, and also the fancy-schmanzy market where all the vegetables were so perfect they looked fake. It was early evening, already dusk, and I could see from my car that the doors of the store where I parked were already locked. The Closed sign was up, though I could see a light on inside. Fourteen years ago, when I had felt this same desperation I ended up here at the Shadyside Hardware Boutique, where I bought the green hose. Now here I was again. I got out of the car and went to the front door and pressed my face to the glass and looked in. The store manager was standing at the register, actually the same man who had sold me the hose years ago. He was a rotund, jolly sort of guy in his fifties who wore a green mechanic's-style apron with big pockets on the front and a billboard-type message across the chest that said *The Electrician and I Are Not Just Friends.*

I held the photograph flat against the door-glass and rap-rap-rapped with my knuckles to get his attention. He looked up immediately and peered over his bifocals in my direction. He looked back at the ledgers in front of him, and put the ledgers aside, and walked around the counter to the door. He peered through the glass and looked at me.

He mouthed, "Closed. Sorry." I couldn't really hear him through the door, only the muffled sound of his voice, but I could read his lips well enough.

He turned and started to walk away, and I rap-rap-rapped again until he looked back at me and noticed that I was trying to show him the photograph. I still held it against the glass. I had been in the hardware boutique many times over the years, but I wasn't sure he remembered me.

I shouted through the heavy glass: "I want to build a tombstone." I had not known I was going to say this, or even that I had had such a thought. It seemed eccentric even to me, bizarre even. I would not have been surprised if he had called the cops.

He didn't though. He turned slowly and cocked his head to one side. He hadn't really heard me, though he must have heard some part of what I said. I had been shouting very loud, bellowing you could say. He began to walk back toward the door, very slow, cautious. I was desperate, far more out of my mind than I had known, or than I can describe now. It was luck that such feeling attracted rather than repelled him.

For a long time he stared at the photograph. He looked from it to me and then back to the photograph again. After a long time he nodded his head and looked into my face. He said, "What did you say?" Now he put his ear near the glass to listen to my words. I shouted again that I wanted him to help me build a tombstone, and this time he heard, he understood what I was saying. He knew his ears weren't deceiving him. He opened the door of the Shadyside Hardware Boutique, and I stepped inside, out of the chill.

I said, "I bought a garden hose from you. To gas myself with."

He shut and locked the door, then turned so that we faced one another. He said, "No refunds without a receipt."

I said, "No, it was—" and then I saw that he was joking, and the two of us laughed.

He said, "Come on back to the back."

We built the tombstone. Together we did this odd thing. We spoke very little as we worked. He asked me nothing of my motives. He gave me a workman's apron of my own, similar to his but without the gay rights logo. It was made of stiff, heavy canvas, with big tool pockets. It felt very different from the aprons I wore to cook our meals. He measured and sawed some two-by-fours on a table saw. The ringing of the saw in my ears and the fragrance of sweet-scented sawdust in my nostrils might have been magical things. This was a man's world. I had never lived in such a world before, at least so it seemed to me in this strange moment. He showed me how to nail the sawn boards together into a large box. I reached my hand into a barrel of nails and drew out as many as I could hold. I placed some of them into my mouth and tasted the sweet metallic oil. I took up a hammer with a handle made of ash and balanced it in my hand. From my mouth I drew first one nail and then the next and the next, as I went about my work, at this man's direction. I banged my thumb and fingers with the hammer until finally all the nails were in the pine. I tested the box, and it held firm.

The man with me showed me how to extend the sides upward to form wooden wings. He rummaged through a series of sheets of tin until he found one I could cut to the right length with a pair of tin snips. With this strip of sheet metal I fashioned the head, the mold that would eventually become the head of the tombstone-statue. When the cement was poured—the bag emptied into a plastic tub, the sand and water mixed in with a boat paddle—together the two of us shoveled the wet cement into the form of the crude angel-boy that we had created in the back room of the hardware boutique. We painted the wings with white paint. With a dowel rod I drew a face into the wet cement. A joy I had not felt for fourteen years swam into my heart as I fashioned Robin's sweet closed eyes, as I remembered having seen them in sleep, and a trace of his pickerel smile, a shallow dimple in his cheek. On the wide breast of the tombstone I etched in his name, I wrote this day's date—his birthday, and in an odd way my own birthday as well. I thought of Annie eating pumpkin soup with her support group. I thought of Susan out in Oregon. No wonder Annie loved her, wept for fear of her passing. They were denizens of the same world, sisters even in betrayal. Now I stood in my world, in communion with one of my own, wearing our canvas aprons. I told him my secrets, my fears, my love for my wife. He held me as no one else could have. Our hands were covered with cement. I was tired and banged up from our work.

LOUIS D. RUBIN, JR.

 The Man at the Beach

From the top of the ferris wheel at Folly Beach you could see a long way in all directions, up the beach to where it was woodland along the shore and beyond that the black and white rings of Morris Island lighthouse tower, northward to the flat marshland beyond the wide creek that separated Folly from James Island, and to the south the ocean, green-blue to the far-out horizon beyond which lay nothing but water all the way to the coast of Africa. It was almost like being in an airplane, except that there was the steel grid of the giant wheel that, though it revolved, was anchored securely to the earth.

The amusement park was across the way from the pavilion. We headed for it as soon as my father parked the car. Uncle Leo's car was right behind, and Maynard and Elaine hurried across to join us. Uncle Leo and Aunt Sophie were not really our uncle and aunt, but we had always called them that. There were five of us in all—my sister and my little brother, Maynard and Elaine, and myself. Maynard, at 13, was the oldest, and my brother, who was seven, the youngest. Each of us had money for three ride tickets and an ice cream cone when we were done. My brother went straight for the merry-go-round, as he always did. There was one horse that was his favorite, painted red with a silver mane and saddle. He would climb aboard it and grasp the reins securely, use all three of his tickets one after the other, then buy his ice cream cone and rejoin my parents on the beach in front of the pavilion.

What we liked were the electric cars. There were several dozen of them, and when the current was turned on they all glided around the circle. The cars were powered by electricity. They had metal rods that thrust up from the cockpit like the mast on a sailboat, and as the rod atop them made contact with the electric grid there were continual flashes and sparks and a strong odor of ozone, much like the atmosphere of a violent thunderstorm on a summer day. The cars had thick rubber bumpers, and steered very loosely, and the trick was to bump into one car and send it spinning into the path of another. But if you were not careful, and sometimes even if you were, someone was apt to run into your car, and before you knew it you were caught in the melee, frantically turning the steering wheel while your car slid sideways out of control.

Maynard and I got into one car. My idea was to move to the outside of the circle and stay out of trouble, but Maynard saw an opportunity to ram into the side of the car bearing my sister and Elaine, and we steered toward it, only to be bumped from behind, pushed sideways directly across their path, and promptly sent flying again. My sister and Elaine were laughing at us, but then someone rammed into their car and off they went, too. When the cars stopped moving and the ride was over, my sister proposed that we switch places. She would ride with Maynard, and Elaine with me. So we changed over, and Maynard and I dueled with each other, bouncing against each other's cars again and again as we made the circle, while the girls shrieked and laughed. Finally Maynard's car sent ours sliding halfway across the track, and we spun round until finally I gained control and was about to return the favor, when the flow of electrical current ceased and the cars slowed to a halt.

Then we went to the ferris wheel, and as the open gondola rocked back and forth we went rising up, seated four abreast, over, down, then up again, until the ferris wheel stopped while we were at the very zenith of the orbit and, suspended in the air and swaying slowly, we hung in space for a long minute, gazing at the ocean, the beach, the land. A bank of gray-white cloud was over the sky to the west. There was a freighter far out at sea, so far that we could see only the super-structure above the horizon. It seemed to be without a hull, only a white cabin and masts and a stack with a smudge of smoke. The Mor-ris Island lighthouse tower was clearly in view. Then the ferris wheel resumed its revolution, and we dropped downward, until we could see only the tip of the lighthouse tower, and in a moment it was com-pletely out of sight.

We walked over to the pavilion, bought our ice cream, then went down to the beach. Our parents were seated in folding chairs, beneath striped beach umbrellas. Uncle Leo had on his bathing suit. My father never went swimming; before his illness he had been a strong swimmer, and used to venture far out beyond the breakers, but though he had mostly recovered from the operation on his head he was for-bidden to go into the ocean for fear of ear infection. He and my mother and Aunt Sophie sat in the beach chairs watching us as, run-ning ahead of Uncle Leo, we sprinted for the surf.

We stepped out, dodging the incoming waves, until the water was up to our waists. Though it was a very hot July afternoon, the sea seemed chilly at first, but after a moment we became used to it and settled down into the water with only our heads above the surface. Uncle Leo, however, continued out toward the breakers, striding out to an oncoming comber, then diving through the wall of the rising water as it broke over his head, to emerge well beyond it. Maynard, who could swim very well, followed him out. I could not swim at all, and I stayed with my sister and Elaine, my head above the water, let-ting the current sweep around me, occasionally pushing myself up to let the swell of an incoming wave go past. My brother, I saw as I looked shoreward, was seated in water up to his waist in a gully at the edge of the ocean's margin. I waved to my father and mother and Aunt Sophie, and my mother waved back.

After a while Uncle Leo went back onto the beach. The four of us stayed in the surf, with everyone swimming around except myself. What I did was to move about, my arms outstretched so that my hands were just touching the bottom, and my body buoyed by the salt water, pretending to myself that I was a ferryboat, traveling back and forth, pausing occasionally to dock, and repeating under my breath the bells and the whistle signals, just as the boy in *Tom Sawyer* did with the Big Missouri. It was enjoyable to push myself about in the surging water, giving way as the waves swept around me, but always keeping a hand, or sometimes just a finger or two, in touch with the coarse sand of the submerged beach, gently but firmly maintaining my way even as my legs and my trunk swayed in the ebb and flow.

Later we left the water and went back up onto the beach. My little brother stayed on in the gulley. He seemed to be trying to splash minnows into a pool he had dug. When we reached the place where our parents were seated, we saw that a man was standing there talking to them. He was wearing white duck trousers with rust stains on them and a yellow polo shirt and was blond-headed and somewhat red of face, though his skin was deeply tanned. The man was doing most of the talking, with my father and Uncle Leo nodding and occasionally responding, "Oh, yeah?" and "Is that right?" The man seemed to be telling about a voyage or airplane trip or something that he had been involved in and was going into considerable detail, though I could not tell exactly what it was he was saying.

"That your boy?" the man asked Uncle Leo, pointing to me.

"No, that's his boy," Uncle Leo replied. "That's my boy over there," with a gesture toward Maynard, who was standing off to the side listening.

"Going to show you a trick, son," the man said to me. He came over to where I stood, lay down on his back in the sand, and held his arms out in front of him. "Now you run and jump right into my hands, and I'll flip you over, and you'll come right down on your feet."

I looked at him uneasily. I was not sure just what it was that he wanted me to do, and not especially eager to try it.

"Don't be afraid," he said. "Just run straight to me, and throw yourself right at my hands. I'll catch you. It won't hurt."

I looked at my father. I stepped back a little way, and ran, not too fast, toward the man, half throwing myself, half falling upon him. He had to lower his hands to catch me, but he grasped me about the waist, and I felt myself being lifted and tossed up and over, so that my legs went over my body and head and I came down on my feet a foot or so beyond the man's head, having executed a somersault in the air.

"How's that?" the man asked. He looked at Maynard. "You want to try it now?"

Maynard nodded. He came running toward the man, launched himself in a swan dive toward the man's arms, and was taken up and tossed in a flying somersault, head over heels, landing upright several yards beyond.

"That's the way!" the man said. "Just run hard and throw yourself at me. I'll do the rest." Still lying with his back on the sand, he turned his face to me. "Now you come try it again. Run hard."

This time I came at him faster, and dove toward him. Once again, but more smoothly, I felt myself being taken in his strong hands and tossed up and over, into the air, and some distance beyond him. As I did I again smelled a strong, raw odor, not exactly unpleasant but quite sharp. It must be whiskey, I thought.

"Can I try it?" my sister asked.

"I think you'd better not," my mother said.

"I won't let her fall," the man promised.

"Can't I?" my sister repeated.

"Do you think it's all right?" my mother asked my father.

"I think so," he replied.

"Very well, but be careful," my mother told my sister.

Now it was my sister's turn to go sailing in a cartwheel above and beyond the man. Then Elaine tried it, and for a while we took turns, one after the other, somersaulting in the air. The man did not seem to tire. My little brother, who had come to watch, decided he wanted a turn, and because of his lightness the man flipped him far into the air and he came down, squealing with delight, well beyond where any of us had landed.

"Now, that's enough!" my mother called. "You'll wear the poor man out."

"That's all right," the man told her. "I'm doing fine." He sat up. "Here," he said, this time to Maynard, "let me show you another one. Come here and just stand right over my chest." He lay on his back again. Maynard went up, placed his feet on either side of the man's torso, and the man put a hand around each of Maynard's shins and raised him straight up in the air, over his head. "How's that?" he asked as he held Maynard three feet above him, firmly and without seeming to strain at all. Maynard giggled. Then the man tossed him deftly sideways and up, and he came safely down on his feet.

"My turn," my little brother said. Each of us followed. The man's hands were very firm in their grip, and I had no difficulty at all holding my balance, though when he tossed me away I stumbled as I landed and fell to my knees before I could regain my equilibrium.

"You're real strong, mister," my little brother said.

"I'm all right," the man said, grinning at my parents and Aunt Sophie and Uncle Leo. "You're pretty strong, too, I bet."

"Uh huh." My brother flexed his biceps determinedly. The adults laughed.

"That's enough acrobatics for now," Aunt Sophie said.

"Were you really a pilot?" Maynard asked the man. Maynard knew everything about airplanes and pilots. He had books about them, and built balsa models that were highly exact in detail. When he grew up, he said, he wanted to be an airplane designer.

"Sure am," the man said, making a change in tense. "Flew in the Dole Pineapple Derby, Seattle to Honolulu. Finished third, right behind Martin Jensen."

"How come you didn't win?" my sister asked.

"Cracked cylinder head about 400 miles out. Slowed us down and we finished out of the money. We were ahead till it happened. Flew a hundred feet above the ocean most of the way. Had only five gallons of gas left when we landed."

"What kind of plane did you have?" Maynard asked.

"Beechcraft 17R. Got a picture of it in my living room."

"Do you still have it?" my sister asked.

The man shook his head. "Sold it the next summer, when we went barnstorming in Mexico." He pronounced it as if it were spelled Mehico. "Too heavy for that."

"What kind of plane do you have now?" Maynard asked.

"Don't have one right now." The man turned to our parents. "How about if I take these kids up to the pavilion and buy them an ice cream cone?"

"That's awfully nice of you," my mother said, "but they've already had some ice cream, and we've really got to be going home." She and Aunt Sophie rose to their feet. Uncle Leo and my father took down the beach umbrellas and began folding the canvas chairs and towels.

"Where did you go in Mexico?" I asked the man.

"Mexico City, Guadalajara, Tampico, Chihuahua—everywhere. Ran out of gas a hundred miles east of Chihuahua, had to land in a cornfield. Nearest gas was 50 miles away. Had to pay a man to go get it by horse and wagon. Spent three days waiting there till he got it and brought it back. Had to live on frijolas and cornmeal. Got sick from drinking the well water, was in the hospital in El Paso for a month."

"Come on, Maynard," Uncle Leo called. "We've got to get going. It's going to rain before long." There were dark clouds coming into view now over the dunes to the northwest.

We said goodbye, but the man came along with us. He began talking to my father. "How about doing me a favor on your way home? Turn right just past Mazo's and go two blocks. My place is right there. Little white house, all by itself. You can't miss it. How about stopping by and telling my wife I'll be home later?"

"Well, uh, we're sort of in a hurry . . . ," my father said.

"Won't take you but a minute. Sure would appreciate it. I got some business at the pavilion. My wife'll be real worried about me."

"Well—," my father said.

"Just go right in, and make yourself at home. There's an ice chest with fresh milk and soft drinks under the cot in the hall. Just help yourself. Take the kids in, too. Got pictures of airplanes on the walls."

"We won't go in," my mother said. "We'll just leave word if your wife is home. Come on," she told me. "Let's be going."

"Have you got any from the Pineapple Derby?" I asked. I had read about that in a book of mine entitled *Minute Epics of Flight.*

"Pineapple Derby? Got a picture of myself wearing one of them leis," the man said. "Put them around our heads soon as we landed." Then, to our parents, "Go right in the house, make yourself comfortable." He turned to me. "You go in and see the pictures. Next summer when you boys and girls come back over here I'll take you for a ride. Take you all over the island, and over to Charleston, and out over the ocean. Won't charge you a thing. You folks, too," he added, addressing the adults. "I'll have my license back next May."

"That's very nice of you," Aunt Sophie said. "Come on, Maynard. We've got to go."

"So long now," the man said. "You just come over and ask for me at Moffett Field, right off the highway a mile the other side of the bridge. That's where I'll be. I'll have my license back," he said again.

He went on into the pavilion, while we walked toward the automobiles, carrying the umbrellas and the chairs. Though the sun was still shining, a bank of dark clouds was rising toward mid-sky, in the shape of a giant anvil.

"How about that?" I said to Maynard. "A real pilot. He was in the Pineapple Derby."

"The Dole Pineapple Derby only had two planes to finish," Maynard said. "All the others were lost at sea. Martin Jensen was second. He said he came in third."

"Maybe he got it mixed up with another race." Maynard was probably right; he knew all those things by heart.

"Besides," Maynard added, "that was in 1927. He said he flew in a Beechcraft 17R. They didn't start making Beechcraft planes until a couple of years ago."

"You think he was lying about being a pilot?"

"I don't know," Maynard said.

"I think he just got his dates mixed up," I insisted. "If he was making it up, how come he's got pictures?"

Maynard only shrugged.

"He was a mite loaded, wasn't he?" Uncle Leo remarked to my father as we reached the automobiles.

"To the gunwales." My father laughed. "He was feeling no pain."

"Do you suppose he really does have a house on the back road?" Aunt Sophie asked.

"We can find out," my mother said. "It won't hurt to deliver his message, I suppose."

"I'll bet his wife will know what kind of business he has at the pavilion," Aunt Sophie said.

My mother chuckled. "If it is his wife." She turned to us. "Be sure you brush all the sand off before you get in the car."

"Come on, get in," Uncle Leo said to Maynard and Elaine. "If we're going to stop by his house we'd better be moving. We'll be caught in the rain if we don't." By now the sun was hidden behind the edge of a mass of gray clouds. It was hot and the air felt sticky. I thought I could hear a rumble of thunder off in the distance, though it might have been an airplane.

We got into our car and drove off. The cars had been sitting in the sun all afternoon long with the windows closed and were very hot. Past Mazo's Grocery we turned right and headed down a sandy road with crushed shell spread along the ruts.

"Are you going to go in his house?" my sister asked my parents.

"No, we'll just deliver the message," my mother said.

"I'd like to see the picture of his plane," I said. The man had said that he was in the picture with the plane, wearing a lei. If he was, I ought to be able to recognize him. Maybe there was another Pineapple Derby besides the famous one in 1927.

We drove past pine trees and a few houses, until we came to a small bungalow with white asbestos shingling, off by itself, with stands of pine trees on either side. There was an old bicycle near the front door, and alongside the house a couple of washtubs and several rusted 20-gallon barrels. The place seemed deserted.

My father stopped the car, and we got out. Uncle Leo pulled up behind us and got out of his car. "I'll go see if anyone's home," he said. It was so hot in the car that all of us also got out, and we stood together in front of the house. We could hear the thunder growling off to the west, and the sky was dark.

Uncle Leo walked up to the front door and knocked. He waited. No one came to the door.

"Nobody seems to be home," he said.

"Let's go look," said my mother. She went up to where Uncle Leo was standing. Uncle Leo knocked again. After a moment he tried the front door handle, and it opened. "Anybody home?" he called. There was no answer. He closed the door.

My mother went to the door and opened it again. She peered inside. "I don't see anyone," she announced.

"Maybe we ought to leave a note," Aunt Sophie suggested.

"No, there's no use in that," Uncle Leo told her.

"Can I go in and see the airplane pictures?" I asked.

"No," my father said. "You stay right here."

"But he told us to," I argued. "He wanted us to go in and see the pictures."

"I don't care," my father said. "You just stay outside."

Then, as we stood there, a woman appeared from around the side of the house, with a little girl.

Quickly my mother stepped back from the door. "Your husband asked us to stop by and tell you he was going to be late," she said to the woman.

The woman barely nodded. She was small, with light hair, and dressed in a faded green blouse and a pair of yellow slacks. She was wearing sandals, and her toenails were painted pink.

"He said he had some business at the pavilion," my mother explained.

I looked at the little girl. She seemed to be about eight years old, and with long blonde hair and blue eyes. Her face was almost expressionless; her eyes gazed at us.

They must have been around back, I thought. I had the conviction, which grew on me, that no matter how plausible our reasons for having come, we were intruders. There was a blanched look to the little girl, and to her mother as well, which seemed to go along with the fading colors of the clothes they wore and the chalky siding of the house, as if the weather had bleached them all to a drab, neutral tone. The girl and her mother stood there impassively, while around them the afternoon was growing dark with the heavy thunderclouds that now entirely obscured the sun. The air was oppressively thick, and the imminent approach of the storm gave a forlorn and even desperate cast to yard, house, and inhabitants.

I took it all in—the weatherworn look of the small house, the coming storm, the absence of the man at the beach, the presence of the woman and little girl who had to wait for him to come home—as with a sense of a terrible weariness. Why did what I now saw appear so squalid and wretched? We must seem like part of the coming storm to them, I thought: a band of strange people suddenly materialized at their front door. I felt that if there were in fact photographs of airplanes on the wall, then actually to see them would only confirm the shame.

"Well, let's go," Uncle Leo said after a moment. We returned to the automobiles and got in. As I did, I looked back and saw the woman and the little girl still standing there watching us.

As we drove off down the road, the wind began blowing strongly, and the sand swirled about us. Then the rain came. It came in torrents, driving at the car windows as we turned into the highway, sweeping across the road. All about us the thunder boomed and the lightning flashed. My father drove very slowly, peering through the windshield as the wiper blade beat back and forth to clear a narrow field of vision through the streaming water.

"She didn't even so much as say thank you," my mother remarked after a minute. My father, concentrating his attention on the road ahead, made no comment.

"Is that man going to take us for a ride in his airplane?" my little brother asked.

"No, he was just talking," my mother said.

"He was real strong," my brother said. "He threw me way, way up in the air."

"I smelled whiskey on his breath," my sister said.

I watched out the window at the salt marsh alongside the road. The storm had begun to slacken in ferocity, though the rain was still falling steadily. The marshland, which in sunlight was sharp and brightly defined, seemed blurred and diffuse in detail. I tried to make out the shape of the lighthouse tower in the distance, for I knew that usually it was visible across the marsh, but the rain and haze were too thick. Through the back window, I could see Uncle Leo's car coming along behind us, headlights burning. He too was driving carefully through the downpour, keeping well to the rear.

"Why do you think he lost his pilot's license, Daddy?" I asked.

"I don't know," my father said.

"How do you know he did?" my mother asked.

"He said he was going to get it back next May," I told her, "so he must have lost it."

"Maybe it was because he tried to fly when he was drunk," my sister proposed.

"I don't think so," I said. "He'd have more sense than to do that."

"Well, he was drinking plenty today," my sister insisted, "because I could smell it on his breath."

"He wasn't drunk, though," I said. "Was he, Mother?"

"It depends on what you mean by drunk," my mother said. "I don't think he was no longer in control of his actions. He was just feeling real good."

"Maybe he wasn't a pilot at all," my sister said. "He might have been pretending."

"I bet he was!" I declared. "He couldn't have just made all that up. Could he, Daddy?"

"I don't know," my father replied.

"What difference does it make?" my mother said. "It's really none of our affair."

"I bet he *was* a pilot!" I insisted.

"I bet he wasn't," my sister said.

"Oh, shut up!" I told her.

"That will do," my father said. "I don't want to hear any more about it."

I thought of how Maynard and I had steered the little electric cars around the metal floor at the amusement park, and had tried to ram into each other's car, while Elaine and my sister had laughed and shrieked each time the rubber fenders collided and the cars were jolted from their paths, while the sparks flashed overhead. The rain continued to come down, and my father drove carefully. Occasionally an automobile would come along in the opposite direction, materializing abruptly out of the downpour with headlights turned on for visibility, and pass by in a rush. The thunder seemed further away now, and there were no more flashes of lightning. Soon the darkness lifted a little, and it was possible to see objects off in the distance. My father kept his eyes on the road.

LEE SMITH

 Between the Lines

"Peace be with you from Mrs. Joline B. Newhouse" is how I sign my columns. Now I gave some thought to that. In the first place, I like a line that has a ring to it. In the second place, what I have always tried to do with my column is to uplift my readers if at all possible, which sometimes it is not. After careful thought, I threw out "Yours in Christ." I am a religious person and all my readers know it. If I put "Yours in Christ," it seems to me that they will think I am theirs because I am in Christ, or even that they and I are in Christ *together*, which is not always the case. I am in Christ but I know for a fact that a lot of them are not. There's no use acting like they are, but there's no use rubbing their faces in it, either. "Peace be with you," as I see it, is sufficiently religious without laying all the cards right out on the table in plain view. I like to keep an ace or two up my sleeve. I like to write between the lines.

This is what I call my column, in fact: "Between the Lines, by Mrs. Joline B. Newhouse." Nobody knows why. Many people have come right out and asked me, including my best friend, Sally Peck, and my husband, Glenn. "Come on, now, Joline," they say. "What's this 'Between the Lines' all about? What's this 'Between the Lines' supposed to mean?" But I just smile a sweet mysterious smile and change the subject. I know what I know.

And my column means everything to folks around here. Salt Lick community is where we live, unincorporated. I guess there is not much that you would notice, passing through—the Post Office (real little), the American oil station, my husband Glenn's Cash 'N Carry Beverage Store. He sells more than beverages in there, though, believe me. He sells everything you can think of, from thermometers and rubbing alcohol to nails to frozen pizza. Anything else you want, you have to go out of the holler and get on the interstate and go to Greenville to get it. That's where my column appears, in the Greenville *Herald*, fortnightly. Now there's a word with a ring to it: fortnightly.

There are seventeen families here in Salt Lick—twenty, if you count those three down by the Five Mile Bridge. I put what they do in the paper. Anybody gets married, I write it. That goes for born, divorced, dies, celebrates a golden wedding anniversary, has a baby shower, visits relatives in Ohio, you name it. But these mere facts are not what's most important, to my mind.

I write, for instance: "Mrs. Alma Goodnight is enjoying a pleasant recuperation period in the lovely, modern Walker Mountain Community Hospital while she is sorely missed by her loved ones at home. Get well soon, Alma!" I do not write that Alma Goodnight is in the hospital because her husband hit her up the side with a rake and left a straight line of bloody little holes going from her waist to her armpit after she yelled at him, which Lord knows she did all the time, once too often. I don't write about how Eben Goodnight is all torn up now about what he did, missing work and worrying, or how Alma liked it so much in the hospital that nobody knows if they'll ever get her to go home or not. Because that is a *mystery*, and I am no detective by a long shot. I am what I am, I know what I know, and I know you've got to give folks something to hang on to, something to keep them going. That is what I have in mind when I say *uplift*, and that is what God had in mind when he gave us Jesus Christ.

My column would not be but a paragraph if the news was all I told.

But it isn't. What I tell is what's important, like the bulbs coming up, the way the redbud comes out first on the hills in the spring and how pretty it looks, the way the cattails shoot up by the creek, how the mist winds down low on the ridge in the mornings, how my wash all hung out on the line of a Tuesday looks like a regular square dance with those pants legs just flapping and flapping in the wind! I tell how all the things you ever dreamed of, all changed and ghostly, will come crowding into your head on a winter night when you sit up late in front of your fire. I even made up these little characters to talk for me, Mr. and Mrs. Cardinal and Princess Pussycat, and often I have them voice my thoughts. Each week I give a little chapter in their lives. Or I might tell what was the message brought in church, or relate an inspirational word from a magazine, book, or TV. I look on the bright side of life.

I've had God's gift of writing from the time I was a child. That's what the B. stands for in Mrs. Joline B. Newhouse—Barker, my maiden name. My father was a patient strong God-fearing man despite his problems and it is in his honor that I maintain the B. There was a lot of us children around all the time—it was right up the road here where I grew up—and it would take me a day to tell you what all we got into! But after I learned how to write, that was that. My fingers just naturally curved to a pencil and I sat down to writing like a ball of fire. They skipped me up one, two grades in school. When I was not but eight, I wrote a poem named "God's Garden," which was published in the church bulletin of the little Methodist Church we went to then on Hunter's Ridge. Oh, Daddy was so proud! He gave me a quarter that Sunday, and then I turned around and gave it straight to God. Put it in the collection plate. Daddy almost cried he was so proud. I wrote another poem in school the next year, telling how life is like a maple tree, and it won a statewide prize.

That's me—I grew up smart as a whip, lively, and naturally good. Jesus came as easy as breathing did to me. Don't think I'm putting on airs, though: I'm not. I know what I know. I've done my share of sinning, too, of which more later.

Anyway, I was smart. It's no telling but what I might have gone on to school like my own children have and who knows what all else if Mama hadn't run off with a man. I don't remember Mama very well, to tell the truth. She was a weak woman, always laying in the bed having a headache. One day we all came home from school and she was gone, didn't even bother to make up the bed. Well, that was the end of Mama! None of us ever saw her again, but Daddy told us right before he died that one time he had gotten a postcard from her from Atlanta, Georgia, years and years after that. He showed it to us, all wrinkled and soft from him holding it.

Being the oldest, I took over and raised those little ones, three of them, and then I taught school and then I married Glenn and we had our own children, four of them, and I have raised them too and still have Marshall, of course, poor thing. He is the cross I have to bear and he'll be just like he is now for the rest of his natural life.

I was writing my column for the week of March 17, 1976, when the following events occurred. It was a real coincidence because I had just finished doing the cutest little story named "A Red-Letter Day for Mr. and Mrs. Cardinal" when the phone rang. It rings all the time, of course. Everybody around here knows my number by heart. It was Mrs. Irene Chalmers. She was all torn up. She said that Mr. Biggers was over at Greenville at the hospital very bad off this time, and that he was asking for me and would I please try to get over there today as the doctors were not giving him but a 20 percent chance to make it through the night. Mr. Biggers has always been a fan of mine, and he especially liked Mr. and Mrs. Cardinal. "Well!" I said. "Of course I will! I'll get Glenn on the phone right this minute. And you calm down, Mrs. Chalmers. You go fix yourself a Coke." Mrs. Chalmers said she would, and hung up. I knew what was bothering her, of course. It was that given the natural run of things, she would be the next to go. The next one to be over there dying. Without even putting down the receiver, I dialed the beverage store. Bert answered.

"Good morning," I said. I like to maintain a certain distance with the hired help although Glenn does not. He will talk to anybody, and any time you go in there, you can find half the old men in the county just sitting around that stove in the winter or outside on those wooden drink boxes in the summer, smoking and drinking drinks which I am sure they are getting free out of the cooler although Glenn swears it on the Bible they are not. Anyway, I said good morning.

"Can I speak to Glenn?" I said.

"Well now, Mrs. Newhouse," Bert said in his naturally insolent voice—he is just out of high school and too big for his britches—"he's not here right now. He had to go out for a while."

"Where did he go?" I asked.

"Well, I don't rightly know," Bert said. "He said he'd be back after lunch."

"Thank you very much, there will not be a message," I said sweetly, and hung up. I *knew* where Glenn was. Glenn was over on Caney Creek where his adopted half-sister Margie Kettles lived, having carnal knowledge of her in the trailer. They had been at it for thirty years and anybody would have thought they'd have worn it out by that time. Oh, I knew all about it.

The way it happened in the beginning was that Glenn's father had died of his lungs when Glenn was not but about ten years old, and his mother grieved so hard that she went off her head and began taking up with anybody who would go with her. One of the fellows she took up with was a foreign man out of a carnival, the James H. Drew Exposition, a man named Emilio something. He had this curly-headed dark-skinned little daughter. So Emilio stayed around longer than anybody would have expected, but finally it was clear to all that he never would find any work around here to suit him. The work around here is hard work, all of it, and they say he played a musical instrument. Anyway, in due course this Emilio just up and vanished, leaving that foreign child. Now that was Margie, of course, but her name wasn't Margie then. It was a long foreign name, which ended up as Margie, and that's how Margie ended up here, in these mountains, where she has been up to no good ever since. Glenn's mother did not last too long after Emilio left, and those children grew up wild. Most of them went to foster homes, and to this day Glenn does not know where two of his brothers are! The military was what finally saved Glenn. He stayed with the military for nine years, and when he came back to this area he found me over here teaching school and with something of a nest egg in hand, enabling him to start the beverage store. Glenn says he owes everything to me.

This is true. But I can tell you something else: Glenn is a good man, and he has been a good provider all these years. He has not ever spoken to me above a regular tone of voice nor raised his hand in anger. He has not been tight with the money. He used to hold the girls in his lap of an evening. Since I got him started, he has been a regular member of the church, and he has not fallen down on it yet. Glenn furthermore has that kind of disposition where he never knows a stranger. So I can count my blessings, too.

Of course I knew about Margie! Glenn's sister Lou-Ann told me about it before she died, that is how I found out about it originally. She thought I *should* know, she said. She said it went on for years and she just wanted me to know before she died. Well! I had had the first two girls by then, and I thought I was so happy. I took to my bed and just cried and cried. I cried for four days and then by gum I got up and started my column, and I have been writing on it ever since. So I was not unprepared when Margie showed up again some years after that, all gap-toothed and wild-looking, but then before you knew it she was gone, off again to Knoxville, then back working as a waitress at that truck stop at the county line, then off again, like that. She led an irregular life. And as for Glenn, I will have to hand it to him, he never darkened her door again until after the birth of Marshall.

Now let me add that I would not have gone on and had Marshall if it was left up to me. I would have practiced more birth control. Because I was old by that time, thirty-seven, and that was too old for more children I felt, even though I had started late of course. I had told Glenn many times, I said three normal girls is enough for anybody. But no, Glenn was like a lot of men, and I don't blame him for it—he just had to try one more time for a boy. So we went on with it, and I must say I had a feeling all along.

I was not a bit surprised at what we got, although after wrestling with it all for many hours in the dark night of the soul, as they say, I do not believe that Marshall is a judgment on me for my sin. I don't believe that. He is one of God's special children, is how I look at it. Of course he looks funny, but he has already lived ten years longer than they said he would. And has a job! He goes to Greenville every day on the Trailways bus, rain or shine, and cleans up the Plaza Mall. He gets to ride on the bus, and he gets to see people. Along about six o'clock he'll come back, walking up the holler and not looking to one side or the other, and then I give him his supper and then he'll watch something on TV like "The Brady Bunch" or "Family Affair," and then he'll go to bed. He would not hurt a flea. But oh, Glenn took it hard when Marshall came! I remember that night so well and the way he just turned his back on the doctor. This is what sent him back to

Margie, I am convinced of it, what made him take up right where he had left off all those years before.

So since Glenn was up to his old tricks I called up Lavonne, my daughter, to see if she could take me to the hospital to see Mr. Biggers. Why yes she could, it turned out. As a matter of fact she was going to Greenville herself. As a matter of fact she had something she wanted to talk to me about anyway. Now Lavonne is our youngest girl and the only one that stayed around here. Lavonne is somewhat pop-eyed, and has a weak constitution. She is one of those people that never can make up their minds. That day on the phone, I heard a whine in her voice I didn't like the sound of. Something is up, I thought.

First I powdered my face, so I would be ready to go when Lavonne got there. Then I sat back down to write some more on my column, this paragraph I had been framing in my mind for weeks about how sweet potatoes are not what they used to be. They taste gritty and dry now, compared to how they were. I don't know the cause of it, whether it is man on the moon or pollution in the ecology or what, but it is true. They taste awful.

Then my door came bursting open in a way that Lavonne would never do it and I knew it was Sally Peck from next door. Sally is loud and excitable but she has a good heart. She would do anything for you. "Hold on to your hat, Joline!" she hollered. Sally is so loud because she's deaf. Sally was just huffing and puffing—she is a heavy woman—and she had rollers still up in her hair and her old housecoat on with the buttons off.

"Why, Sally!" I exclaimed. "You are all wrought up!"

Sally sat down in my rocker and spread out her legs and started fanning herself with my *Family Circle* magazine. "If you think I'm wrought up," she said finally, "it is nothing compared to what you are going to be. We have had us a suicide, right here in Salt Lick. Margie Kettles put her head inside her gas oven in the night."

"Margie?" I said. My heart was just pumping.

"Yes, and a little neighbor girl was the one who found her, they say. She went over to borrow some baking soda for her mama's biscuits at seven o'clock A.M." Sally looked real hard at me. "Now wasn't she related to you all?"

"Why," I said just as easily, "why yes, she was Glenn's adopted half-sister of course when they were nothing but a child. But we haven't had anything to do with her for years as you can well imagine."

"Well, they say Glenn is making the burial arrangements," Sally spoke up. She was getting her own back that day, I'll admit it. Usually I'm the one with all the news.

"I have to finish my column now and then Lavonne is taking me to Greenville to see old Mr. Biggers who is breathing his last," I said.

"Well," Sally said, hauling herself out of my chair, "I'll be going along then. I just didn't know if you knew it or not." Now Sally Peck is not a spiteful woman in all truth. I have known her since we were little girls sitting out in the yard looking at a magazine together. It is hard to imagine being as old as I am now, or knowing Sally Peck— who was Sally Bland then—so long.

Of course I couldn't get my mind back on sweet potatoes after she left. I just sat still and fiddled with the pigeonholes in my desk and the whole kitchen seemed like it was moving and rocking back and forth around me. Margie dead! Sooner or later I would have to write it up tastefully in my column. Well, I must say I had never thought of Margie dying. Before God, I never hoped for that in all my life. I didn't know what it would do to *me*, in fact, to me and Glenn and Marshall and the way we live because you know how the habits and the ways of people can build up over the years. It was too much for me to take in at one time. I couldn't see how anybody committing suicide could choose to stick their head in the oven anyway—you can imagine the position you would be found in.

Well, in came Lavonne at that point, sort of hanging back and stuttering like she always does, and that child of hers Bethy Rose hanging on to her skirt for dear life. I saw no reason at that time to tell Lavonne about the death of Margie Kettles. She would hear it sooner or later, anyway. Instead, I gave her some plant food that I had ordered two for the price of one from Montgomery Ward some days before.

"Are you all ready, Mama?" Lavonne asked in that quavery way she has, and I said indeed I was, as soon as I got my hat, which I did, and we went out and got in Lavonne's Buick Electra and set off on our trip. Bethy Rose sat in the back, coloring in her coloring book. She is a real good child. "How's Ron?" I said. Ron is Lavonne's husband, an electrician, as up and coming a boy as you would want to see. Glenn and I are as proud as punch of Ron, and actually I never have gotten over the shock of Lavonne marrying him in the first place. All through high school she never showed any signs of marrying anybody, and you could have knocked me over with a feather the day she told us she was secretly engaged. I'll tell you, our Lavonne was not the marrying sort! Or so I thought.

But that day in the car she told me, "Mama, I wanted to talk to you and tell you I am thinking of getting a d-i-v-o-r-c-e."

I shot a quick look into the back seat but Bethy Rose wasn't hearing a thing. She was coloring Wonder Woman in her book.

"Now, Lavonne," I said. "What in the world is it? Why, I'll bet you can work it out." Part of me was listening to Lavonne, as you can imagine, but part of me was still stuck in that oven with crazy Margie. I was not myself.

I told her that. "Lavonne," I said, "I am not myself today. But I'll tell you one thing. You give this some careful thought. You don't want to go off half-cocked. What is the problem, anyway?"

"It's a man where I work," Lavonne said. She works in the Welfare Department, part-time, typing. "He is just giving me a fit. I guess you can pray for me, Mama, because I don't know what I'll decide to do."

"Can we get an Icee?" asked Bethy Rose.

"Has anything happened between you?" I asked. You have to get all the facts.

"Why *no!*" Lavonne was shocked. "Why, I wouldn't do anything like that! Mama, for goodness' sakes! We just have coffee together so far."

That's Lavonne all over. She never has been very bright. "Honey," I said, "I would think twice before I threw up a perfectly good marriage and a new brick home for the sake of a cup of coffee. If you don't have enough to keep you busy, go take a course at the community college. Make yourself a new pantsuit. This is just a mood, believe me."

"Well," Lavonne said. Her voice was shaking and her eyes were swimming in tears that just stayed there and never rolled down her cheeks. "Well," she said again.

As for me, I was lost in thought. It was when I was a young married woman like Lavonne that I committed my own great sin. I had the girls, and things were fine with Glenn and all, and there was simply not any reason to ascribe to it. It was just something I did out of loving pure and simple, did because I wanted to do it. I knew and have always known the consequences, yet God is full of grace, I pray and believe, and his mercy is everlasting.

To make a long story short, we had a visiting evangelist from Louisville, Kentucky, for a two-week revival that year. John Marcel Wilkes. If I say it myself, John Marcel Wilkes was a real humdinger! He had the yellowest hair you ever saw, curly, and the finest singing voice available. Oh, he was something, and that very first night he brought two souls into Christ. The next day I went over to the church with a pan of brownies just to tell him how much I personally had received from his message. I thought, of course, that there would be other people around—the Reverend Mr. Clark, or the youth director, or somebody cleaning. But to my surprise that church was totally empty except for John Marcel Wilkes himself reading the Bible in the fellowship hall and making notes on a pad of paper. The sun came in a window on his head. It was early June, I remember, and I had on a blue dress with little white cap sleeves and open-toed sandals. John Marcel Wilkes looked up at me and his face gave off light like the sun.

"Why, Mrs. Newhouse," he said. "What an unexpected pleasure!" His voice echoed out in the empty fellowship hall. He had the most beautiful voice, too—strong and deep, like it had bells in it. Everything he said had a ring to it.

He stood up and came around the table to where I was. I put the brownies down on the table and stood there. We both just stood there, real close without touching each other, for the longest time, looking into each other's eyes. Then he took my hands and brought them up to his mouth and kissed them, which nobody ever did to me before or since, and then he kissed me on the mouth. I thought I would die. After some time of that, we went together out into the hot June day where the bees were all buzzing around the flowers there by the back gate and I couldn't think straight. "Come," said John Marcel Wilkes. We went out in the woods behind the church to the prettiest place, and when it was all over I could look up across his curly yellow head and over the trees and see the white church steeple stuck up against that blue, blue sky like it was pasted there. This was not all. Two more times we went out there during that revival. John Marcel Wilkes left after that and I have never heard a word of him since. I do not know where he is, or what has become of him in all these years. I do know that I never bake a pan of brownies, or hear the church bells ring, but what I think of him. So I have to pity Lavonne and her cup of coffee if you see what I mean, just like I have to spend the rest of my life to live my sinning down. But I'll tell you this: if I had it all to do over, I would do it all over again, and I would not trade it in for anything.

Lavonne drove off to look at fabric and get Bethy Rose an Icee, and I went in the hospital. I hate the way they smell. As soon as I entered Mr. Biggers' room, I could see he was breathing his last. He was so tiny in the bed you almost missed him, a poor little shriveled-up thing. His family sat all around.

"Aren't you sweet to come?" they said. "Looky here, honey, it's Mrs. Newhouse."

He didn't move a muscle, all hooked up to tubes. You could hear him breathing all over the room.

"It's Mrs. Newhouse," they said, louder. "Mrs. Newhouse is here. Last night he was asking for everybody," they said to me. "Now he won't open his eyes. You are real sweet to come," they said. "You certainly did brighten his days." Now I knew this was true because the family had remarked on it before.

"I'm so glad," I said. Then some more people came in the door and everybody was talking at once, and while they were doing that, I went over to the bed and got right up by his ear.

"Mr. Biggers!" I said. "Mr. Biggers, it's Joline Newhouse here."

He opened one little old bleary eye.

"Mr. Biggers!" I said right into his ear. "Mr. Biggers, you know those cardinals in my column? Mr. and Mrs. Cardinal? Well, I made them up! I made them up, Mr. Biggers. They never were real at all." Mr. Biggers closed his eye and a nurse came in and I stood up.

"Thank you so much for coming, Mrs. Newhouse," his daughter said.

"He is one fine old gentleman," I told them all, and then I left.

Outside in the hall, I had to lean against the tile wall for support while I waited for the elevator to come. Imagine, me saying such a thing to a dying man! I was not myself that day.

Lavonne took me to the big Kroger's in north Greenville and we did our shopping, and on the way back in the car she told me she had been giving everything a lot of thought and she guessed I was right after all.

"You're not going to tell anybody, are you?" she asked me anxiously, popping her eyes. "You're not going to tell Daddy, are you?" she said.

"Why, Lord, no honey!" I told her. "It's the farthest thing from my mind."

Sitting in the back seat among all the grocery bags, Bethy Rose sang a little song she had learned at school. "Make new friends but keep the old, some are silver but the other gold," she sang.

"I don't know what I was thinking of," Lavonne said.

Glenn was not home yet when I got there—making his arrangements, I supposed. I took off my hat, made myself a cup of Sanka, and sat down and finished off my column on a high inspirational note, saving Margie and Mr. Biggers for the next week. I cooked up some ham and red-eye gravy, which Glenn just loves, and then I made some biscuits. The time seemed to pass so slow. The phone rang two times while I was fixing supper, but I just let it go. I thought I had received enough news for *that* day. I still couldn't get over Margie putting her head in the oven, or what I had said to poor Mr. Biggers, which was not at all like me you can be sure. I buzzed around that kitchen doing first one thing, then another. I couldn't keep my mind on anything I did.

After a while Marshall came home and ate, and went in the front room to watch TV. He cannot keep it in his head that watching TV in the dark will ruin your eyes, so I always have to go in there and turn on a light for him. This night, though, I didn't. I just let him sit there in the recliner in the dark, watching his show, and in the pale blue light from that TV set he looked just like anybody else.

I put on a sweater and went out on the front porch and sat in the swing to watch for Glenn. It was nice weather for that time of year, still a little cold but you could smell spring in the air already and I knew it wouldn't be long before the redbud would come out again on the hills. Out in the dark where I couldn't see them, around the front steps, my crocuses were already up. After a while of sitting out there I began to take on a chill, due more to my age no doubt than the weather, but just then some lights came around the bend, two headlights, and I knew it was Glenn coming home.

Glenn parked the truck and came up the steps. He was dog-tired, I could see that. He came over to the swing and put his hand on my shoulder. A little wind came up, and by then it was so dark you could see lights on all the ridges where the people live. "Well, Joline," he said.

"Dinner is waiting on you," I said. "You go on in and wash up and I'll be there directly. I was getting worried about you," I said.

Glenn went on and I sat there swaying on the breeze for a minute before I went after him. Now where will it all end? I ask you. All this pain and loving, mystery and loss. And it just goes on and on, from Glenn's mother taking up with dark-skinned gypsies to my own daddy and his postcard to that silly Lavonne and her cup of coffee to Margie with her head in the oven, to John Marcel Wilkes and myself, God help me, and all of it so long ago out in those holy woods.

ELIZABETH SPENCER

 The Everlasting Light

Kemp Donahue was standing at the window one December afternoon, watching his daughter Jessie come up the walk. Without reason
or warning, his eyes filled with tears.

What on earth?

She came closer, books in her old frayed satchel, one sock slipped
into the heel of her shoe, looking off and thinking and smiling a little.
Kemp scrubbed the back of his hand across his eyes.

Why had he cried? Something to do with Jessie?

Jessie was not at all pretty (long face, uneven teeth, thin brown hair)
and though Sheila, Kemp's trim and lovely looking wife, never men-
tioned it, they both knew how she felt about it. But what did pretty
mean?

Jessie, now in the kitchen rummaging in the fridge, was into everything at school. She sold tickets to raffles, she tried out for basketball.
Once rejected for the team, she circulated announcements for the
games, and lobbied for door prizes.

Kemp came to the kitchen door. "What's new, honey?"

"Oh, nothing. Choir practice."

Mentioning it, she turned and grinned, ear to ear. ("Smile," her mother admonished. "Don't grin.")

Jessie loved choir practice. Non-churchgoers, the parents had decided a few years back it would be in order to send Jessie to Sunday School a few times. To their surprise, she liked it. She went back and back. She colored pictures, she came home and told Bible stories, she loved King David, she loved Joshua, she loved Jesus, she loved Peter and Paul. Sheila and Kemp listened to some things they didn't even know. ("Good Lord," said Sheila, hearing about the walls of Jericho.)

"Choir practice," Kemp repeated.

Sheila was out for the evening at one of her meetings. She was a secretary at the history department at the university. Twilight was coming on. "Are you eating enough?" asked Kemp. He wanted to talk to his daughter, just him and her. What did he want to say? It was all in his throat, but he couldn't get it out. "Honey . . . ," he began. Jessie looked up at him, munching a tuna sandwich in the side of one jaw. ("Don't chew like that," Sheila said.) "Honey . . . ," Kemp said again. He did not go on.

After a lonely dinner at the cafeteria Kemp drove up to the church and wandered around. The churchyard was dark, but light was coming from the windows, and the sound of singing as well was coming out. It was very sweet and clear, the sound of young voices. At the church, there were two morning services. At the early, nine o'clock service, the young choir sang. At the 11:15 service, the grown-up choir took over, the best in town, so people said.

Kemp did not go in the church, but stood outside. He crept closer to the church wall to listen. They were singing Christmas carols. He knew "Silent Night" and "Jingle Bells" and that silly one about Rudolph. But as for the others, they had a familiar ring, sure enough, and he found himself listening for Jessie's voice and thinking he heard it.

O little town of Bethlehem,
How still we see thee lie
Above thy deep and dreamless sleep
The silent stars go by.

Still in thy dark streets shineth
The everlasting light. . . .

"Everlasting light. . . ." That stuck in Kemp's mind. He kept repeating it. He strained to hear the rest. What came after little town, and dreamless sleep and silent stars? He was leaning against the wall, puzzling out the words until the song faded, and he could even hear the rap of the choir director's wand, and his voice too. Another song?

Kemp looked up. A strange woman was approaching the church and was looking at him. She was stooped over and white-haired and every bit of her said he'd no business leaning up against the church wall on a December night. He straightened, smiled and spoke to her and hastened away, pursued by strains of

Away in a manger, no crib for a bed,
The little Lord Jesus. . . .

At breakfast the next morning, Kemp said, "Tell me, Jessie, what's that Christmas carol that says something about 'the everlasting light' . . . ?"

Jessie told him. She knew the whole thing. She was about to start on "Joy to the World," but her mother stopped her. "Your eggs are getting cold as ice," she pointed out firmly.

"Why don't we all go to church tomorrow," Kemp proposed. "We can hear them all sing."

Sheila valued her Sunday sleep more than average, but she finally agreed and the Donahues, arriving in good time, listened to all sorts of prayers and Bible readings and music and a sermon too. Everyone was glad to see them. Jessie wore her little white robe.

"Well, now," said Kemp when they reached home. "Maybe that's how Sunday ought to be."

Sheila looked at him in something like alarm.

Sheila was from New England, graduate of one of those schools people spoke of with awe. Kemp was Virginia born and though it seemed odd for a Southern family, he had never been encouraged to attend church. Kemp did audits for a Piedmont chain of stores selling auto parts; he drove a good bit to various locations. Driving alone, he found himself repeating, "dark streets . . . the everlasting light. . . ." He especially liked that last. Didn't it just *sound* everlasting? Then, because they didn't have one, he had sneaked and borrowed Jessie's Bible. It took him a long time, but he found the story and relished the phrases: ". . . the glory of the Lord shone round about them. . . ." That's great! thought Kemp.

One week more and it would be the weekend of Christmas. Sheila said at breakfast, "Now, Jessie, you're certainly going to the Christmas party at school?"

"I have to go to choir practice," said Jessie.

"No, you do not," said Sheila. "It won't matter to miss one time. Miss Fagles rang up and said she especially wanted you. There's some skit you wrote for the class."

"They did that last year," said Jessie. "Anyway, I told Mr. Jameson I'd come."

"Then tell him you can't."

"I don't want to," said Jessie.

Sheila put down her napkin. She appealed to Kemp. "I am not going to have this," she said.

Kemp realized he was crucial, but he said it anyway. "Let her go where she wants to."

Sheila went upstairs in a fury. She had always wanted a pretty daughter who had lots of boyfriends begging for her time. "She's impossible," she had once muttered to Kemp.

Church on Christmas and Easter was what even the Donahues usually attended, and this year was no exception. The church was packed and fragrant with boughs of cedar. They heard carols and once more the stories of shepherds and angels read from the pulpit. They heard the choir and told Jessie later how proud they were of the way she sang. "But you couldn't hear me for everybody else," said Jessie.

It was at dinner a day or so later that she said: "The funniest thing happened the last night we practiced right before Christmas. This man came in the back of the church and sat down, way on the back row in the dark. We were singing carols. But then somebody noticed him and he was bent way over. He kept blowing his nose. Somebody said, 'He's crying.' Mr. Jameson said maybe he ought to go and ask him to leave, because he was probably drunk, but then he said, 'Maybe he just feels that way.' I guess he was drunk, though, don't you?"

*   *   *

Through years to come, Kemp would wonder if Jessie didn't know all the time that was her dad, sitting in the back, hearing about the 'everlasting light,' welling up with tears, for her, for Christmas, for Sheila, for everything beautiful. Someday I'll ask her, he thought. Someday when she's forty or more, with a wonderful job or a wonderful husband and wonderful children, I'll say, Didn't you know it was me? And she won't have to be told what I mean, she'll just say, Yes, sure I did.

WALTER SULLIVAN

Losses

It was true that except for a little heaviness around her mother's waist and hips, she and her mother were the same size, but her mother was forty, the very worst possible age if you didn't count people who were older than that, and there was no way that she was going to wear her mother's dress to the funeral. Because of the controversy about what she was going to wear, they were running late. They should have been in the parish hall already, waiting with all of Addie's aunts and uncles and cousins to greet the people who had come to pay their respects, but the argument had delayed them. They were standing instead in her mother's bedroom, Addie still in her slip, her mother holding the plain black dress with a round, old-fashioned looking neckline and buttons down the front that wasn't going to do a thing for Addie's figure, which was, for better or worse, the best part of Addie's appearance. Besides good legs and hips and breasts, she had a round face and a short, wide nose, which weren't helped much by her straight brown hair that hung to her shoulders. In her mother's dress, all the best parts of her would be disguised, not to mention the fact that she would look like the dork of the century.

But her mother, who was feeling put upon already, who, to tell the truth, felt put upon most of the time, was insisting. She had had it all to do, she was telling Addie. Every detail of the funeral, every arrangement had been up to her. Not one of her five siblings, all of whom lived out of town, had offered to fly in early and help her. She had chosen the casket; she had called the priest; she had named the pallbearers and selected the music and hired the musicians and ordered the flowers. She would have sent Addie to buy a suitable dress if she had thought of it, but it was too late now, and Addie could not go to her grandmother's funeral in a miniskirt or jeans or shorts or a school uniform, which, Addie had to admit, was all her closet had to offer.

"Put it on!" her mother said. "Move! We should have left ten minutes ago."

"Screw that!" Addie said, and almost before the words were out of her mouth, her mother slapped her. The blow was hard. The force of it jolted Addie's head, the sound of it made her ears ring. As seconds passed, the burning pain in her cheek got worse instead of better. She wanted to run, but her mother was between her and the door, her hand raised as if she were about to strike again, and Addie had to surrender. She stepped into the dress, pulled it up over her shoulders, and tried without success to deal with the excess material. Even though her image in the mirror was blurred by her tears, she could see that she looked as bad as she had thought she would. The dress was loose around her hips; the hem fell to the middle of her knees; the cut of the dress was all wrong, not to mention the fact that given her brown hair and gray eyes, black was not her best color. But worse than the dress was the red print of her mother's hand where her mother had slapped her. Addie touched it, rubbed it gently, feeling the heat of it, but it wouldn't go away. At the sight of it, brightly delineated on her cheek, her tears that had begun to subside, started up again.

"No!" she said. "No! Look at my face! You can't make me go looking like this!"

"We'll hide it," her mother said. "We'll use powder. But you'll have to stop crying."

"No!" Addie said again, but even to her own ears, her voice lacked conviction. There was no use fighting. She had lost once more. Damn it, she thought, what was happening to her now was what always happened although before today, it had been years since her mother had slapped her. Even when her grandmother had been alive and watched over her after school until her mother got home from work, her mother had paid too much attention to her. "You need a brother or a sister," Addie's friend, Roberta Northington, had told her. "Then there would be somebody to share your mother's hassling."

True, Addie had thought, she probably needed one of each, but she knew that what she really needed was a father. Other girls, and boys too, she supposed, although boys didn't talk much to girls about what happened at home, knew how to work their parents individually. When it came to getting permission or confessing a crime that was bound to be discovered, they knew which parent to go to. Addie had had her grandmother who, some members of the family said, had been a second parent to her, but it wasn't the same. Addie's grandmother would probably have been more strict than her mother. In any event, when it came to what punishment Addie would receive or how late she would be allowed to stay out or what places she would be allowed to go, her mother made the decision. One day Addie had asked her grandmother about her father. Addie thought she could remember him, but only barely. Her recollection was of a man of uncertain build and undefined features who could have been anybody. She could remember the time he left; she was positive of that. Others in her family might have sensed an emptiness in the house, a void that her father once had filled, but Addie, who was three at the time, remembered activity, people, and, in spite of her mother's tears, excitement. Her grandmother had been in their house most of the time. Two of Addie's aunts had come to give her mother their shoulders to cry on.

Addie's grandmother had said only that he had left, which, Addie learned as she grew older, was about as much as anybody knew. There had been, as she understood it, no preamble; no arguments between him and Addie's mother; no complaints about the way he was treated. If there had been another woman, nobody in the family was aware of it, but he had planned his departure so carefully and disappeared so quickly and completely, he might have had a dozen girl friends without anyone suspecting it. He had hired a lawyer to make over whatever they owned jointly to Addie's mother. She got the house with some years to go on the mortgage, a few shares of stock that in the long run didn't amount to much, a bank account that contained a few hundred dollars. He drove off in the new Camry, leaving her the Ford Escort, and covered his tracks so well that Addie's mother was never able to find him and make him pay child support or alimony.

But why? Addie had always wanted to know. If he had loved her mother enough to marry her in the first place, why didn't he love her enough to stay with her? What had changed from the time he asked her to marry him until the day he left? The answer, of course, was Addie. She didn't like to think so, but maybe he had left because he hadn't liked her. Maybe he had hated being a father so much that he didn't want to risk hanging around in case Addie's mother had another baby. It didn't make sense, as the hollow tones of their voices showed, when her mother and grandmother told her that her father had loved her. If he had, he wouldn't have left, and she wished he hadn't. He had deprived her of the only chance she had had of having a father. Or a stepfather either for that matter. Her mother had men friends who took her out. She was, Addie had to admit, not bad looking for a woman her age. But no man in his right mind would marry someone with such a gloomy disposition.

It was all right for her to cry at the visitation, all right for her to cry at the funeral. Everybody else was crying too, more or less, and everyone assumed that she had loved her grandmother deeply. *Oh, Addie,* they said using the line that had become standard in the family, *she was like a second mother to you, wasn't she? Oh,* they said, *of course you loved her. You were even named after her.* And this gave Addie one more reason to weep in anger.

"Why, Adelaide was a saint's name," her mother told her once when she had complained about being named that. Her mother told her what the saint had done. Unlike many females who became saints protecting their virginity, Adelaide, who had lived a million years ago, had simply been persecuted. Addie hadn't listened very carefully. There were, Addie knew, hundreds of saints, almost all of whom had better names than Adelaide. Half the girls in her class, probably half the Catholic girls in the world were named Mary, although you had to put something else with it like Mary Dolores or Mary Frances so you could keep one Mary straight from another. But there were other good saints' names: Katherine and Elizabeth and Dorothy and Joan, any one of which, Addie thought, would have been acceptable. She would have even settled for Monica or Teresa. For years, she had planned to change her name when she got to be sixteen, and although she had been sixteen now for several months and hadn't changed it yet, she still meant to do it as soon as she decided what she wanted to be called instead of Adelaide.

Miserable because of the dress she was wearing, miserable because she believed that everybody could tell that she'd been slapped, miserable because her tears would not stop coming, she sat through the music, the readings, the blessings, the homily. Then, when it all should have been over, the holy water sprinkled, the casket censed, the procession on the way to the cemetery, the priest stopped the service to invite friends and relatives to come forward and share their memories of Adelaide. They went: aunts and uncles, a neighbor, even a cousin who, to Addie's certain knowledge, had hardly known her grandmother at all. Addie paid no attention to them. She had known her grandmother too well to need to hear what anybody else had to say about her, and at a time like this, nobody ever told the truth anyway. Not the whole truth at least. They related only the nice things, but there had been more than that to her grandmother.

Addie longed to get this part of the day finished, and soon it was. She and her mother, the crowd of relatives and friends were out of the church into the warmth and the glowing sunlight of a late April day. There was some milling around, some confusion about where the various members of Addie's grandmother's big family would ride. Addie's aunts and uncles had all come by plane, and not all of them had rented automobiles. Somebody decided that Addie's grandmother's children and their spouses would ride in the first two limousines. There was a third limousine, but it could not possibly carry Addie and all her cousins. All right! Addie thought. If she could make herself sufficiently inconspicuous, she might manage to get left behind. She could walk home, change clothes, listen to music. There was a chance her mother wouldn't even miss her. She placed herself against the wall of the church, just outside the door, but Mrs. Witherspoon, who had lived across the street from Addie's grandmother, apprehended her.

Mrs. Witherspoon was short and fat and gray, and her flowery perfume, faint and innocuous, gave her the smell of an old lady. "Well, Addie," she said. "What a sad day for you, child." She stared at Addie's damaged cheek and, for a moment, was silent. Then she glanced at the now full limousines, and looked back at Addie. "Where are you riding?"

Damn! Addie said to herself. If she could have thought of a good lie, she would have told it. She hesitated too long. "Hm," she said, "uh. . . ."

"Then you must ride with me," Mrs. Witherspoon said. "We can have a visit."

Addie thought some words that would have made Mrs. Witherspoon faint if Addie had spoken them. Just what I need, she said to herself. She wished now that she had elbowed her way into the third limousine.

The ride to the cemetery was as bad as Addie had expected. For most of the trip, Mrs. Witherspoon talked a blue streak: about Addie's grandmother, about the funeral mass, about Addie's aunts and uncles whom she had known since they were children. But she could not keep herself from glancing now and then at Addie's cheek, and when she did, she lost the thread of her own conversation.

"You are all right, aren't you, Addie?" she asked once, and Addie said that she was.

Later, Mrs. Witherspoon said, "I guess your mother is taking this hard. I know how close your mother was to Adelaide."

This time Addie could avoid answering for now they were at the cemetery, and Mrs. Witherspoon was diverted by the familiar names that she saw on the tombstones.

"Now," Mrs. Witherspoon said when they were parked and out of the car, "Of course, you want to be with your family during the service. I'll meet you back here after the interment."

Addie had had plenty of time to prepare for this. "Thank you," she said, "but I'd better not. I think I'd better stay close to my mother."

A lie, a lie, but who was counting? Certainly not Mrs. Witherspoon who gave a plump and approving smile. Addie smiled back and was free to do what she wanted to.

Addie's mother was seated under the canopy in the front row beside the open grave. Other relatives were arranging themselves according to rank as they had when they boarded the limousines. Addie joined them. She had stopped crying when she left the church. From the way Mrs. Witherspoon had looked at her, she knew that there must be some vestige of her mother's handprint on her cheek, but her cheek had long ago quit hurting. She was calm now and deeply angry. Looking at the back of her mother's head while the priest shook his aspergill and sprinkled dirt on the coffin, she felt her profound and bitter fury grow until it encompassed almost everything: not only her mother, but her dead grandmother too, her aunts and uncles and cousins, and the priest and Mrs. Witherspoon and the other mourners. She hated them all too much to stay around them. As the priest began his final blessing, she stepped back and took herself slowly away, past one tombstone and then another. Nobody saw her go, or, if anyone did, nobody cared. No one called her name. No one attempted to impede her. She hid behind the wing of a stone angel and waited until the grave was filled and the last of the crowd had left the cemetery.

Well, she thought, well. This was the best moment she had had all day. She was still angry, she still felt the outrage of all her mother had done to her, but she felt free too. She could say anything that she wanted to say and she said a few things that she wouldn't have dared say around her family and enjoyed saying them even though there was no one to listen. She hummed a tune she had heard on the radio that morning before she began to get grief from her mother. She looked around once more to be sure everyone else had left. Then she went and sat by her grandmother's grave in the chair her mother had occupied during the burial. Addie wanted to get her own thoughts straight, to get clear in her own mind what she thought of her grandmother. She wanted to balance the bad things she remembered against the good things that had been said about her grandmother at the church, but she was having trouble getting her memory to work the way she wanted it to. There weren't any big moments of agony that she held against her grandmother. It was just that she had hated having to go to her grandmother's house with its dark woodwork and fat furniture and porcelain dolls and dogs on every table and glass vases that you had to watch out for.

She had to go there every afternoon until she was twelve and could go to her own house, and she had despised it. She couldn't listen to music while she was there; her grandmother said what Addie liked was noise and she couldn't abide hearing it. Addie couldn't talk on the phone. Or rather she could, but she wasn't permitted to linger in her grandmother's bedroom, and the only other phone in the house was in the living room where her grandmother would hear everything she was saying. She and her grandmother didn't talk. When you got home from school, there were things you needed to say; whether what had happened to you that day was good or bad, you needed to tell somebody. Sometimes she tried to tell her grandmother about a teacher who had given the class too much homework or about a girl who had got in trouble for saying something her friends thought was funny or about the dogs that Sister Marie Clare tried to chase off the playground. Addie's grandmother had never listened. On the rare occasions when she had, she missed the point. Finally, Addie gave up. She ate the peanut butter sandwich her grandmother made for her, drank the milk her grandmother poured. Her grandmother wouldn't allow her to serve herself. She was, her grandmother said, too messy. There had been nothing to do but to try to read or study or to give up and watch the *Oprah Winfrey Show* with her grandmother. When Addie complained, her mother told her that her grandmother was not by nature very demonstrative, that, being old, she was not interested in the things that interested young people. "She's giving up a part of her own life to keep you," Addie's mother said. "If I didn't have her, I don't know who I'd turn to."

Suddenly, Addie realized that she was no longer alone. A man whom she recognized as someone who worked for the funeral home was coming toward her. He had taken off his coat and tie and unfastened several buttons of his shirt. Addie could see his tanned throat and some curly dark hair on his chest. The hair on his head was curly and dark too, and he was handsome in the slightly threatening way that the Italian boys she saw at church were handsome, but he was older.

"Hey," he said when he got to the edge of the canopy. He smiled and showed her nice teeth. "I thought everybody had gone. You miss your ride or something?"

For a moment, Addie wasn't sure what she ought to do. She absolutely did not speak to strange men, and she didn't know this one's name; she certainly had not been introduced to him. But knowing where he worked, having seen him around the funeral home must count for something. She decided not only to answer but to tell the truth. "Actually, I hid. I didn't want to ride with them."

"Wow," the man said. "But I'll tell you what. You can ride with me. Just wait until I load up these chairs. I'll get the one you're sitting on last, but I have to take them all back to the funeral home."

Addie knew what her mother would say about this, her grandmother too if she could still use her vocal cords. The idea of Addie's being alone with a man in the cemetery where dark deeds might be hidden by the tombstones, where there was nobody around to hear her cries for help should she need to make them, would cause them to shudder with anxiety. That the man worked at the funeral home, that Addie remembered seeing him there would make no difference to Addie's pessimistic mother who could discover something to be fearful of at a meeting of the PTA. All the more reason to ride in the truck, Addie thought. She hadn't wanted to go home on the bus anyway.

"Okay," Addie said. "Why not?"

The man told her his name was Frank. She told him hers.

He repeated it. "Addie," he said, "St. Adelaide. You Catholic girls are all named for saints. Catholic boys too, I guess, but I don't pay much attention to them."

"What are you?" Addie asked.

"Everything," Frank replied. "We get them all. Catholics, Protestants, Jews. No Muslims yet since I've been working there. I fit in with every drill. I'm whatever the trade calls for."

She had to lift her mother's skirt to make the high step into the truck. It slid up exposing most of her thigh. Frank was watching. So what, Addie thought. This was a kind of revenge for her having to wear the dress in the first place. Besides, yesterday she had come to the funeral home directly from school. The skirt of her uniform fit snugly around her waist and over her hips; it stopped at the top of her knees. Frank would have known already that she had good legs if he had been paying attention.

Unlike the outside which was clean, the inside of the truck was dusty. It smelled of tobacco smoke and the plastic covers on the seats. Addie settled into one of them and tried to deal with the excess material of her mother's dress. Frank drove slowly down the winding cemetery road. He told Addie that he was really glad to meet her. He said that he had almost introduced himself yesterday at the funeral home, but he was afraid his boss wouldn't like it. There was a note of maturity in his voice, a kind of confidence in the way he looked at her and smiled that made Addie feel triumphant. She examined the muscular outline of his arm beneath his shirt, his strong, blunt hand that rested on the gearshift. He was dangerous, Addie told herself, not really believing that he was, but feeling the excitement that came with thinking so. For a moment, she was glad that she was wearing her mother's dress, taking it into this situation that would make her mother faint if she knew about it. She wished that there were some way that her mother could know, could see what she was doing and not be able to stop her.

They were silent for a while. Frank turned onto the busy street that led back to the center of town. He offered her another bright smile. "You in a hurry?"

Not I, she thought, but whether she ought to be was another story. The family was going to Addie's grandmother's house after the funeral. They were doubtless there now, and given the crowd, there was a chance that her mother had not yet missed her. There was a better chance that she had; Addie decided to enjoy herself since she was going to catch hell anyway.

"No," Addie said. "Take your time. You can let me out back at the church if you want to."

"Well." Frank looked at her. "I was thinking. . . . How old are you?"

Remembering that he had seen her in her school uniform, she took a few seconds to decide how big a lie she could get away with. "Eighteen," she said, "I'm about to graduate."

"That's terrific," Frank said, "I'm not in a hurry either. How about if we stop somewhere? Have a beer. Get to know each other."

The exciting sense of danger that she had felt when she first got into the truck came back. It was a thrill in her breast, a kind of painful joy that made her stomach tighten, but she was also frightened. She hesitated. She needed someone to help her decide. The freedom in which she had been rejoicing had, for now at least, become a burden.

"Hey," Frank said, peering at her in a questioning way that made her realize that she was frowning. "Lighten up. We'll just have a beer, and I'll take you home. It's no big deal."

Maybe not for him, Addie thought, but it was, or would be if she did it, the biggest deal that she had ever been involved in. All of her mother's admonitions, all of her years of Catholic schooling, all the cautionary tales about girls who had come to bad ends argued against it. She was about to say no, to tell Frank to take her home, but he spoke first.

"How about it, Adelaide?"

The sound of her name made her flinch. Much of the fury that she had felt in the cemetery returned and gave her courage. "Why not?" she said, and even though her anger continued to burn, almost immediately, she wished she hadn't.

In the middle of the afternoon, the bar was almost empty. Across from the booth where Frank and Addie sat, a man was drinking what she supposed was whiskey. At a table, a man and a woman were eating sandwiches. Frank asked her what kind of beer she wanted, and she had to think quickly to remember a brand that she had seen advertised. The only times she had ever drunk beer was when, at the house of friends, they were able to sneak a bottle out of the refrigerator. She told Frank that she wanted Budweiser.

"Nah," he said, "we can do better than that. I'll get us something good from Australia."

The beer came in tall blue cans, and it tasted worse than she remembered. The first sip burned in her throat and made her eyes water.

"You like it?" Frank said.

She nodded and sipped again.

"You know," Frank said, "when I first saw you yesterday, I thought what a beautiful girl you were, how very attractive."

"Well," she said, then remembered her manners. "Thank you."

Frank told her that he was from Illinois, that he was a musician, that he played guitar and sang and wrote songs. He had come to Nashville to try to start his career. He was looking for a recording contract, a publisher. What he needed most, he said, was a good agent.

"I'd like to hear you sing," Addie said. "I'd like to hear some of your songs."

Could this be true? she wondered. She thought maybe it was, although ordinarily, she did not like country music. But maybe Frank's was different. She was willing to give him the benefit of the doubt.

Having finished her beer—the taste had become less objectionable as she drank—she found that both her fear and her anger were almost gone. She was feeling peaceful.

Frank ordered more beer, and soon she had to go to the bathroom. It felt good to walk, but different. She looked down at the floor to be sure it was where she thought it was and considered it funny that she had to do this. She managed to deal with her mother's dress in the stall, then said *Hey* to the face she saw in the mirror. *Look where we are*, she said to her reflection, *Look what we're doing*. It seemed the grandest thing in the world that she should be in this bar drinking beer with an attractive and talented man who was older than she. She felt as if she really were eighteen or maybe even older. She thought briefly of her mother and what was in store for her when she got home, but that part of her future seemed a thousand years away, and given her newly discovered maturity, she was confident that from now on she could deal with her mother. She was sure that she was where she ought to be, doing what she ought to be doing, and she was delighted.

Back at the booth, she found another can of beer beside the one she had left half finished.

"I needed one," Frank said, "so I got one for you too. But you've fallen behind. You'd better drink if you want to catch up with me."

Well, why not? she thought. She drank, then lifted the can and drank again. She looked at Frank, at his prominent nose, his flat cheeks, his dark eyes. In the rest room, she had thought of things that she might say to him, questions she might ask him about his life—she knew that men liked to talk about themselves—but she could no longer remember them. The failure of her memory struck her as funny, and she giggled.

"You know," Frank said, "you really are attractive. There was a girl I knew in high school. She looked a lot like you, but she wasn't as pretty. I was in love with her, but she wouldn't give me the time of day. She wouldn't even speak to me."

How sad, Addie thought. This had never happened to her. The boys she had had crushes on had at least been nice to her. Feeling more grown up than ever, she put her hand on top of Frank's.

"I'm so sorry," she said for if she looked like the girl who had broken Frank's heart, it seemed that she ought to apologize. "I would never have done you that way, Frank." She paused. Then she said, "I would have spoken to you." Seeing that this was funny, though she hadn't meant it to be, she began once more to giggle.

"I wish it had been you," Frank said. "But you're here now. Better late than never." He lifted her hand and kissed it.

For an instant, she was inclined to think this was funny too, but then she was struck by the great seriousness of it. Nobody had ever kissed her hand before; she had never seen any hand kissed except in the movies. This moment was like a scene out of one of her mother's novels that Addie read sometimes when she was grounded. It was sweet and sad, and it brought tears to Addie's eyes.

"Let's drink up," Frank said. "We ought to get out of here."

She didn't want to leave. She wanted to stay and listen to the light rock of the piped in music, to look at the interesting array of bottles behind the bar, to let Frank kiss her hand again. She thought that this was the best moment of all her life. She told herself that she had never been so happy.

"How about it, babe?" Frank said. "You ready?"

She wasn't, but if to leave was what he wanted, she couldn't refuse him.

To hold the moment, she took another two or three swallows of her beer. Now this can was almost empty. "All right," she said and smiled what she intended to be a generous and slightly superior smile. She was letting him have his way. She was indulging him.

First, Frank had to go to the bathroom. She went too and bumped against a table on her way. She was definitely unsteady. She had to move her legs more carefully, think more seriously about where she was going to put her feet than when she had come this way—when? Thirty minutes, an hour ago? She had lost her sense of time. It seemed to her that she had not been in the bar very long, but she had drunk two tall cans of beer and almost all of another. She had more trouble with her mother's dress this time. When she looked in the mirror, she had to squint to make her blurred face come into focus. She didn't look quite right to herself. It was her mouth, she decided. Her smile that she hadn't realized she was wearing was slightly crooked. So what? she thought. However she looked to herself, Frank thought she was beautiful.

When they got outside, she was astonished to find that the sun was setting. Through her happiness, she felt a stab of concern. She thought of how furious her mother was going to be. In her mind, she saw her mother's face flushed and twisted with anger. For the briefest instant, she was frightened. Then she thought that this too was funny.

"Hey," Frank said, "let me in on the joke."

She was laughing so hard she could barely reply. Finally, she managed to say, "That was no joke. That was my mother."

She had difficulty getting into the truck. On her first try, she missed the step. Halfway through the door, she paused involuntarily, her body caught in a curious equilibrium. Frank put his hands on her behind and pushed, and she dropped into the seat. Frank had to remind her to fasten her seat belt. Even in the fading afternoon, the world outside the truck looked strangely bright. The late sun glinting off other cars hurt her eyes. She closed them but had to open them again to keep from being dizzy. The truck seemed stuffy, airless. She considered rolling down the window, but to do so, she would have to lift her hand and this seemed too formidable an effort. Well, now, she thought and relaxed against the seat. In spite of a slight queasiness, she still felt peaceful. She was glad that she was where she was, sitting beside Frank.

She must have closed her eyes again and kept them closed for a few minutes, because Frank had stopped the truck and cut off the engine. Where were they? At first glance, she saw a grassy field that slanted down to a busy road where drivers had turned on their lights against the falling darkness. Then she turned her head and saw, to her surprise, that they were back in the cemetery. This wasn't right. Maybe Frank had thought she wanted to come back here. She didn't like being here. She needed to tell Frank that he had made a mistake, but his seat was empty. He opened the door on her side and startled her.

"Come on, babe," he said. "Get out. We need to make ourselves comfortable."

"No," she said and found it hard to make her tongue form the word. She was vaguely aware that her mind was not working very well, but it was working better than her body. "Listen," she said, the sound of the word strange to her own ears. "It's not here. I mean, this is not the place."

"It's a great place," Frank said. "Most people don't know how to appreciate cemeteries."

He put his hands under her arms and lifted her out of the car. "Can you stand up?" he said.

She wasn't sure. She thought she could, but he didn't let her answer.

He kissed her. She felt his tongue between her lips, and she didn't want it there. She tried to pull away. She wanted to tell him to stop, but he was too strong for her. He lifted the skirt of her mother's dress, pulled it up above her waist, slid his hand inside her pants and squeezed her buttock. No! No! No! she thought. She got her lips free and attempted to say no, but she was sobbing too hard to say anything. She was crying harder than she had cried all day, harder than she had ever cried in her life. She wanted somebody to come and help her. If her mother were here, she would know how to make Frank stop what he was doing. She was on the ground now, and Frank was on top of her. In her pain and desperation, she wished that her grandmother could come back if only for this moment. Addie tried to call her and managed to form the word. "Adelaide!" she heard herself shout, though she had never before called her grandmother this. Adelaide! Adelaide! she thought and perhaps said, Adelaide, please come! But of course she didn't, and at last Frank was finished.

"Oh," she said. "Oh." Each word was prolonged by a sob. Oh, she thought, what was she to do now? She needed to find her pants; she needed something to wipe herself with. Her pants were around one of her ankles, torn beyond further wear. She used them to clean herself, sponge away her own blood and what Frank had left when he caused her to shed it. She threw the soiled rag away and leaned against a tombstone and vomited.

Frank was beside her, touching her, his arm around her shoulder. "Too much brew," he said. "That will happen sometimes."

"Stop," Addie said. She wanted to run away, but it was dark now and she was in the middle of the cemetery. She was cold and grieved and deeply frightened. She was trembling so violently that she couldn't move if she had had the courage to.

"Look," Frank said, "don't take it so hard. It had to happen sometime."

She shook her head, but in the darkness, he probably didn't see it.

"Come on," he said. "I'll take you home." He laughed. "I'm in trouble too, you know. I'll probably get fired for all the time I've been gone from the funeral home."

She had to let Frank lead her to the truck and help her into it. She leaned against the door as far away from him as she could get. As they drove out of the cemetery, their lights catching here and there the monuments and the statuary, she tried to tell herself that what had happened to her had not happened. In her mind, she tried to go back to the afternoon, to the time when her relatives were still sitting under the canopy and Mrs. Witherspoon was still waiting at the edge of the crowd, ready to take Addie home, if Addie had asked her. She wanted time to stop there. She wanted to retrieve that moment and try again, to start her life over. Thinking of what she should have done and of how different things would be now if she had acted differently deepened her sorrow. Oh, God, she thought. Oh, God. She wanted to die, except that the thought of being put in a casket and buried beside her grandmother was too horrible. Oh, God, she thought again. What was she going to do now? Maybe she was going to die whether she wanted to or not. There was a good chance that her mother was going to kill her.

They drove through the waning rush hour traffic, among the anonymous headlamps of passing cars. People moved along the sidewalks, waited at the corners for busses. Frank stopped for a traffic light, and two girls passed in front of the truck. They were talking and laughing. They were happy, or at least it seemed to Addie that they were, and she envied them bitterly.

"You'll have to tell me where you live," Frank said. "I can't take you home unless I know where to take you."

When she heard his voice, she pressed herself more firmly against the door. She didn't answer.

"How about it, Adelaide? Where are we going?"

"The church," she said, her voice high and thin. "Take me to the church."

"There's nobody there now. The church is locked."

"The church," she said again.

"Okay," Frank said, "it's your funeral."

He stopped in front of the doors where she had stood with her family a few hours ago, where she had talked to Mrs. Witherspoon. "Listen," he said, "it's what everybody does now, Addie. When you think back on it in a day or two, you'll remember that you enjoyed it."

She wanted to say something awful to him, to tell him what a scum he was, to let him know how much she hated him, but she couldn't come up with the words, and if she had, her throat was too tight for her to speak them. Still weak and trembling, she got out of the truck and stood with her back against the cool stone of the church. She would have gone inside, but she knew Frank was right. The building was locked and dark except for the uncertain glow of a few candles. That she couldn't enter didn't matter. She would have gone in to rest, not to pray. There was only one thing she wanted, only one thing that she would have prayed for, and that was a prayer that could never be answered now. What was done was done. No prayer that was said now could change it.

She was not ready to go home. Even her mother's sympathy, should she offer it, would be enough to break Addie's heart. She would prefer to be slapped again, but she wasn't ready for that either. From the darkness around the corner, she heard what sounded like a shuffling of feet, the scrape of leather against concrete, and suddenly she was almost as afraid as she had been of Frank in the cemetery. She remembered that the church operated a soup kitchen, and in good weather, homeless people often slept in the churchyard. Most of them were unshaven men in dirty clothes who smelled of vomit and alcohol, the way she herself smelled now, she supposed. She was frightened of them even when she was with her mother or one of her classmates, scared of them even in the brightest light of day. She heard the scraping noise again. She saw a shadow, or thought she did, a movement in the darkness. For a moment, her legs were too weak to lift her feet. But when the noise came again, closer this time, she started running.

She ran toward a streetlight, moved under it, and turned the corner. She raised the hem of her mother's dress and ran away from the church and whatever lurked in its shadows. She ran down sidewalks and across streets. She ran past fences and hedges and under trees. She ran as she had never run before, hearing the sound of her own footsteps, feeling the cool of the night on her face and in her lungs, tasting in her damp mouth her deep weariness. She ran until she came to her own house where beside the front door a light was burning. She ran up the driveway and down the walk. She ran up the steps and across the porch. Here she paused and waited for courage to go in, feeling in her throat the sharp edge of her frantic breathing and in her breast the inexorable beat of her wounded heart.

ALLEN WIER

Excerpts from the Novel *Tehano*

FROM CHAPTER IV

Knobby Cotton: Born a Slave

(June of 1832, born; September of 1862, a runaway)

From the time of his birth in a slave cabin, Knobby Cotton had been lanky as a child's drawing of a stick person. When the midwife handed him to his momma, Hester, for the first time, she looked at her first baby—her skinny, only baby—and said, "Chile, you all arms and legs." But what most folks saw was his stick out ears, his stick up shoulders, his jut out elbows, his jut up knees, the balls of his heels on back of his long feet. "Knobby is what you is," Hester said. She named him Samuel, after her daddy, but everybody always called him Knobby.

Nighttime, when she got back from the field, Hester made hoe-cakes and syrup, sometimes fixed dumplings, made rice or baked yams in the ashes, and after they had eaten, Grandfather Samuel told stories about Africa, about the wise turtle and the wily spider, and about the snake, Damballa, revered by some as a god. Grandfather said that Damballa was no god, but that his stories were still good. After Grandfather's stories, Knobby's mother rocked him in the rocking chair Grandfather Samuel had made the month before Knobby was born and sang to him:

> You was hatched from a buzzard's egg,
> My lil knobby colored chile.
> Mastah's chile born rich and free,
> You God's skinny gift to me
> In this po slave cabin home.

Grandfather Samuel, before he got so old, had hunted down lost cattle for Noble Plantation with as much determination as our Lord and Saviour sought his lost sheep. In those olden days many plantation owners in Alabama, Mississippi, and Louisiana made their living from cattle and kept their slaves on horseback working as cow-keepers.

Grandfather Samuel had been captured by slave raiders in West Africa when he was twelve. He remembered his home and many African words, and he kept his memories alive by telling his stories. The oldest slave in the quarters and the only one who had been born in Africa, Grandfather Samuel was revered by all the slaves. Sure-handed and strong as a man half his age, he thatched the roofs of the slave cabins and he made the calabash drums for Sunday afternoon after-school singing. He had his own Bible and he had the *Watt's Hymnal* with the song words everybody learned. Grandfather Samuel's first master, Leonard Viress up in Delaware, taught Grandfather Samuel (who was then called John) to read and to write his name. When Master Viress learned that his slave had gotten hold of a Bible and was reading Scriptures on his own, the master was furious. He attempted to cut off Grandfather's thumb and first finger, but Grandfather stood up his full height and aimed his eyes down at Leonard Viress and said *You will have to take my life to take my thumb.* Master Viress settled for burning Grandfather's Bible and wetting the ashes down to a paste that Viress made Grandfather eat while the slave owner kept a gun pointed up at Grandfather's mouth.

"From the day those long-haired, red-faced slavers had put me down in the dank hold of their ship my life had become ashes. Weeks in that dark hold, on dark water, under dark skies, everything gray and dead, gone to ashes. What waited for me after my dark ocean passage? The ashes of lonely mud hearths in slave cabins. Every breath I took, every bite I chewed, tasted ashes. When I learned to read there was a small flame amongst the ashes and I would not let my master extinguish that light. So it was that my Saviour turned to ashes, too. The Word manifested itself in ashes, and I took ashes for my nourishment, my first communion, take, and eat, my body and my blood. Slave, you are ashes to ashes. On the slave's tongue, the taste of cremated hope, the bitter residue of nigger combustion."

Grandfather's second owner was Judah Grivot, a rice planter in Louisiana.

"There I learned the true nature of a tyrant, learned to ignore the earthly stings of club and whip. I spent my days from dawn to dusk standing in muddy water, breathing rising swamp stink, squint-eyed against the sun's reflected stare, mindful always of water moccasins. My feet festered with water poisoning and ground itch, my legs burned with chigger bites, I ached all night long. I first loved a woman there, but vowed I would not be a slave husband, would not be a slave father."

Grivot was shot and killed in a duel in New Orleans. His childless widow, Marie, inherited the plantation and all the slaves, sold everything and moved away. Grandfather was taken to a slave pen in New Orleans and put on the auction block.

"Master Noble came along and asked me, 'What can you do?' and I said I can ride a horse and I can herd cattle."

"When had you learned to ride a horse?" young Knobby asked.

Grandfather smiled and continued his tale without answering the boy's question. "I did not want a rice planter buying me. Master Noble did not look inside my mouth or even lift my shirt to see if I bore the whipping scars of obstinacy."

Grandfather became the best cow-keeper and horseman on Noble Plantation. "I took to horses as an angel to his harp. I learned horse language. Ropes and knots did what I told them."

When Master Noble died and his son took over the plantation, Grandfather persuaded young Master Noble that if he spared the whip his slaves would work harder for him. Grandfather let the slaves believe he had cast a spell over young Master Noble to make him end their floggings. Grandfather's knowledge of herbs and healings brought slaves to his cabin late at night. He had stopped the floggings and he ministered to their needs; they called him the conjure man.

"Down in the swamp I learned the hoo-doo conjure ways and then I put those dark spirits in the service of our Saviour, Lord Jesus."

Slaves on Noble Plantation were treated much better than most slaves. They had ample cornmeal and syrup, even meat, and those who wanted could plant gardens by their cabins. They were given plenty of tallow candles for light. Their cabins had wooden floors, windows with wooden shutters, and partitions to separate families who lived together. The Master gave them passes to visit other plantations, and he built the chapel where Samuel read Scriptures and the slaves sang hymns and on Sunday afternoons had their school. Thanksgiving, Christmas, Easter, and the Fourth of July they were given days off and treats of cake bread, coffee, and roasted hens and pigs. For cotton picked beyond his quota, a slave on Noble Plantation got a cash bonus. Buying or selling, the Master kept slave families together. Only the Master, not the overseer, was allowed to use the whip, and Master did not flog unless he had a runaway, which he didn't have often. But the best-treated slave is not free. Grandfather told Knobby he could never trust any white person.

"Remember the Israelites, Knobby. We are biding our time, lying in wait, until the Lord will raise us up to smite our white enemy and set ourselves free. Thus saith our Lord, grandson, 'I will deliver thee out of the hand of the wicked, and I will redeem thee out of the hand of the terrible.' "

On Noble Plantation, Grandfather again fell in love.

"I did not want to see my wife flogged, I did not want to love a family and risk being sold apart. But young Master Noble promised me he would not separate his slave families and my love was strong, so I married and made children. My daily prayer begs Jesus help Master Noble keep his promise and, so far, Jesus has answered my prayers. But a life of ashes is habited to wreckage and ruin, and my fears have never had a moment's repose."

When cotton displaced cows on Noble Plantation, as it did over most of the south, the master put most of his slaves in the fields. Knobby's daddy, William, outpicked every slave on Noble Plantation. He outpicked every slave in Marion County, every season for as long as memory, and earned his family a last name.

When Knobby was born, William was in his prime, and he might have gotten his son beside him in the fields and made a first-rate picker out of Knobby, had William not died of a fever the first winter after the boy was born. They buried William in the nigger cemetery close by Grandfather Samuel's wife, Sara, who had been at rest a year, both her hands torn off by the saw teeth of the cotton gin, all the cotton crimson when she bled to death.

Sara and William buried left only Grandfather Samuel and Hester and Knobby in the cabin, so the master sectioned off the room with a plank wall and moved in a slave named Hamp and his wife Rachel and their children Fanny and Rose and Lily.

One night Hester's corn shuck mattress chattered loud enough to wake everyone in the cabin, Hamp climbing heavily onto the space where William had lain before he died.

Of a sudden Grandfather Samuel said that slave's name, "Hamp." He didn't say it loud and he didn't say it soft, but there was something like bones gnawed between his teeth when he said it, and the fire that had gone to coals jumped up bright on Rachel and Fanny and Rose and Lily peering around the partition, four round faces stacked on top of one another like four full moons shining down.

And before that flare of the fire dimmed again it brightened also the blade of Hester's cooking knife that Grandfather Samuel held in his big fist and pointed as a finger at Hamp.

"I am the minister of God to even thee, Hamp, for good. But if thou do that which is evil, be afraid; for I beareth not the sword in vain: for I am the minister of God, a revenger to *execute* wrath upon him that do evil," Grandfather Samuel said.

"No, conjure man, don put no cus on me. I gots all dese chillun and dis woman in de bed wid me an I jis natchul lookin fo mo room fo my res." Hamp was on his knees on Hester's mattress, his hands up as if to ward off blows from Grandfather Samuel, so afraid was he of the conjurer's power.

"Ye are of your father the devil, and the lusts of your father ye will do," Grandfather Samuel said.

Ever after that night Hester built her fire on the left side of the mud fireplace and Rachel built hers on the right side and they took care not to let their fires touch and no words passed between the two families.

In spite of his big-knuckled, long-fingered hands, Knobby was no picker. He was a throwback to Grandfather Samuel, the cow-keeper and drover.

"Yes sir, Grandson, your way is with the livestock, especially horses. I will pass along to you the secret language of horses."

While he was still so small Grandfather Samuel had to lift him up onto a pony's back, Knobby rode every horse in the stable. About the only "toy" the boy ever had was a length of rope he twirled and threw. He roped gateposts, hogs, hens, other children, cattle, and, eventually, horses. But before he ever put a rope on a horse, he learned to talk to horses. He watched their eyes and their ears as Grandfather Samuel taught him, and he learned to know what was in a horse's heart.

Because they had smaller, quick fingers many of the women and children were the best pickers, but Knobby always dragged home a mostly empty basket, his long fingers pricked bloody by the hard cotton pods. Master Noble encouraged Knobby's gift with livestock and took him out of the fields where he said Knobby was of little use to him. Knobby was put to work feeding all the animals and milking the cows and mucking out all the stalls. He grew tall and strong, the muscles beneath his dark skin rolling like the muscles of the horses he tended. Under Grandfather Samuel's tutelage, Knobby trained new horses, trained the big jumper the Master bought for his daughter. Grandfather taught Knobby never to "break" a horse. Grandfather hated the word.

"Same way a Master tells the overseer to gain control of a black man—break him, break his will. Now, Knobby, sometimes you *can* make a creature do your bidding by force of might—a horse or a man. But if you treat a horse, or a man, with respect, he will do your will because he wants to. Our Lord and Saviour gave us free will in the garden. He could have made us love him, could have made us do right, from the start. Look how big his stick is—be easy for God to break man. Harder to love us into heaven."

FROM CHAPTER VIII

Knobby Cotton: An Uncommon Duet
(September–October, 1862)

So two naked adults, a man and a woman, dark-skinned humans whose recent ancestors had run down the beaches of West Africa, ran that night down a narrow passageway between rows of warehouses, and then across an open field that seemed to the runners endless land, and then into the sucking mud alongside a dark bayou, water they entered almost without sound.

The warm bayou offered little relief from the muggy heat. In the water they moved with the water, moved steadily and without speech, Elizabeth at rest in the crook of Knobby's arm that he kept held up, keeping dry the sack with what was left of the biscuits, ham and apples Bohannan had given him the day before. Knobby rested in the water's slow current, letting it carry them along. All the world was shades of black. Beneath the starless and impossibly tall sky and beyond the moving darkness they were in were the dark shapes of trees and an occasional barn or house. That shoreline was here and there dotted with a yellow light, then of a sudden went ragged and wild with the fur of cypress, willow, and mossy oak, and no more lights burned.

After they had been for a long time in the darker dark of swampy forest primeval, at the first faint delineation of light to the east, Knobby pulled them into a muddy wallow that was neither fully land nor fully water.

"I wish we had a big sack of pepper," he told Elizabeth, "but if they get after us the hounds going to have almost as hard a time tracking over all this wet as if we peppered their noses."

"I don't want no dogs after me, Knobby Cotton, didn't ask noway for that kind of run-off-and-hide."

"It'll be all right, girl." He started to say the Lord was with them and would watch over them, but he didn't.

"It's already not all right."

Glad he had left the Lord out of it, Knobby coated his body and Elizabeth's with mud to shield them from gnats and mosquitoes, against the mud he patted leaves and moss to hide them in with the forest. In this protective coloring they clung all the hours of daylight to the low forked limb of a thick-leaved oak like patient larvae in a cocoon. Well after nightfall, they left the water for the woods and flew fast and far.

For the next two days and nights they portioned out biscuits and ham, bites of apple; they drank pooled rainwater. And every step of the way Elizabeth complained. By night they moved; working against the north star, Knobby kept them walking mostly west, with wide circles around marshland and distant buildings. It was hard to judge, but he hoped they'd gotten thirty or forty miles away from New Orleans.

"You call this free, Knobby Cotton, I be pleased to take myself back to Noble Plantation or some such proper house."

"Well you can't do that. No telling what kind of master you'd have been sold to in New Orleans. You're so pretty some man might have bought you for his fancy lady. We're going to Texas and live free."

"I'm too dark black to be pretty, an las time I heard, Texas was a slave state same as Mississippi."

"No, it's not the same, not the same as anyplace else." To ease her complaints, Knobby put his arms around her, but she would have none of that.

"You don't be kissing on me out here with me all smeared over in mud batter to fry in the sun. You can kiss on me when I'm good and ready. When I's had me a bath and something sweeter smelling than swamp gas coming off my skin."

After that, Elizabeth went into a long pout. She grudged Knobby every move she made, but she made them all the same, she didn't have much choice.

Like birds they lived on blackberries and hid in trees, but they did not chirp or sing; they watched and listened for any sign of humans. When they came to a bayou or a muddy place that held water, they drank, and Knobby put back their mud coverings that dried and flaked off as they walked.

After two more nights of walking, both of them shaky with hunger, their naked bodies bug bitten and thorn scratched in spite of their baked mud shells, Knobby woke in the shade of the brush arbor he'd made of palmetto palms to hide them from the daylight. Judging from the slant of light, it was not yet midday. The top of one far off cypress tree gave off a blue different from the blue of sky. Knobby knew that different blue as rising woodsmoke and woodsmoke might mean food cooking. He leaned over to shake Elizabeth awake, but her eyes were already open wide.

"Come on," he whispered, "I see something." But Elizabeth lay, motionless, staring into his eyes. "Elizabeth, what's the matter with you?" He bent and lifted her to a sitting position. She acted paralyzed. "Elizabeth?"

Finally, she blinked, licked her lips, spoke in a husky whisper,

"Knobby, I was froze solid, I couldn't move a muscle, couldn't make speech."

"You're just scared," he said. "Be a fool not to be scared."

"No, I bein rid by a ghost. Someone whispered my name this mornin, while we slept and it wasn't you. He's settin on my chest right now, pressin so heavy I can't hardly draw breath."

Knobby sighed. He made himself wait a moment before he spoke. He hated all these superstitions. "Elizabeth, let me help you up," he said as gently as he could. She took his hand and her arm trembled. She really was wobbly. He was amazed that her imagination could so affect her body. He got her to her feet and she fell against him.

"My legs is like the mud they smeared with, got no stand up in me."

"You're scared and hungry. My legs don't work so well either— nobody walks well on an empty stomach."

"Knobby, we got to put red pepper by the window, keep this ole ghost off me."

He laughed in spite of himself. "I'm so hungry, if we had any red pepper I'd just eat it. Besides, we don't have any window."

Elizabeth looked around as if she was just remembering they were no longer on Noble Plantation. *Wherever* they were, it was just woods. She squeezed his arm, and he released her. She stood on her own now and she smiled. "Pends how you look on it, Knobby. We got no window or we got windows all aroun."

Whatever ghost had waylaid her, Elizabeth was shed of him now. She stayed close behind as Knobby led the way through the sun-dappled bushes and vine-wrapped trees, slowly zigzagging them closer to the smoke. At a narrow bayou they rested and tried to quiet their hungry stomachs by filling them with water. Knobby was scared to be moving during daylight, but he was too hungry not to follow the cloud of smoke, and by early afternoon they hid in a thicket just out of sight of a bats and boards shack in a clearing in the woods—the shack's chimney sending up the blue smoke Knobby had spotted earlier. So close were they to the shack that afternoon breezes brought to them the smell of bacon and the faint slap of a slammed door, followed by the yawps of a hound off after some bloodscent. When the hound bayed and bayed again, Knobby let out his held breath because the dog was growing more distant, hunting away from their hiding place in the thicket.

Knobby left Elizabeth to wait in the thicket and he worked his way silently between the trees toward the little farm shack. He crept close enough to see a gray-headed, bony man hitch an even bonier mule to a harness. The legs of the man's overalls were rust-colored with the dust of red clay. The man shouldered a shovel and an axe, put on a straw hat with a brim so frayed it looked like it was fringed, then plodded in heavy, brass-toed brogans, slowly after the mule toward a field of parched-looking corn. The baying hound, silent now with long tongue lolling, loped out of the woods to lie in the cool dirt before the house, a brown lump so motionless that Knobby would have taken it for a rock had he not just seen the animal walk three circles before dropping to the earth. From inside the house came singing, a woman's voice so pure and strong it was all Knobby could do not to join in when she sang:

All my trust on Thee is stayed,
All my help from Thee I bring;
Cover my defenseless head
With the shadow of Thy wing.

While Knobby crouched in his spying place, the voice from inside the house serenaded him. His stomach growled so he feared the woman would hear it over her loud singing.

The sun was almost overhead when the singer came outside. The woman was too young-looking to be the wife of the skinny, old man who had traipsed off behind the mule. She wore a bonnet and carried a basket and a bucket, and she hummed as she walked toward the field behind the house, the field in which the man and his mule were two small, dark shapes, leaning forward as if into a strong wind. The dark curve of the plow between them looked like some kind of hook that hitched them together as they inched forward.

The woman stopped humming, cocked her head, turned back and yelled, "Grover, you wuthless houn, come on wuth me."

There was a long moment in which nothing whatsoever happened, then the dog slowly stirred, his front legs pushing up step by step while his behind stayed put. Then he pulled himself forward and the stiff hind legs came along. Once he was up on all fours, the dog stretched, the middle of his back dipping down until his belly disappeared in the high grass. Then he was off behind the woman, the tip of his upcurled tail dancing merrily just above the grass.

Good dog, Knobby thought, almost out loud. *Git on out of here with your nose and your growl and bark and most especially with your bite.*

Keeping the board house between himself and the woman, Knobby walked in a half-crouch, toward the door. When the woman stopped and switched her basket and bucket each from one hand to the other, Knobby stopped too. His heart beat so it made his chest ache and he was dizzy enough he thought he might fall down. Then the woman went on without looking back and he ran the rest of the way to the house. His hand on the wood latch, he held his breath, then pushed on the door. He had to force the door to move on its leather hinges. The boards scraped loudly against the packed dirt floor. From here, in the doorway, he could not see the woman. When nothing happened, he bent under the low doorframe and went on in. Heat rose up his naked body so sudden he took it first for fear, then he joined the heat to the woman's cookstove. The room was dark and smokey, the ceiling not much above his head. A lingering smell of bacon from the cookstove made his stomach buckle. His bare feet so quick and light they barely touched the ground, he ran to a crude pine cabinet and opened it. *Forgive me, Lord, that I'm a thief, help me not get caught.* He grabbed a feedsack dress and a worn pair of overalls. On the warm stovetop he found a stack of corn dodgers and one sweet potato. He had a moment's guilt—he knew this one potato was the woman's lunch. Then he dropped the bread and potato onto the folded square of the dress he carried on top of the overalls. There were three eggs in a basket on a roughhewn table and he dropped them onto the dress and folded it over the food. One small window in the room—it had no glass, but opened with a solid, pine shutter—looked out on the field where the man and mule still leaned into the space before them. They pulled forward steadily, then played out behind the stalks and leaves of corn, then eased backward only to move forward again. The hound sat beside the woman's basket on the ground. Where was she?

Knobby whirled and ran through the door and almost collided with the woman who was coming back in.

Less than a foot apart they stood and stared at one another. This close, she didn't look so young. Her face, in spite of the bonnet, was sun-freckled and wrinkled, her lips scabbed and cracked. In her dark hair were threads of silver as bright in the sun as a knife's freshly honed edge. She wore a feedsack dress like the one Knobby had just stolen; her mudstained feet were bare. She didn't move a muscle, but her eyes got bigger, from the inside out, the dark pupils steadily opening up like a flower bud in the sun. Her head was tipped back good so she could look up at Knobby.

What a sight I must be, Knobby thought. He held the bundle of stolen clothes and food down below his waist, covering his nakedness as well as possible. Patches of mud and an occasional leaf still stuck to his skin and hair, and dried mud tightened the skin around his eyes and mouth. Were there still wild Indians around here, he thought, she'd like as not take me for a heathen savage in war paint. *If she screams*, he thought, *Oh, if she screams.*

"Mistress," he said softly, his finger to his lips, "Mistress, please." *Oh, please, Lord Jesus.*

Her eyes pulsed and her lips twitched, but still she did not scream.

"Mistress, I ain't gonna tell you no lie. I've had a bad time here of late. My woman and I haven't eaten since day before yesterday. We are freed slaves but some highwaymen stole everything, took all our clothes and our freedom papers included. They whipped my woman and were going to sell us back to being slaves and we slipped off in the dark and been hiding away."

The woman looked around her, as if she were trying to figure out just where she was. She made a croaking noise in her throat.

"Mistress, my nakedness shames me and it shames my woman as well." Knobby let the overalls unfold from his hand and he held them against his stomach, tried to stand with his naked legs behind the unfolded legs of the overalls. "I heard your pretty song this morning, your song, *Jesus, Lover of my soul.* Mistress, we sing to the same Lord, He's the Master of us all. He gave you a voice pretty as a bird, pretty as any one of His singing birds."

"We got no money fer slaves to do our chores, you kin see that," the woman said, her sweet, singing voice gone husky. "But my man wudn't hold wuth hepin no runaways." She looked over her shoulder as if her husband might hear her from the far off field he plowed. "He wudn't hold wuth nuthin might bring down militia patrols on us. They call theirselves prairie rangers but they is jist prairie bandits. They come acheckin right reg'lar, huntin cajuns and niggers alike, scootin all round hyar after trouble."

Knobby looked over *his* shoulder, too, back through the dim room of the house and out the bright square of the window which held the small, dark shapes of the man and the mule. They still moved from right to left, their give and take against the stubborn soil as unchanging as some ocean wave God might have misplaced when He made the world, one perpetual tide God had breathed in motion in a small, red-clay field of dying corn far from any sea.

Knobby wasn't sure how long he and the woman stood and stared at one another. He knew it couldn't have been as long as it seemed. Her lips trembled as if she were about to speak or cry out, and before she could utter sound, with no idea why he was doing it, very softly, Knobby began to sing:

Jesus, Lover of my soul,
Let me to Thy bosom fly,
While the nearer waters roll,
While the tempest still is high:

The woman tilted her head sideways, just the way a bird on a limb will tilt its head, and as if she had no control over her own lips and tongue and throat and lungs, she joined Knobby in singing:

Hide me, O my Saviour, hide,
Til the storm of life is past;
Safe into the haven guide;
O receive my soul at last.

They both stopped, their chests heaving. The woman grabbed her bonnet off her head and bunched it up in her fists. "You git offen this place, you hear? Run on fast and don't you never come back."

Thank you, Lord, thank you. Knobby took a step past the woman, so close he breathed in the mingled musks of their frightened bodies, eased past her sideways so he wouldn't turn his naked backside to her. He was about to run when she touched his upper arm.

"Here," the woman said, thrusting her bonnet, still wadded in one fist, into his hand. Squinting up, she said, "Hits a hot sun." He took the bonnet, and she said, angry sounding, "Fer yer woman."

Knobby glanced toward the tiny man struggling in the far field.

And for the first time, the woman smiled, spreading her badly cracked lips to reveal crooked, brown-stained teeth. Her sudden, wide smile gave her an addled look. "Huh," she rasped, "He won't miss no bonnet. He never pays me no mind."

"If you please, Mistress, one thing more?"

The woman neither shook her head nor nodded—she simply waited, one eyebrow arched slightly.

"How close to the Gulf are we, Mistress?"

The woman gave an involuntary smile, little more than a twitch of her lip muscles, then she said, "This place ain't got no name. You done passed Labadieville. Hit's back a good piece to Thibodaux and a hard way across the marsh to New Iberia. I aint never been to the Gu'f."

Knobby had never heard of Labadieville, and it wasn't on Joseph's map. After all these miles of walking, Knobby had decided there was precious little on Joseph's map.

"How far to Texas?" he asked. *What matters*, Portis Goar had said, *is how a man sits a horse*.

The woman shook her head. "I know you got to cross the marshland and some days later, the Sabine River," she said. "And I wager Sabine ain't nar as purty as hit sounds. And I know hit's a lifetime of a'walking away."

In less than a minute Knobby was running through the woods, the spontaneous duet in the clearing already a strange dream he could not clearly remember.

Contributors

RICHARD BAUSCH is the author of five story collections and eight novels, including *Take Me Back*, *In the Night Season*, and *Real Presence*. Born in Georgia in 1945 and raised in Maryland and Virginia, he was educated at Northern Virginia Community College, George Mason University, and the Iowa Writers' Workshop. He is the Heritage Professor of Writing at George Mason University and lives in rural Virginia.

MADISON SMARTT BELL is the author of numerous works of fiction, including the novels *The Washington Square Ensemble*; *Waiting for the End of the World*; *Straight Cut*; *The Year of Silence*; *Doctor Sleep*; *Save Me, Joe Louis*; *Ten Indians*; and *Soldier's Joy*, which received the Lillian Smith Award in 1989; and two collections of short stories: *Zero dB* and *Barking Man*. His novel *All Souls' Rising* was a finalist for the 1995 National Book Award and the 1996 PEN/Faulkner Award. Born in Tennessee, he is a graduate of Princeton University and Hollins College and now lives in Baltimore and is director of the Kratz Center for Creative Writing at Goucher College.

DORIS BETTS, current chancellor of the Fellowship of Southern Writers, is the author of *The Gentle Insurrection and Other Stories, The Astronomer and Other Stories, Heading West, Souls Raised from the Dead, The Sharp Teeth of Love,* and other books of fiction. She is a recipient of the American Academy of Arts and Letters' Medal of Merit for the Short Story and is Alumni Distinguished Professor of English at the University of North Carolina at Chapel Hill.

FRED CHAPPELL, a native of Canton, North Carolina, is the author of many works of fiction, including the novels *It Is Time, Lord; The Inkling; The Gaudy Place; I Am One of You Forever;* and *Brighten the Corner Where You Are.* He has also written many books of poetry, including *The World between the Eyes, Midquest, Spring Garden,* and *Family Gathering.* A recipient of the Bollingen Prize and the Aiken Taylor Prize and numerous other honors, he teaches at the University of North Carolina at Greensboro.

ELLEN DOUGLAS, winner of the Fellowship of Southern Writers' first Hillsdale Prize for Fiction in 1989 and a literature award from the American Academy of Arts and Letters in 2000, has written many novels, including *A Family's Affairs; Where the Dreams Cross; A Lifetime Burning; The Rock Cried Out;* and *Can't Quit You, Baby;* as well as the nonfiction work *Truth: Four Stories I'm Finally Old Enough to Tell.* She has served as Writer-in-Residence at the University of Mississippi, Millsaps College, and the University of Virginia and currently lives in Jackson, Mississippi.

SHELBY FOOTE is a historian, novelist, and playwright. Among his novels are *Shiloh, Love in a Dry Season,* and *Jordan County: A Landscape in Narrative.* He is also author of *The Civil War: A Narrative,* for which he won the Fletcher Pratt Award, and *Stars in Their Courses: The Gettysburg Campaign.* He was a commentator for the Ken Burns documentary *The Civil War* and has been honored with three Guggenheim Fellowships and a Ford Foundation grant. He was born in Greenville, Mississippi, and now lives in Memphis.

GEORGE GARRETT, a prolific writer and editor, has written many books of fiction, including *The Finished Man; Whistling in the Dark;*

Do, Lord, Remember Me; An Evening Performance: New and Selected Stories; Death of the Fox; and *The King of Babylon Shall Not Come against You.* He has also written many books of poetry, including *Days of Our Lives Lie in Fragments: New and Old Poems.* He has been honored with the Prix de Rome, fellowships from the Ford Foundation and the *Sewanee Review,* and the PEN/Malamud Award for short fiction. He is Henry Hoyns Professor of Creative Writing at the University of Virginia.

ALLAN GURGANUS is author of the novels *Plays Well with Others* and *Oldest Living Confederate Widow Tells All,* which was awarded the Sue Kaufman Prize from the American Academy of Arts and Letters. His collection of stories and novellas *White People* won the Los Angeles *Times* Book Prize. A grouping of four novellas, *The Practical Heart and Other Necessary Tales,* is to be published in 2001. Translated into fourteen languages, Gurganus' work is read widely abroad. After decades of seeking his fortune elsewhere, he was returned to his native North Carolina, to a village of five thousand souls with one major cross street.

BARRY HANNAH is the author of *Geromino Rex; Airships; The Tennis Handsome; Ray; Never Die; Bats out of Hell;* and *High Lonesome.* His latest book, *Yonder Stands Your Orphan,* is to be published in 2001. He is Writer-in-Residence at the University of Mississippi and lives in Oxford.

WILLIAM HOFFMAN is the author of eleven novels, including *The Trumpet Unblown, Yancey's War, The Land That Drank the Rain, Furors Die, A Death of Dreams,* and *Tidewater Blood* and the story collections *Virginia Reels; By Land, By Sea; Follow Me Home;* and *Doors.* He has won many honors, among them the Best American Short Stories Award, the O. Henry Prize, the Lytle Prize, the Balch Prize, the Goodheart Prize, the Dos Passos Prize, the Fellowship of Southern Writers' Hillsdale Prize, and the Hammett Prize. He and his wife live in Charlotte Court House, Virginia.

MADISON JONES is the author of *A Cry of Absence; Nashville 1864: The Dying of the Light;* and other novels. He has received many honors, including the Ingersoll Foundation's T. S. Eliot Award, the Michael Shaara Award for Civil War Fiction, the Harper Lee Award, the

Andrew Lytle Short Story Award from the *Sewanee Review,* and fellowships from the Rockefeller Foundation and the Guggenheim Foundation. He was educated at Vanderbilt University and the University of Florida, has taught at Miami University of Ohio and the University of Tennessee at Knoxville, and is now Writer-in-Residence Emeritus at Auburn University.

MICHAEL KNIGHT has published fiction in *Esquire, GQ, The New Yorker, Story, Virginia Quarterly Review,* and other magazines. His first two books—the short story collection *Dogfight and Other Stories* and the novel *Divining Rod*—were published simultaneously in 1998. He teaches at the University of Tennessee at Knoxville.

WILLIAM HENRY LEWIS was born in Denver in 1967 and grew up in Washington, D.C., and Chattanooga. He is author of a collection of stories, *In the Arms of Our Elders.* He has published plays, nonfiction, poems, and short fiction, which has appeared in journals and anthologies, including *Speak My Name, Bedford Guide for College Writers,* and *Short Stories of 1996.* His fiction has been honored by the Zora Neal Hurston/Richard Wright Foundation and the Virginia Commission for the Arts, and he was the first recipient of the Fellowship of Southern Writers' Prize for New Writing. He has taught at almost every educational level and now teaches creative writing and literature at College of the Bahamas on New Providence Island.

JILL MCCORKLE was born in Lumberton, North Carolina, and graduated from the University of North Carolina and Hollins College. She is the author of several books of fiction, including the novels *The Cheer Leader, Ferris Beach, Tending to Virginia,* and *Carolina Moon* and the story collections *Crash Diet* and *Final Vinyl Days.* She has taught at the University of North Carolina at Chapel Hill, Tufts University, Harvard, and Bennington College.

LEWIS NORDAN has published numerous short stories in magazines, three short story collections, four novels, and a recent memoir, *Boy with Loaded Gun.* The novel *Wolf Whistle,* a fictionalized account of the Emmet Till murder, has won many prizes, including the Southern Book Critics Circle Award for fiction. The novel *Lightning Song* won the Hillsdale Prize of the Fellowship of Southern Writers. His other books include *Music of the Swamp, The Sharpshooter Blues,* and

Sugar among the Freaks. Mr. Nordan is married to Alicia Blessing Nordan. They live in Pittsburgh and have three grown sons.

LOUIS D. RUBIN, JR., is a literary critic, historian, editor, and novelist. His works of fiction include *The Golden Weather, Surfaces of a Diamond,* and *The Heat of the Sun.* His numerous nonfiction books include *Thomas Wolfe: The Weather of His Youth; The Faraway Country: Writers of the Modern South; Small Craft Advisory: A Book about the Building of a Boat; The Mockingbird in the Gum Tree; A Writer's Companion;* and *A Memory of Trains: The Boll Weevil and Others.* He is the Distinguished Professor of English Emeritus at the University of North Carolina at Chapel Hill and the founder of Algonquin Books.

LEE SMITH was born in Virginia, graduated from Hollins College, and was a professor of English at North Carolina State University for many years. She has published two collections of short stories and eight novels, including *Fair and Tender Ladies, Oral History,* and *The Last Day the Dogbushes Bloomed.* Her many awards include the Lyndhurst Prize; the Lila Wallace—*Reader's Digest* Award; the Fellowship of Southern Writers' Robert Penn Warren Prize for Fiction; and, in 1999, an Academy Award in Fiction from the American Academy of Arts and Letters.

ELIZABETH SPENCER is the author of many books of fiction, including the novels *This Crooked Way, The Voice at the Back Door, The Salt Line, The Snare,* and *The Night Travellers* and the collection *The Stories of Elizabeth Spencer.* Her most recent book is a memoir, *Landscapes of the Heart.* She has received many awards and honors, including five O. Henry Awards, the American Academy of Arts and Letters Award of Merit Medal, and the John Dos Passos Award for Literature. Born in Carrollton, Mississippi, she lived for many years in Montreal and now resides in Chapel Hill, North Carolina.

WALTER SULLIVAN, novelist, teacher, and literary critic, is author of the novels *The Long, Long Love; Sojourn of a Stranger;* and *A Time to Dance.* He has also written a memoir, *Allen Tate: A Recollection.* His critical works include *Death by Melancholy: Essays on Modern Southern Fiction; A Requiem for the Renascence: The State of Fiction in the Modern South;* and *In Praise of Blood Sports and Other Essays.*

Educated at Vanderbilt University and the University of Iowa, he is Emeritus Professor of Literature and Fiction Writing at Vanderbilt.

ALLEN WIER is the author of the novels *Tehano* (forthcoming in 2001), *A Place for Outlaws*, *Departing as Air*, and *Blanco* and a collection of stories, *Things about to Disappear*. In 1997 he received the Chubb LifeAmerica Robert Penn Warren Award from the Fellowship of Southern Writers, and he is also the recipient of a Guggenheim Fellowship, a grant from the National Endowment for the Arts, and a Dobie-Paisano Fellowship from the Texas Institute of Letters. He teaches at the University of Tennessee in Knoxville, where he holds the English Department's distinguished teaching chair.